A
FASHIONABLE
FATALITY

Books by Alyssa Maxwell

Gilded Newport Mysteries
MURDER AT THE BREAKERS
MURDER AT MARBLE HOUSE
MURDER AT BEECHWOOD
MURDER AT ROUGH POINT
MURDER AT CHATEAU SUR MER
MURDER AT OCHRE COURT
MURDER AT CROSSWAYS
MURDER AT KINGSCOTE
MURDER AT WAKEHURST
MURDER AT BEACON ROCK

Lady and Lady's Maid Mysteries
MURDER MOST MALICIOUS
A PINCH OF POISON
A DEVIOUS DEATH
A MURDEROUS MARRIAGE
A SILENT STABBING
A SINISTER SERVICE
A DEADLY ENDOWMENT
A FASHIONABLE FATALITY

Published by Kensington Publishing Corp.

A
FASHIONABLE
FATALITY

ALYSSA
MAXWELL

KENSINGTON
PUBLISHING CORP.

www.kensingtonbooks.com

KENSINGTON BOOKS are published by

Kensington Publishing Corp.
119 West 40th Street
New York, NY 10018

All Kensington titles, imprints, and distributed lines are available at special quantity discounts for bulk purchases for sales promotion, premiums, fundraising, educational, or institutional use. Special book excerpts or customized printings can also be created to fit specific needs. For details, write or phone the office of the Kensington Special Sales Manager: Attn. Special Sales Department. Kensington Publishing Corp, 119 West 40th Street, New York, NY 10018. Phone: 1-800-221-2647.

Library of Congress Card Catalogue Number: 2022945813

The K with book logo Reg. U.S. Pat. & TM Off.

ISBN: 978-1-4967-3491-4
First Kensington Hardcover Edition: February 2023

ISBN: 978-1-4967-3494-5 (ebook)

10 9 8 7 6 5 4 3 2 1

Printed in the United States of America

To the members of the newly renamed South Florida Fiction Writers, who have been a vital part of my writing journey from the very beginning, always a source of strength, wisdom, and community. Thank you!

CHAPTER 1

The Cotswolds, England
September 1921

Phoebe never learned. In recent years, that much had become clear. Try as she might to gain wisdom from her experiences, some inner stubbornness refused to allow life's lessons to sink in. Take today, for instance. What had begun as an exciting and hopeful morning as she'd set out to visit her newly remarried sister and spend time with her baby nephew had ended here, in Julia's drawing room, with a slender Frenchwoman rapidly clucking her tongue in disapproval as only Frenchwomen could.

"Ah, *non, non, non.* Julia"—the woman pronounced it Zhoo-lee-a—"how right you are about your poor sister. But we shall fix her, *non?*"

Not only had Phoebe not known she needed fixing, she didn't *want* fixing. Moreover, this pronouncement had been made before she and this individual had even been introduced. The woman, at least ten to fifteen years older than Julia, possessed a sharp, discerning gaze, the eyes nearly black in color; a straight, pert nose and a pointed chin; and she wore her cropped dark hair in soft waves drawn back from her face. She had come at Phoebe just now like a bombardment, making short work of the carpet between them, her hands outstretched and a look of almost painful dismay on her face.

Call it *hope*, that tenacious inner quality that had set Phoebe up for today's abasement. Julia, formerly the Viscountess Annondale but now, due to her second and much happier marriage, the Marchioness of Allerton, had telephoned a week ago to invite Phoebe to Allerton Place for an extended weekend. Julia rarely telephoned. No, that wasn't true. She telephoned all the time to speak with their younger sister, Amelia, or with Grams or Grampapa. But as for Phoebe . . .

She had accepted the invitation eagerly . . . but she had forgotten there would be strings attached. She had forgotten that nothing was ever easy between Julia and her.

The Frenchwoman now began plucking at the attached sash that circled the waist of Phoebe's dress. "It is too wide for this year. So passé. Cut it off! Either a thin belt, or nothing and allow the fabric to skim the figure. Do you see?"

No, Phoebe didn't see. She liked this frock. Very much, and she had seen something just like it on the pages of the April edition of *La Mode*. With its pintucked blouson bodice, wide silk sash, and velvet piping, all in varying shades of russet, she thought it not only charming but suitable to her coloring and shape. Judging by their expressions, however, Julia and her mystery friend had other notions.

And to think, her biggest qualm about coming to Allerton Place had been the expected presence of Julia's mother-in-law, Lucille Leighton, Dowager Marchioness of Allerton. It must be admitted that the elder Lady Allerton had a way of vexing everyone within hearing range with her frequent complaints. But she and her late husband's aunt, Lady Cecily, not only had taken up residence at the Dower house since Julia and Theo's wedding but were currently on a tour of the West Country and weren't expected back until early next month.

As it turned out, though, Phoebe hadn't escaped criticisms and complaints.

Fingering a curve of blond hair where it swooped away from her face and curled over her ear, Julia strode closer. A tolerant smile tilted her lightly rouged lips. "Phoebe, I'm delighted to introduce you to Mademoiselle Gabrielle Chanel. Coco, my sister, Phoebe Renshaw."

"Oh. Mademoiselle Chanel, a pleasure," Phoebe managed, though she wasn't sure it was. A pleasure, that is. She offered the woman her hand. She knew Gabrielle Chanel by reputation. Actually, by Julia having discovered Maison Chanel's clothing designs only a few years prior—during the war when the designer had been featured in *Harper's Bazaar*. Julia had immediately decided the modern, clean lines and soft jersey fabrics were perfect for her long, lean figure.

Julia wore one such suit today, a waistless, calf-skimming dress in royal blue covered by a jersey cardigan, the sleeves loose-fitting and three-quarters in length. A flowing beige jacket and darker pleated skirt swayed around Mademoiselle Chanel's slight figure when she moved, as did the long strands of pearls around her neck, transforming what might have been a frumpy ensemble into an elegant statement.

Phoebe's murmured greeting brought on another clucking of Mademoiselle Chanel's tongue. The woman forewent shaking hands and instead shook her head and waggled her forefinger. Her gaze dropped to Phoebe's feet—would she find fault in the leather pumps as well?—

and slowly slithered back up to her face. She commented to Julia, "I would have known this was Phoebe even if you had not told me. She is very much as you described her."

"I'm afraid she is," Julia replied brightly, as if Phoebe weren't there. "That's why I was so excited for the two of you to meet. In your hands, there will finally be hope for my little sister." She turned one of her patented enchanting smiles on Phoebe, though its effects on her were rather less fruitful than with most people. "Phoebe, surely you remember I had the wonderful fortune of meeting Coco during Theo's and my honeymoon."

With the war a memory and France continuing to heal, Julia and Theo had decided to travel through the country with a stopover in Paris before continuing south to Marseilles and then Monte Carlo. The family had received postcards along each stage of the trip, including a gushing report of meeting the fashion designer and spending an afternoon at her couture shop at 31 Rue Cambon in Paris.

Phoebe forced a smile. "Yes, I remember. It's lovely to meet you, Mademoiselle."

"*Mais non*, it is Coco to my friends. And next time, you must accompany your sister to Paris, yes?" She pronounced the city's name in the French way: Par-ee. "Oh, what we couldn't do for you at Maison Chanel." Once again, she plucked at Phoebe's frock, tsking and sighing.

Phoebe was saved from further assessment by the arrival of two men who stepped in from the hall laughing at some joke between them. They fell silent at the sight of the women, but only for an instant.

"Phoebe! You made it in one piece." Theo Leighton, Phoebe's new brother-in-law, held out his arms and she gratefully entered his embrace. His comment referred to her preference for driving herself places in her two-seater Vauxhall, much to her grandmother's dismay. "You're looking splendid and none the worse for wear. How did the roads treat you?"

"They were quite passable, although I did notice Eva clutching the seat more than once." Her lady's maid had yet to embrace motor travel, and though she never complained about riding in Phoebe's motorcar, she nearly always emerged with a chewed lip and white knuckles.

"Good, good," Theo said, and hugged her again. "So *very* glad you could join us."

He said this with something of a conspiratorial tone, making Phoebe wonder if he, too, had come under Mademoiselle Chanel's critical scrutiny.

"I wouldn't have missed it," she assured him, "even if it had threated rain and hail all the way."

It *had* been a somewhat challenging drive, if the truth be told. Although the borders of Allerton Place nearly touched the farthest reaches of the Renshaws' estate of Foxwood Hall, their entrances lay in two separate Cotswold villages nearly twenty hilly, twisting miles apart. Which meant Julia didn't simply pop over daily to see her grandparents and siblings, and nor did they in turn embark on the trip here without some thorough planning beforehand.

"Let me look at you." Theo grasped Phoebe's hand and twirled her. "Lovely, as always. You're like a picture in a fashion magazine."

She thought *surely* he must be teasing, that perhaps he had overheard Mademoiselle Chanel's lamenting, until she remembered Theo didn't tease when giving compliments. A more sincere man she had rarely met. It hadn't always been so. He'd come home from the war injured, the poisonous gasses rolling across the battlefields of the Somme having scarred his lungs, face, and hands. Even now, having undergone procedures to restore the skin, the left side of his mouth tugged downward and the flesh beside his

chin and down onto his neck had been left pink and puck-
ered. He had regained the use of his fingers for the most
part, but his occasional coughing remained a source of
concern.

The ordeal had initially left Theo withdrawn and often
ill-tempered, but only temporarily. And to be honest, Phoebe
believed much of his peevishness had stemmed not from
frustration over his wounds but from Julia having nearly
married his elder brother, Henry, and then *actually* marrying Gilbert Townsend, Viscount Annondale, the previous
year.

As for Theo's transformation to the jovial, kindhearted
gentleman who stood grinning before Phoebe now? Again,
it was admittedly due to Julia, and the revelation that it
had been Theo she had loved all along. Now, he had not
only Julia, but also his deceased brother's title of Marquess of Allerton.

But barely a penny to go with it, relatively speaking.

"I hope you brought riding clothes," he added after a
moment.

"I did," she said, "and I'm so looking forward to being
in the saddle again." It had been a rather long while. So
many horses had been taken to the Continent to be used in
battle . . . "I'm glad you kept a few."

"Yes, well, we sold off most of them, as you know, but I
couldn't bring myself to part with all of them. Oh, but
good grief," he exclaimed suddenly, his scarred mouth
contorting, "where are my manners? I see you've already
met Coco." He gestured to the man waiting slightly behind him, who had been watching with an amused gleam.
"Phoebe, I don't believe you've ever met our other guest
for the weekend, Ralph Hewitt-Davies, Earl of Chesterhaven. His brother and I were at Eton and Oxford together. Chessy, this is Julia's sister, Phoebe."

The earl's gaze dipped and rose much as Coco's had

done, although without the disapproval. "Ah, another Renshaw granddaughter. The old Earl of Wroxly certainly has lovely faces to gaze upon at his breakfast table each morning, doesn't he?" *This* earl, Chessy, was approaching middle age yet remained handsome and, at present, deeply tanned. Obviously an outdoorsman. He stood several inches taller than Theo, but something in his bearing suggested he would always seem the tallest man in the room, even if, in fact, he was not. He extended a manicured hand and grasped Phoebe's firmly. "A pleasure, my dear. An *absolute* pleasure."

He continued to hold her hand as he performed another brisk assessment—at least, Phoebe had the sense that he was taking her measure. He might as well, since everyone else had. And she took his. Yes, though he must be approaching forty or perhaps more, he was blond and fit, tall and straight, with broad shoulders and a narrow waist. Yes, an athlete, and an aristocrat through and through. She hadn't needed to be told of his title to perceive that much. He continued to hold her in his gaze, as if he had asked a question and waited for the answer.

She began to grow uncomfortable . . .

"Ahem." Coco was suddenly beside him, looping her arm through his and drawing him away from Phoebe until he had no choice but to release her hand. Coco simpered up at him. "Did you enjoy your tour of the stables? The horse—does it meet with your approval?"

"Chessy is interested in the filly born here a year ago last spring," Theo explained.

"Oh. Are you going to buy her?" Phoebe's stomach sank. She had, in fact, hoped Grampapa might purchase her for the Foxwood Hall stables. It had been three years since the Armistice, and Phoebe hoped they might finally keep a horse or two. She so missed riding along the woodland trails and the fields bordering the tenant farms.

"Yes, the chestnut," the earl confirmed. Though Coco continued to exert pressure on his arm to set him walking, he stood his ground and stared into Phoebe's eyes in a way that nearly brought a blush to her countenance—and would have, several years earlier. "Do I detect a bit of disappointment, Phoebe? Do you want the filly?"

"Oh . . . no." She could make no claim on it, after all, not having ample funds of her own to make the purchase. If only Grampapa had taken the several hints she and Amelia had dropped . . . "She's yours, if you want her."

"*Bon*, then it is settled. Chessy shall have his filly." Coco effectively dismissed Phoebe and appealed to Julia. "It is time for tea, *non*? You English and your tea." She gave a brittle laugh. "We shall adjourn to the garden, if I remember correctly. *Oui*?"

"You are correct. Tea will be served on the terrace. The weather is so lovely today." Julia strolled forward, stopping when she reached Theo and taking his arm, though in a much more relaxed manner than Coco's possessive clutch on Chessy. Neither did Julia glower at Phoebe or flash a warning with her dark blue eyes, as Coco's brown ones currently were.

Curious. Only moments ago, the Frenchwoman had fussed over Phoebe like a mother hen—clucking and all. She couldn't wait to "fix" Phoebe. Now she seemed eager to separate herself—and Chessy—from Phoebe's side as quickly as possible.

Could she be . . . was it possible . . . jealous? Of the little sister with no style?

Eva moved the last of Lady Phoebe's things into the armoire and shut the paneled doors. Turning, she surveyed the guest room and decided its pale wood furnishings and toile fabrics were charming, if ever-so-slightly shabby. But then, much of Allerton Place showed signs of wear, despite it being the family seat of the marquesses of Allerton these many generations.

Well, she supposed that was the point, wasn't it? For so many families, the Renshaws included, the war, taxes, tumbling agricultural prices, the abandonment of the countryside as young people flocked to the cities, and simply time itself had worn great fortunes away much as rivers wear away their own banks.

The marriage of the Marquess of Allerton and Lady Julia Renshaw had brought renewed hope to the estate, as her previous husband had provided most generously for her in his will. And, of course, though he did not yet know it, their son, baby Charles, was Gilbert Townsend's heir and already the master of a vast fortune—one based on business and industry and not on old family money passed down through the generations.

Eva straightened Lady Phoebe's things on the dressing table, arranging the jewelry box, hair accessories, and cosmetics as Lady Phoebe liked them; took one more look around the room; and let herself out. On her way to the service staircase, she noticed the door of another guest room ajar and heard the sounds of someone performing similar tasks to those she had just completed. Curious as to who it was, she peeked in. It wouldn't hurt to get to know the other servants who had traveled here with their employers.

A youngish brunette, about Eva's own age and dressed similarly to Eva—all in black serge with hems that skimmed just below her calves and sleeves reaching to her wrist— was laying out evening clothes across a four-poster bed. Eva checked the locket watch pinned to her bodice and noted the time, though in truth she had already known it was merely midafternoon.

She stuck her head in the doorway and said with a smile, "A bit early for that, isn't it?"

The woman gasped, obviously startled. She whisked her hands to her bosom and dropped the pair of stockings she'd been holding. She said nothing as she focused her gray eyes on Eva with something approaching fear—which in turn startled Eva.

She stepped into the room. "I'm terribly sorry, I didn't mean to frighten you." She held out a hand and went closer. "My name's Eva Huntford, Phoebe Renshaw's maid. We just arrived this afternoon."

While that would have been the other woman's cue to introduce herself, she seemed utterly unaware of the proper response. She ignored Eva's hand and ducked to retrieve the fallen stockings. She shook them out and scrutinized each one as if expecting to find some shocking aberration lurking in the silk weave.

Eva didn't quite know what to do. Try again? Turn around and leave?

The former won out. "Is there anything I can help you with?"

The woman gently laid the stockings on the bed, taking special care that each lay smooth, without the slightest wrinkle or crease. Then, with a sigh, she regarded Eva. "*Bonjour, madame.*"

She murmured on in French for several sentences, only part of which Eva understood. She had studied the language during her years at the Haverleigh School for Young Ladies, which she had attended on scholarship. But before she had quite mastered tense and syntax, an accident at home had made it necessary for her to cut short her lessons and help out on her parents' farm.

Besides, this individual's tone gave no indication of either friendliness or annoyance, nor did her countenance give away her sentiments. Eva had a sense only of an efficient worker with an underlying current of trepidation.

Hmm . . .

"Have you a name?" She shook her head at her own attempt to communicate and then asked the same question in poorly executed French.

"Remie," the other lady's maid replied with a nod that could have been, if one were optimistic, interpreted as cordial.

"Eva." She stuck out her hand again. Remie stared at it an instant, shook it briefly, and turned back to the clothing on the bed.

Eva studied the ensemble Remie had laid out for her mistress—whoever that might be. The evening dress consisted of a beige silk undergown with an overlay of beaded, sheer black chiffon. The front dipped in a low V to a barely existing waistline, while the hem flowed to a short train in back. But for the beading, the garment was sublimely simple yet undeniably elegant, and nothing a woman with a curving figure could ever consider wearing. Lady Julia could manage it, she thought, and even Lady Phoebe, though Eva considered it rather too sophisticated for the latter.

"As I said, it's rather early to be laying out dinner clothes, no?" Not *rather* early, she silently amended, but extremely so. How odd that any woman would want her evening attire lying around collecting dust hours before it was needed.

"Mademoiselle insists," Remie said in English. "She must . . . ap . . . approve, yes?"

Though she barely worked her tongue around the sound of an English R, Eva understood her. "She must approve of what you've laid out? Didn't you agree on what she would be wearing ahead of time? This morning, perhaps?" For the most part, Eva knew what Lady Phoebe would be wearing during every phase of this visit. If Lady Phoebe changed her mind, she and Eva would discuss it in the morning, while Eva helped her dress for the day.

Remie looked perplexed and didn't reply, and Eva realized that, just as she couldn't follow the Frenchwoman when she spoke too fast, neither could Remie follow Eva's English. Footsteps thudded on the runner in the corridor, and Remie looked up, her eyes widening in fear. She went so far as to give Eva a little push.

"You go. Now."

Eva felt half tempted to push her back. "All right. I'll see you later, then, belowstairs, perhaps, for dinner."

"*Oui*, go. *Go*."

The footsteps stopped somewhere outside the room. A door opened and closed, and Remie let out a relieved breath. But the look she sent Eva left no room for doubt. Remie wanted her gone.

She began backing toward the door. "It was lovely meeting you," she lied. "If you need anything . . ."

Remie fluttered her hand in the air. Once Eva had stepped into the corridor, Remie shut the door on her.

A soft knock brought Phoebe's eyes fully open. "Good morning, my lady," Eva singsonged as she shouldered her way into the room with a tray. "I hope you slept well."

Phoebe turned onto her back, stretched, yawned, and sat up. "Hard to say. I had a sense of being annoyed all night long."

Eva laughed. "I can't say I blame you, after what you told me last night."

As Eva had helped ready Phoebe for bed the night before, they had talked about Phoebe's first hours here at Allerton Place, and how Gabrielle Chanel had treated her first like a badly dressed doll in need of repair and then as a cast-off plaything. The reason for this transition had been obvious to Phoebe: Ralph Hewitt-Davies. Coco had made it clear he belonged to her, while he had made it abundantly obvious he might like to know Phoebe better.

She gave a shudder and acknowledged the next few days would stretch out interminably.

"It was trying at every turn," Phoebe replied, curling her hands into loose fists and rubbing the sleep from her eyes. Eva set the tray on the bedside table and caught Phoebe's hands in her own.

"Don't do that, you'll end up with red eyes, and how will that look to the others?"

"As if I could care how I look to the others. Julia was no better than her friend, talking about me as though I weren't in the room. I don't know why she invited me." She took the cup and saucer Eva handed her after pouring tea and adding cream and sugar in the exact quantities Phoebe liked. "On second thought, I believe I do. The contrast between us makes her appear all the more beautiful."

"Now, now. It's true Lady Julia—or Lady Allerton, I should say—is a beautiful woman, but you're equally lovely in your own way."

Phoebe almost pushed out a sardonic laugh but decided instead to let it go. Her lady's maid was far too loyal and loving to ever recognize Phoebe's faults, except to point out when she was about to make a regrettable choice.

"So, do you know what's on the agenda for this morning? A ride perhaps?" Eva went to the armoire and began thumbing through. Coming to the frock they had decided on for today, she stopped and turned with a questioning look in her eyes.

"No riding that anyone mentioned." Phoebe reached over to the tray for a slice of toast. "I do hope there will be at some point though. It's been ages. Not to mention one needn't make conversation while riding across a meadow." She nodded at the plum day dress with the double-breasted bodice and square neckline, and Eva took it from the armoire. "How was *your* night after you left me? Any more strange behavior from anyone?"

They had also discussed Eva's experience with the woman named Remie, later identified as Coco's lady's maid. The notion that Coco found fault in everything the woman did didn't surprise her at all.

"No, not from anyone else. But Remie never relaxed, not even for a moment. There were times I wanted to hug her and offer reassurances, if it weren't for the almost permanent scowl across her face." Eva helped Phoebe on with her wrapper.

"It's not right, and if I see Mademoiselle Chanel treating Remie badly, I'm going to say something." Phoebe went to the dressing table, while Eva strolled into the adjoining bathroom to draw her a bath. Over the sound of the running water, Phoebe called to her, "Not that Julia would be of any help. She certainly seems smitten."

Eva came back into the room, an amused light in her eyes. "With Mademoiselle Chanel?"

"Who else? She's like a puppy around her. Agrees with everything she says and hangs on her every word." Phoebe came to her feet and started for the bathroom. "It's one thing to admire someone's work, but quite another to be utterly blind to that person's faults."

"I'm sure if Mademoiselle Chanel proves herself to be less than worthy of your sister's affections, Lady Allerton will soon realize it."

"I wonder." She padded into the bathroom. "Honestly, Eva, I can't say why I'm not going home this very morning."

"I do, my lady. You're worried about your sister and this new friend of hers, and you're staying on to make sure Mademoiselle Chanel doesn't press some kind of advantage that will cause Lady Allerton to regret ever inviting her here."

Some forty minutes later, Phoebe was downstairs and convincing herself she had no choice but to enter the dining room, despite the voices that made her want to retreat back up the staircase. She had seen her nephew, Charles, only briefly yesterday and would far prefer to while away the morning with him. But he had the sniffles, and his nurse insisted he needed rest and quiet.

Into the dining room it was, then. Even several yards from the doorway, she could hear Coco going on about something, half in English and half in French, and from the sounds of it, Julia enthusiastically agreed with everything she uttered. Phoebe entered the room to find all four of them—Julia and Theo, Coco and Chessy—seated around the table and finishing off their breakfast. Good, then she needn't linger long. The toast and jam she'd consumed upstairs would keep her in good stead until luncheon, or elevenses, as Julia had become fond of enjoying.

"Good morning, sleepyhead," Julia said upon catching sight of her in the doorway. The men stood in greeting, then resumed their seats.

Coco glanced up from the remnants on her plate and just as quickly leaned closer to Chessy. She twittered in his ear, prompting him to chuckle. Phoebe felt a wave of heat sweep across her face. Whatever they whispered might have nothing to do with her, but why must they make it *appear* they were mocking her?

"Sit," Julia commanded her. "I'm glad you're up. I've a surprise for you today."

Phoebe did as she was bidden. A footman brought her a cup and saucer from the buffet, and she helped herself from a pot on the table. "What kind of surprise?"

"You'll see." Julia's gaze traveled to the others. Their eyes crinkled as if at a private joke. All but Theo's. He'd taken on a pensive expression, not altogether approving of whatever Julia had cooked up. Phoebe wondered why. What further humiliations were in store for her today? At least no one had insulted her outfit—yet.

"This color is flattering on you."

The compliment, spoken in an offhand way, almost be-grudgingly, came from Coco. Phoebe's eyebrows shot up and she skewed her lips skeptically to one side. Then she remembered her manners. "Thank you. Coming from a famous designer, that's very encouraging."

Coco waved her hand. "Ah, not so very famous. Not yet. But mark my words, in a few more years . . ." She held out both arms as if to encompass the world. "That is why I am in England, to make more women aware of Maison Chanel."

"I thought you were in England to see my homeland," Chessy muttered, and Phoebe compressed her lips to stifle a chuckle.

The next few minutes passed in small talk, until a commotion from the front hall caught their attention. Soon more voices joined the first few, until it seemed a small crowd had descended on Allerton Place.

Julia, frowning, set her napkin on the table. "What in the world? Phoebe, you didn't arrange another of your house tours and didn't tell me, did you?" She came to her feet, prompting the men to do the same. Theo looked mys-tified. Chessy appeared eager to see who their unexpected company could be.

Phoebe shook her head. "Don't look at me."

Coco came to her feet as well. "*This* surprise is mine, Julia. I have invited a few guests of my own. I hope you will be pleased, *non*?"

Judging by the shocked expression on Julia's face, Phoebe guessed the answer to that.

CHAPTER 2

Eva followed Remie and Hetta, Lady Julia's maid, from the service yard into the garden proper. They had been summoned minutes ago, but Eva was hard-pressed to guess why. Beyond the terrace, a stone walkway led onto grassy paths that intersected raised flower beds delineated by box hedges.

What would normally be a scene of carefully ordered tranquility was at this moment noisy, cluttered chaos. Walking beside Hetta, Eva cast her a sideways glance, and saw her own confusion mirrored in the Swiss woman's clear blue eyes. Nearly a dozen individuals, including several footmen along with others she had not seen before, milled along the pathways calling out orders and asking questions. Equipment, which Eva soon recognized as cameras on tripods accompanied by lighting enhancers—round or square metallic reflectors so large, Eva's outstretched arms would mark the circumference—were set up at three points in the garden. A pavilion some twenty feet square had sprung up just to the right of the terrace steps.

She spotted Lady Phoebe near the pavilion, looking as

baffled as Eva felt. Meanwhile, Lady Allerton and the Frenchwoman, Mademoiselle Chanel, were striding from group to group, Mademoiselle Chanel in the lead and waving her arms about as she spoke, and Lady Julia following closely at nearly a trot.

Her husband, the Marquess of Allerton, and the Earl of Chesterhaven, whom Phoebe had described as tall, blond, and unmistakably aristocratic, were nowhere in sight. She didn't blame them. Except for the footmen and one other man she assumed to be a photographer, judging by his proximity to one of the cameras, the rest were all women.

Eva was about to comment to Hetta, whose English had been coming along swimmingly during the past couple of years, but before she could summon the words, Mademoiselle Chanel spotted them and gave two sharp claps of her hands.

"Come, come. What takes you so long, ah?" She pointed to the pavilion. "In there. Claudette will tell you what to do."

Wondering who on earth Claudette was, Eva stood her ground before this slim Frenchwoman with cropped brunette hair and elegant features, who issued commands like a seasoned general. "I don't understand."

"*Non,* but you will. You are a lady's maid, *oui*?"

"I am."

"Then your services are needed." Mademoiselle Chanel gave another clap. "Quickly!"

Lady Allerton hurried over, circling a card table that had been brought out from the drawing room and was now being stacked with an assortment of cases and a triptych dressing-table mirror. "If you wouldn't mind terribly, Eva, Mademoiselle Chanel *could* use your assistance. You, too, Hetta. Your help would be most appreciated." She spared a glance for the third lady's maid, Remie, and offered an uncertain smile. "You may all consider it a favor to me."

"Really, Julia, how you speak to your help." Mademoiselle Chanel shook her head and tsked. "You pay their wages, do you not?"

Leaving Lady Allerton to sputter in reply to that, Eva, Hetta, and Remie filed into the pavilion, enclosed by canvas on three sides with its front flaps tied open. Inside, several racks held clothing, while three open trunks waited to be unpacked. There were also two ironing boards with a pair of irons waiting on a coal-burning heater. In a rear corner, a folding screen offered a few feet of privacy. Eva now had her first clue as to what she and the other lady's maids would be doing. She wondered how on earth all this had been set up so quickly, for when she arose that morning and glanced out her garret window, the gardens had been empty.

"*Oui, bon*, you are here." A woman who clearly took her fashion cues from Mademoiselle Chanel approached them with a brisk stride. Her hair was a bright chestnut and cropped short, and her clothing, consisting of a frock and jacket, were loose-fitting yet impeccably suited to her shape and size. Even her features bore some similarity to Mademoiselle Chanel's, although this woman's nose turned up with an elfin tilt. But where Mademoiselle neared middle age, this woman was young and fresh-looking, her eyes bright, her complexion smooth, her cheeks rose-tinged. "I am Claudette Renault, Mademoiselle's clothing mistress. Come, we have much work to do."

She gestured to the trunks. One appeared filled with dark-hued evening dresses. Another held Mademoiselle Chanel's signature jerseys. The third housed an assortment of shoes and boxes of what Eva assumed were accessories.

"First, we must rearrange what is already hung." Though her words were heavily accented, it was clear to Eva she had enough command of the English language to hold a conversation.

Hetta tapped Eva's shoulder. "What does she say? What are we to do?"

Hetta had grown up speaking German in her native Switzerland, and although French was also spoken in that country, obviously that had not been the case in Hetta's region. And to expect the poor woman to now comprehend English spoken with a heavy French accent? That was too much to ask. Eva set about interpreting.

They had just begun rearranging garments according to fabric, color, evening or daywear, when Lady Phoebe entered the pavilion and signaled to Eva. She drew her outside.

"I'm so sorry about this, Eva. Julia apparently approved it, but no one asked me if I wished my lady's maid to be put to work for Mademoiselle Chanel's fashion photos. I'll gladly make your excuses if you like."

"Actually, your sister did ask if we minded," Eva replied, raising a hand to shield her eyes from the sun, "and truly, I don't. And you know Hetta would do anything for her Lady Allerton. It's all rather interesting, really. Such dresses and suits, my lady! I've seen several already I thought would be perfect for you."

"That may be, but it still isn't right. That woman has taken over. Do you realize all these people"—she swept her arm in a wide arc to encompass the garden and those milling through it—"will all be staying here? Without ever asking Julia or Theo."

"I didn't realize." Eva drew a hand to her bosom, indignant on Lord and Lady Allerton's behalf. "What does your sister have to say about it?"

"Not much. She was clearly taken aback earlier. She can't be at all pleased. You know how Julia can be about matters of protocol and etiquette. Yet she said nothing at the time and seems to be going along with it now."

"And your brother-in-law?"

"Has made himself scarce, as you can see. Theo only wants Julia to be happy, and if this invasion makes her happy, he's all too willing to tolerate it. To a point." Lady Phoebe gave a significant lift of her brows. "I've little doubt *Mademoiselle* will end up crossing a line, and then Theo, and perhaps even Julia, will toss her out as she deserves."

Eva studied her mistress against the backdrop of gardens and activity. "You truly don't like her, do you?"

"I didn't like her yesterday, and I like her less today. But you were right. I'll stay on because I don't trust her, and I don't want to see Julia hurt by her."

"*Mademoiselle! Mademoiselle!*" The clothing mistress waved impatiently at Eva, who didn't need to ask what she wanted.

"It seems I've been missed. You keep watch out here, and I'll keep an eye on things in there." She inclined her head toward the pavilion. "If I hear anything odd or nefarious, especially to do with Mademoiselle Chanel's immediate plans, I'll let you know."

"Thank you, Eva. Just . . ."

"What, my lady?"

Lady Phoebe grinned. "Don't work too hard for them."

Phoebe went to the steps, intending to go up and watch the commotion from the terrace, but she made it no farther. Coco stood at the top along with two other women, both young, slender, and uncommonly attractive. One stood practically toe-to-toe with Coco, forcing the latter to raise her chin to meet the younger woman's gaze. Like the clothing mistress, this woman had chestnut hair—but darker and longer, swept up with combs at the sides to hang in glorious waves between her shoulder blades. Her eyes were large and heavily lashed, her eyebrows bold, her cheekbones high. A countenance so classic and striking, Phoebe could barely pull her gaze away, had she wished to. But at this moment, she didn't wish to. She was far too interested in what was being said.

The other young woman—a girl, really—hovered a few feet away, eying the pair as they carried on their debate. She, too, possessed a unique beauty, but of an utterly different variety from the first. A redhead, she was also tall and slender, but where the darker-haired woman's features were pronounced and dramatic, the redhead's were soft, still childlike, her face heart shaped with a chin punctuated by an indent no larger than Phoebe's pinky finger. She also noticed that while the brunette wore one of Mademoiselle Chanel's signature jersey outfits, the redhead was dressed for riding in breeches and boots.

Where the former looked distinctly French, the latter struck Phoebe as quintessentially English. The dark-haired woman and Coco were all but yelling now in rapid French, making it difficult for Phoebe to comprehend, though she considered herself fairly fluent. The redhead looked on as if not understanding a word, and yet . . . Phoebe had the distinct impression the girl knew exactly what fueled the argument and was merely waiting for it to end before getting on with things.

Whatever those things might be.

Eva reappeared at the edge of the pavilion. "What on earth is that all about?"

Phoebe tried to concentrate on the words. She replied in whispers. "I believe they are clothing mannequins. The one arguing with Mademoiselle Chanel is upset by the presence of the other." She listened another few moments, then nodded to Eva. "It would seem the brunette is Mademoiselle Chanel's favorite, the one she uses for many of her shows and photographs. The other . . . the redhead . . . is new."

Julia came up beside her and gazed up at the spectacle on the terrace, as many of the others in the garden were doing as well. "Oh dear, this won't do."

"Do you understand what they're saying?" Phoebe asked her.

"I know all about it." Julia gestured at the brunette. "That is Suzette Villiers."

She spoke as if this should explain everything, but Phoebe understood no more than before. She exchanged a glance with Eva, who only shrugged and disappeared back inside the pavilion. Phoebe asked her sister, "And who is Suzette Villiers?"

"Why, only Maison Chanel's principal clothing mannequin. She's famous in France, very sought after by all the fashion houses. Jeanne Lanvin would *love* to steal her away. But Suzette is loyal to Coco."

Phoebe tipped her face up and regarded the pair. "Then why the sharp words?"

"You see the other mannequin, the redhead? Well, that's India Vale. A nobody, really."

Phoebe nodded, beginning to comprehend. The established mannequin feared being supplanted by the younger nobody. Then a recollection struck her. "Wait, is her father Steffen Vale, the horse breeder?"

Julia nodded. "The very same. He and Chessy know each other well. Chessy's purchased a number of horses from the Vale stables. Anyway, Coco and Chessy ran into India at a party in London. Apparently, Coco took one look at India and decided she wanted her not only in photos but in the fashion show she's planning to hold back in London next month."

"Do her parents know about this?" Despite the glamour associated with modeling high-fashion clothing, mannequins were yet considered rather less than respectable.

"I certainly doubt it. But it's none of my business, is it?"

Phoebe watched the altercation another moment before commenting, "I'm guessing Coco didn't bother to explain the change to Mademoiselle Villiers. Until now, that is."

Julia sighed. "That would appear to be the case."

They both fell silent as the encounter on the terrace escalated in volume and erratic hand motions. Phoebe half feared one might inadvertently strike the other with all the gesturing they were doing. The redhead, Miss Vale, continued observing silently. Phoebe believed she detected a slight smile lifting the girl's lips.

"This is getting out of hand." Frowning, Julia folded her arms across her chest. "It's a good thing Lucille and Cecily aren't here to witness it. They'd both have the vapors, and at their ages, that could prove dangerous. Why is Coco tolerating this? Why didn't she put a stop to it at once?"

"A fair question," Phoebe agreed. "Here's another. Why have *you* allowed all these people here? Did you know Coco intended overrunning your home and using it as a backdrop for her clothing business? Not to mention as a battleground between rival fashion mannequins?"

"Well . . . this *has* all been a surprise." Julia made a visible effort to smooth the last of her frown lines and assume a serene expression that didn't fool Phoebe one bit. "But I'm excited at the prospect of these photos being taken here. You know I'm a huge admirer of Coco."

"You balked at Foxwood Hall being opened to house tours last spring."

"That was different."

Phoebe plunked her fists on her hips. "How?"

"That was for money." Julia scoffed as she said that last word.

"So is this. It's for the purpose of increasing Maison Chanel's profits. Why is that all right, but trying to bring in funds to help our villagers and tenant farmers was wrong?"

"Really, Phoebe, I shouldn't have to explain myself to you. Allerton Place is my home now—mine and Theo's—and if we're both content to have these people here, it's no one else's business."

Phoebe blew out a breath. "Fair enough. But I can't help feeling this woman is running roughshod over you, and I don't understand why you're letting her."

"Your nose is out of joint because she criticized your frock yesterday." Julia raised an eyebrow and shot Phoebe a significant look. "And with good reason. Instead of pouting you might be grateful someone like Coco Chanel took notice of you and bothered to offer some advice. Her opinions can only improve you."

"Oh, good heavens, Julia." Phoebe tossed her hands in the air and walked away. The terrace had quieted in the past moment or so, although the expressions Phoebe glimpsed assured her the tension remained. Slowly Coco's staff resumed their tasks, the women in the pavilion returning to sorting through the clothing, and the photographer moving through the garden, making adjustments to his tripods and checking his cameras.

The drawing room doors opened and an older woman stepped out. Phoebe judged her to be around fifty, though her hair—also bobbed, like Coco's—showed more dark blond than gray. Her clothing immediately caught Phoebe's eye, and admiration. Loose trousers swayed with each step beneath a shirtwaist worn out and belted at the waist. A silk scarf knotted above the right shoulder lent a spot of color to the monochrome gray outfit. The overall effect was one of easygoing confidence with a touch of devil-may-care defiance. Phoebe found herself smiling.

The woman went straight to Suzette Villiers's side and placed a hand on the mannequin's shoulder as she spoke. Her expression raised brackets beside her mouth and formed crow's feet beside her eyes, yet with a warmth that suggested amiability came naturally to her. Suzette tossed her hair and attempted to shake off the older woman, but the woman persisted, and finally Suzette shrugged. She went to the garden table and threw herself down into the closest chair. The blonde then approached the red-haired mannequin, and the pair came down the steps together.

Phoebe moved off a bit, yet remained near the pavilion, eager in spite of herself to see what would happen next. One thing she had to admit, it gratified her to see how Maison Chanel seemed to be run primarily by women.

"Phoebe!" The voice—deeply male and warmly famil-iar—called down from the terrace.

With a gasp, she forgot everything else going on around her and broke into a grin of delight. "Owen."

They met halfway up—or down—the stairs, and if Phoebe worried about teetering on the step, Owen's strong embrace held her steady. She wrapped her arms around him in turn, but only for a moment, for they weren't alone and Phoebe felt the gazes suddenly converge upon them. From over his shoulder she saw Suzette Villiers studying them with a speculative quirk of her brow. She and Owen eased away from each other but grasped hands to main-tain contact.

"What are you doing here?" She was a little breathless, her voice filled with laughter. She stared up into his dark eyes, shadowed by wisps of black hair swept onto his

brow by the breeze. He smelled of wind and open countryside, and she guessed he had just arrived in his prewar
Morgan Runabout, a three-wheeled motorcar built for
racing.

"Didn't your sister tell you?"

Ah, the surprise Julia had spoken of this morning. This
must be it, forgotten in all the disarray. "No, she didn't,
not in so many words. How did you manage to get away
from the mills?"

Unlike most men of his class—the heir to an earldom
due to his elder brother's death in the war—Owen involved himself in business. He owned several woolen mills
in Yorkshire, and did quite well, although the recent labor
union demands presented constant battles. Owen was a
fair man. Not a man to be taken advantage of, but neither
did he refuse his workers their due.

"She telephoned several days ago to invite me." He
seemed puzzled. "I thought you knew."

"This morning she told me she had a surprise for me.
When all of these people showed up . . ." She swept her
hand in an arc encompassing the garden. "I thought for an
instant they were the surprise, until I realized she was as
baffled by their sudden appearance as I was."

He scanned the garden. "What the devil is going on
here?"

Phoebe filled him in. She left nothing out, not even Coco's
unflattering comments yesterday, to which he grew sym-
pathetically indignant, brushed a kiss across the back of
her hand, and told her she always looked beautiful to him.

To him. Those two simple words filled her with an inor-
dinate amount of joy. But especially today, and here, it
seemed all that mattered. Not whether his opinion was
shared by anyone else, but simply that he deemed it so.

She found she had lost interest in the activity in the garden. "Let's go in. Have you eaten? I'm sure we could find you something." She checked her wristwatch. "Or luncheon is in about an hour, if you'd rather wait."

"Too long." He linked her arm through his, letting his hand rest on hers in the crook of his elbow. "Let's go see what we can muster."

They continued up the steps, but then Phoebe brought them to a halt. "Are you staying on?"

He hesitated, his gaze roaming her face, no doubt detecting her sudden qualms. "I'd planned to. Julia invited me to. Is that . . . a problem?"

"I . . ." She scrunched her features, considering. "It's not a problem for me, exactly. But . . ."

"Yes?" He took on a worried look and seemed slightly wounded.

"It's my grandparents," she quickly explained. Phoebe and her siblings had always lived at Foxwood Hall, but after the death of their mother years ago, and then the death of their father during the war, her grandparents, the Earl and Countess of Wroxly, had become their guardians. "They won't know about this, and with Lucille and Cecily gone away, well . . . that leaves only Julia as chaperone, and, Owen, you know my grandparents. They're highly likely to disapprove."

His lips curled. "But as you said, they won't know about this."

"No, not yet, but they're bound to find out. They always do and . . ."

"You don't wish to upset them."

"No, I don't." She could see that he understood. She didn't *fear* displeasing Grams and Grampapa, not as she would have as a child. But they were of the old school, and she loved them too much to wish to cause them unhappiness. She ran her hand along his shoulder and down his arm, detecting the muscle beneath his coat sleeve. "But I don't wish you to leave, either."

"Then I won't. And neither will I do anything that would distress your grandparents." He pressed his palm to her cheek and gently raised her face to meet his. He kissed her tenderly, then pulled back and smiled. "Except that. There will be lots of that, I'm afraid."

CHAPTER 3

Eva flinched as the argument that had begun on the terrace burst into the pavilion. She had just hung up an evening gown that Hetta had finished ironing, and as Mademoiselle Chanel and the two mannequins strode straight toward her, their expressions inspired an apology to bubble up inside her, though for what, she didn't know.

All this hullabaloo over two young ladies who couldn't be any older than Lady Phoebe. And these clothes! Eva glanced around the pavilion, wondering why they needed so many outfits for only two mannequins. How long did they plan to be at Allerton Place? And would they leave everything out here at night? Eva doubted it, and fully expected to be pressed back into service at the end of the day—and again, tomorrow morning.

Mademoiselle Chanel sauntered to a rack and chose a gown seemingly at random, then practically flung it at the brunette before pointing toward the privacy screen. The brunette, Suzette Villiers, as she had overheard Lady Julia call her, slunk off, sulking, the gown draped over her arm. Mademoiselle Chanel's sour expression transformed as she turned toward the redhead. In the time she had been outside, her russet hair had been done up in a braid coiled at the back of her head, with spiraling tendrils framing her face. Taking the girl's hand, Mademoiselle led her to a rack that held an assortment of frocks suitable for luncheons, garden parties, or an afternoon of boating. Together they went through silks, jerseys, and chiffons, and made a selection. They then chose a hat and suitable shoes.

"Suzette, are you ready?" Mademoiselle Chanel called out.

"*Les boutons*," was the reply, impatient and rather shrill. Mademoiselle Chanel rolled her eyes.

Eva understood enough French to realize the gown buttoned up the back and Miss Villiers was having trouble reaching them. "I'll go," she offered, and Mademoiselle Chanel waved her on.

Suzette offered Eva a scowl as she stepped behind the screen, so Eva repeated the words "*les boutons*" and added the appropriate hand motions. Suzette whirled around, her head tilted and her foot tapping, a wordless order for Eva to get on with it. She did, working each tiny, silk-clad button deftly into its equally miniscule hole. The gown hugged Suzette's every dip and curve, such as they were on that slender form, and draped around her legs like a midnight waterfall.

Suzette brushed past her with no more than a nod, but Eva took it as thanks. The woman strode past Mademoiselle Chanel without a glance and left the pavilion. The redhead took her place behind the screen. Eva made to leave the small space, but Mademoiselle Chanel blocked her path.

"You will help her, *oui*?"

"Of course, Mademoiselle." Eva turned toward the young woman. "Would you like me to wait on the other side while you disrobe?"

The girl shrugged and said, very much in the King's English, "It makes no difference to me."

With that, she unbuttoned the short jacket that covered her shirtwaist. Eva helped her off with those, and then, the girl having perched on the small stool in the corner, Eva tugged off her riding boots. Next, she exchanged her breeches for a dark pair of stockings Mademoiselle had chosen for her.

Eva held the frock low while the mannequin stepped into it. Of creamy yellow, it buttoned across one shoulder and skimmed the hips, cinched ever-so-slightly with a low-slung belt, and fell in pleats to mid-calf. Fawn-colored trim encircled the cuffs and neckline. Lastly, she stepped into a pair of high-heeled oxfords that sported beige patent leather on the toe caps, and Eva placed a large-brimmed picture hat on her head and pinned it in place.

Eva stepped back and surveyed the results. The effect hinted at men's sportswear while remaining completely feminine. "Why, you look utterly charming. Those colors are perfect with your red hair, and the sportiness of the style complements your youth."

The girl beamed at Eva. "Then you think I'll do?"

"Most certainly, Miss . . ."

"Vale. But call me India." She smiled again and stuck out her hand. The familiarity took Eva aback, but she recovered quickly.

"I'm Eva. If you need anything while you're here, you mustn't hesitate to ask me."

"Do you work for Lady Allerton?"

"No, I'm her sister's lady's maid. But she won't mind sharing me, so you mustn't worry about that."

Outside, at the makeshift dressing table, Suzette Villiers sat on one side with a drape covering her gown. Her hair, too, had been arranged in a loose pile of curls atop her head, with tresses draped around her ears. A case stood open to reveal an assortment of cosmetics, more than Eva had ever seen before. Most ladies of the Renshaws' class wore very little makeup, mostly powders to even the complexion, with perhaps a bit of kohl around the eyes and a touch of color on the lips.

Miss Villiers's eyes were closed. Sitting opposite her, a plump young woman, her cheeks pleasingly round, applied color to her cheekbones. This woman must have done the hair on both mannequins as well. She had already outlined Suzette's eyes, making them appear so much larger, though Eva had already thought them large and striking. Her lips were made a startling red, her eyebrows bolder even than Mademoiselle Chanel's. The effect seemed excessive, exaggerated, until Eva remembered no one would see the colors in the photographs, and what might appear overdone in person would translate into much more subtle tones of black, white, and gray.

Soon, Mademoiselle Chanel walked by and signaled to the makeup artist—Marcelle, as India told Eva. Marcelle used a brush to smooth here, set the color there, and sent Suzette on her way—brusquely, it appeared to Eva. Suzette issued a parting rebuke. She spoke in French, and Marcelle replied in kind, but Eva understood the gist.

"You rushed and were careless."

"Not so. You are as beautiful as ever, Suzette." A compliment, perhaps, but Marcelle spoke as if by rote. As if bored. Or perhaps simply weary of the mannequin's surliness.

India took her place in the empty chair. With no one calling her to perform a task, Eva watched each step of the transformation. She had to admit to feeling rather skeptical of India's potential modeling skills. The girl was inexperienced, after all. But by the time Marcelle gave India's face a final, all-over dusting with the powder brush, Eva understood why Mademoiselle Chanel had wished to make the change. India had blossomed from a mere girl into an image rivalling the timeless beauty of a Botticelli painting.

Across the garden, the photographer, a nice-looking young man with a shock of wheat-colored hair that flopped over his brow, shot photos of Miss Villiers, posing her on a bench, beside a statue, beneath a tree. Between each shot, the mannequin scowled, fussed at her clothing, and countered whatever instructions he gave her with what, even at a distance, appeared to be querulous retorts.

Just as abruptly as the makeup artist had done, the photographer waved Miss Villiers away. She glared at him for a long moment before turning on her heel and strutting off.

"Well, I suppose it's my turn now," India said brightly to Eva. "Wish me luck."

The photographer took her hand and drew her to a shady corner of the garden. A low stone wall ran the length of a footpath, and gently he helped her climb onto it. He shot photographs of her sitting with her legs crossed in a jaunty manner, then stretched out along the top of the wall, and then curled beneath her skirt. Prompted by whatever he was saying to her, she smiled as though laughing, tossing her head. She tilted her hat one way and then another, and leaned back on her hands to turn her face toward dapples of sunlight filtering through the trees.

He took her hand again and helped her stand on the wall, and took photos of her taking tenuous steps along the stones, her arms wide as if she walked a tightrope. Instinctively she seemed to know when to stop and how long to hold a pose. All the while she peeked teasingly at the camera. She held out her skirt as if to curtsy, let it drop, kicked her leg, turned about, looking as though she were having the time of her life. As if there were countless people around her and she the center of attention.

Eva shook her head in surprised admiration. The girl was a natural. So fresh and unspoiled. Although, to give credit where it was due, Eva didn't think India would model evening dresses with the same sophistication as Miss Villiers. Surely Mademoiselle Chanel should see the value in having both women and treat each accordingly. She wondered if the tension stemmed from more than a desire to bring in a new mannequin. Perhaps Mademoiselle and Miss Villiers had had a falling out before ever arriving at Allerton Place.

Eva moved off, making her way across the garden to see if she was needed back at the pavilion. Or perhaps she might sneak inside and tend to anything Lady Phoebe needed doing. She had neared the center fountain when she saw Miss Villiers standing beside it, staring across the flower beds to where India continued to pose for photographs. The furious glare and the scowl twisting the brunette's beautiful features sent a chill through Eva.

Phoebe woke at first light the next morning, even before Eva knocked at her door. Despite her lingering annoyance with Coco, Julia, and the situation here at Allerton Place, she sat up in good spirits, eager for the day to begin. Even the sight of the mist-shrouded lawns outside her window couldn't dampen her enthusiasm. Julia had planned a morning ride that would include herself, Phoebe, Theo, and Owen. As there were only five horses left on the estate, that meant one other person could join them. None of the French guests had appeared interested, but India had practically jumped up and down to be included, so their little group was set.

It had been far too long since Phoebe had enjoyed a good canter across the countryside. Certainly her bottom would ache for it later, but she wouldn't complain. With another look out the window she scrutinized the sky, gauzy

gray but hinting at the brightness gathering strength behind it. The sun would burn through, probably by the time
they were saddled up and ready to set out.

Eva helped her don her riding clothes, fastening the
small cameo that had belonged to Phoebe's mother to the
high, ruffled neck of her shirtwaist. Her mother had always affixed the piece to her own riding habit, and Phoebe
continued to wear it for good luck, as if her mother
watched over her and protected her from falls. She had
pulled on fawn breeches and knee-high boots, and donned
a black velvet frock coat. Lastly, Eva helped her on with
the low-crowned top hat, its old-fashioned veil having
been tied into a bow at the back.

"I do wish Amelia could have come," she said to Eva.
Amelia had graduated from the Haverleigh School for
Young Ladies last spring but was presently in London visiting a friend and her family. Their brother, Fox, meanwhile, was back at Eton for the fall term. He'd have loved
the opportunity to ride as well.

Downstairs, Julia, Theo, Owen, and India had gathered
at the buffet, talking and laughing as they made their
breakfast selections. There was the usual fare, but the riders would be eating lightly, and Phoebe saw their plates
held mostly toast and eggs. Owen winked at her in lieu of
a kiss, though he did so with a devilish look that raised a
goose bump or two. He held her chair at the table, conve-
niently beside his own.

While they ate, the woman Phoebe had seen on the terrace the day before, who had seemed to hold such sway
over both clothing mannequins, entered the dining room
and wished everyone a cheerful good morning. Once
again, Françoise Deschamps wore flowing trousers, these
with a light pinstripe that matched the blue of her shirtwaist and the scarf draped over her shoulders. Phoebe had

talked with her at dinner last night and found the older woman possessed an outgoing nature that set others at ease.

Phoebe had also learned, from Julia, that Françoise held a fair amount of power at Maison Chanel and answered only to Coco. Though she must have been approaching her mid-fifties, indicated by gray streaking her blond hair and friendly crow's feet beside her eyes, she spoke and carried herself like a much younger woman. She was older than Phoebe's mother would have been, yet seemed more like the carefree, indulgent aunt everyone wished they had.

The photographer, Narcisse Bienvenue, shuffled in as well, though he approached neither the buffet nor the table. While Coco, Chessy, Françoise and the two mannequins were treated as guests, it appeared the other three Maison Chanel employees were exactly that, and consigned to servants' quarters and the servants' hall belowstairs. He cleared his throat. "Good morning. I see you're ready for your ride. Lady Allerton, I had an idea last night. Perhaps I might take one of your motorcars and rendezvous with the riding party somewhere interesting, to take some photos."

Julia consulted silently with Theo, who shrugged. Julia said, "I don't see why not. Come out to the stables with us and discuss it with the groom. He'll know just the right spot."

"Perhaps I could ride along with Narcisse," Françoise said in her nearly perfect English, only lightly accented. She walked to the table with a plate and cup of fruit. "It sounds like fun. I don't ride anymore, but I do enjoy watching. Horses are such elegant creatures."

"And quite frankly, you're dressed for a picnic in the countryside," Julia pointed out.

"I am, aren't I?" Françoise added cream to the coffee

she had just poured and tucked a strand of bobbed hair behind her ear. "I hope I do not offend with my trousers. But why should men have all the comfort?"

"Indeed. I'm thinking of ordering some pairs of my own." Julia laughed at the notion, but Phoebe could see she meant it.

"Coco could design them for you," Françoise told her. Her use of Gabrielle's moniker spoke of how close the two women were. The other employees never addressed Coco as anything but Mademoiselle.

Julia seemed inordinately pleased with the prospect of specially designed trousers from Maison Chanel.

"What about Coco?" Phoebe asked, suddenly becoming aware of the lack of tension in the room, when it had been so prevalent the entire day before. "And Chessy? Perhaps they'd like to join Narcisse and Françoise for the drive out?"

"Yes, what about Mademoiselle?" India glanced eagerly over at Julia.

"What fun. Yes, we'll include everyone," Julia agreed, then frowned. "I don't know why I didn't think of it myself."

"Coco doesn't care much for horses, to be honest," Françoise informed them. "That's why Chessy didn't jump at the chance to ride this morning." She glanced at India, who would have lost her mount today had Chessy decided otherwise. She flicked her gaze back to the others. "I don't imagine they're even up yet."

Something in the way she spoke those last words dropped an awkward silence over the dining room. Or was it Phoebe's imagination that all of them had interpreted the comment to mean Chessy and Coco had spent the night together, in the same room, despite Chessy having been assigned one of his own. She swept a gaze at Julia, who had tucked her chin and pretended interest in finishing the last bits of scrambled egg on her plate.

"It's early yet," Phoebe said to break the silence. "There's plenty of time for them to join us later."

Suzette Villiers shambled in from the hall. "*Je suis là! Am I late?*" Wearing breeches and boots, she carried a riding hat and gloves and placed them on the table. Her hair fell in a tidy braid down her back. Phoebe and the others stared at her, unsure what to say. "*Pardonnez-moi.* I see I *am* late."

When no one else spoke up, Theo said, "No, it isn't that. There are five of us already, you see."

"*Oui?*" Suzette gazed at him expectantly.

"There are only five horses," he explained. "And last night . . . well . . . you didn't show any interest in coming."

Her beautiful face fell, the expectation slipping away. "Oh. I see."

"It's all right." With the smile of a seasoned hostess, Julia said, "You go. I can ride anytime. You're our guest."

Phoebe traded a glance with Owen, and knew he'd had the same thought as she: Suzette wasn't really a guest. None of these people were, except for Coco and Chessy, who actually had been invited. As for the rest . . . well.

Even so, Julia wouldn't take no for an answer when the brunette tried to demur.

"Please, I insist. I'll spend the morning with Charles and join you all later with Françoise and the others."

Theo looked distinctly saddened by that arrangement. "Darling, you go, I'll . . ."

Julia waved him off. "No, you know the trails much better than I do. Besides, we can ride again tomorrow morning. There, it's settled, no need to say another word about it."

It was decided, then. Phoebe had expected to walk to

the stables, but Theo's motorcar—once his brother's—waited on the drive. Theo slid into the driver's side of the Rolls-Royce Silver Ghost, and Suzette, after angling a brief glance at India, slipped into the passenger seat beside him. That left the back seat for Owen, Phoebe, and India. Phoebe took the middle. As she had predicted, the sun burst through the clouds as they pulled away from the house.

Despite the look Suzette had sent India from beneath her lashes, conversation among the five of them came easily. It struck Phoebe how normal it felt. So much like the way things used to be, before the war, when hunts and rides were frequent occurrences and no one thought twice about them, except how enjoyable they were. It was the sort of thing one didn't know one was missing, until the opportunity came along again. She intended to make the most of it.

At the stables, the groom and his assistant were quick to bring out the horses, saddled and ready to go. Julia and Theo had already settled on which mount would be best for whom—except for Suzette, who took Julia's horse. Phoebe was given a beautiful red dun gelding who turned its head to her in greeting as she walked up to him. She took the time to respond properly, with soft words and a firm patting down his muscular neck. He gave a contented snort and she mounted him smoothly.

With the morning sun warming their backs, Theo led them out of the stable yard and onto a path that narrowed as it entered a woodland. Towering beechwoods, still clothed in summer green, blocked out the climbing sun. It was cooler here, still dew-kissed and holding the last of the night's chill. Beneath the canopy, the beginnings of russet tipped the leaves of smaller elm, oak, and ash. There had been just enough rain recently that no dust rose from the trail, and the horses' hooves thumped comfortably along the ground, but not so much rain they needed to worry about sliding through muck. Riding single file, they broke into a lively trot and Phoebe found her diagonal rhythm as if no time had passed since the last time she'd ridden.

Not so for Miss Villiers, directly in front of her. Suzette bounced with each step and seemed almost to be in a silent struggle with her mount. As if her will and the horse's were at odds, their communication practically nonexistent. Phoebe couldn't help but wonder how many times the mannequin had ridden in her life. It could not have been more than a handful of times, perhaps on the occasional holiday trip. A shame Julia had to give up the morning's ride for someone who should only be trotting in a paddock. Should Phoebe call ahead to Theo and suggest they keep to a slower pace?

She would keep an eye on Suzette and see how she did. Riding between Suzette and Theo, India sat her mount with confidence, her body's motions in perfect harmony with each stride, she and her horse moving as one. Phoebe would have expected no less of Steffen Vale's daughter. She had likely begun riding before she could walk.

The trail wound through the trees for a few miles before bursting into a meadow aflame with late season wild-flowers. The land heaved and rolled, and from their van-tage point the countryside spread out in a patchwork of varying greens and golds, bordered by rambling stone walls and the occasional hedgerow. Thatched or slate roofs of tenant farmhouses peeked up from behind gentle hill-sides, their chimneys sending up friendly curls of smoke.

Closer, a brook caught the sunlight and reflected it to set the overhanging trees glowing. Owen moved up beside her then and reached out a hand. Phoebe reached as well, and their hands caught for the briefest instant. It was enough. A current went through her, filled her with exhil-aration, and, as if by spoken agreement, they spurred their horses forward on a burst of speed.

They left the others behind and cantered along the bank

of the brook. Up ahead, a stone wall divided this meadow from the next, and presented a not-too-difficult challenge for horses and riders. At a shrill whistle from Theo, they slowed their mounts and glanced over their shoulders. He pointed at the wall, then back toward bordering trees, and they took this to mean he intended leading the two mannequins along a safer route that didn't require them to take a jump.

Phoebe turned back to Owen, a broad grin on her face. "Shall we?"

"We most certainly shall."

A canter became a gallop, a heady experience that filled Phoebe with a joy she hadn't experienced in far too long. When they came to the wall, both leaned forward over their horses' necks and took to the air in smooth arcs, clearing the stones with feet to spare and landing firmly on the other side.

They continued another dozen yards or so before slowing their mounts and easing to a walk. "We should wait for Theo," Phoebe said while catching her breath.

Owen didn't reply, but simply stared at her with a broad grin.

"What?" Her hand went instinctively to her hat.

"You," he said, his grin deepening to a tender smile. "Exhilaration suits you."

A delightful warmth suffused her cheeks and she smiled back at him. Then she turned her horse to watch for the others. "There must be a gate near the trees. I can't imagine Suzette attempting the jump."

Owen followed her line of sight. "India isn't having it. She's heading straight for us."

"No matter. She rides well. I'm sure she can handle a wall of this height with her hands tied and her eyes closed."

Theo and Suzette continued toward the trees, but suddenly Suzette changed course. "What is she doing?" Phoebe sat taller in her saddle. "Surely she can't mean to jump? She hasn't the skill. Dear God, Owen, she'll break her neck."

"Little fool." His hands tightened around his reins, knuckles whitening, and he tensed as if ready to surge forward. But he held his ground. Riding straight toward the two women would only make the situation more dangerous for Suzette. For all of them.

"She's gaining on India," Phoebe said unnecessarily, for he could see as well as she that Suzette was kicking her horse hard and urging him forward with shouts.

Owen's eyes narrowed. "What can she be thinking?"

"That she's as good as India," Phoebe said, "even though she isn't. Good heavens, she'd risk so much just to prove a point."

Theo had also changed direction and rode after her. India must have heard the pursuing hooves, for as she neared the wall, she stole a glance over her shoulder. Suzette was almost upon her, riding hard at India's heels. Phoebe shouldn't have been surprised at that. Suzette was riding Julia's horse, probably the swiftest of the five, because Theo would have seen to it that his new wife had the finest mount they could manage.

When India turned back around to gauge the jump, Phoebe saw both concern and anger etched on her features. Suzette pulled up nearly beside her.

"Good grief, does she think she's riding at Aintree Racecourse?" Owen swore with a vehemence that both startled Phoebe and echoed her own indignation that anyone would take such chances with both human and equine life.

Neck and neck now, the two women reached the wall. India's face was a mask of concentration, her hands fisted around the reins. Fear clutched at Suzette's countenance, erasing all traces of her beauty. She reached the wall an instant before India, and as the horse's front hooves left the ground, Suzette squeezed her eyes tight and let the gelding do the work.

Horse and rider made it over in a wobbly arc, and by some miracle landed soundly on the other side and kept going. Owen instantly spurred his horse to a run, and, overtaking Suzette's horse, reached over and snatched the reins from her hands. Several strides later he'd brought them to a halt.

India was not so lucky. With both rider and mount distracted, they'd lost their rhythm, the wordless communication between horse and rider broken. The horse struck its back hooves against the wall and came down on the other side hard, the jolt sending India tumbling headlong over the horse's ears and onto the ground in front of it. At the chaos of hooves and horse and fallen woman, Phoebe's hands flew to her mouth to press back a cry. Then it was over, the horse having come to an uneasy halt, panting and snorting, quivering and shaking its head. Phoebe was off her own horse in a moment and scrambled back toward the wall.

Owen had also dismounted. He was beside her, and then in front, his longer strides swallowing the distance. Theo, too, had jumped from the saddle, made short work of the turf in front of him, and leaped over the wall. The three of them converged on India.

She lay on her side, curled in the fetal position with her head tucked between her shoulders. Her hat lay a few feet away, half crushed on the ground, dented by the horse's hooves. Phoebe knelt beside her and gently brushed tangled locks of fiery red hair back from her face.

"India? Are you all right? Where are you hurt?" For she must hurt. Somewhere, if not everywhere. The girl groaned.

Her eyes came immediately open, a good sign. Phoebe traded looks of relief with Theo and Owen. Owen sent a scathing glare over Phoebe's shoulder, to where Suzette watched them from the saddle.

"The horse," India murmured. And then, with more urgency, "Is he all right?"

While relief poured through Phoebe that India's concerns lay with the horse and not herself, Theo pushed to his feet and went to inspect the animal. Its initial agitation had subsided, and it stood tolerantly as Theo gently assessed each leg, then looked it over carefully. "I think he's fine, but we'll have the veterinary doctor look him over once we've gotten him home."

India, her eyes closing, nodded her thanks.

"Now what about you?" Phoebe said briskly, trying not to frighten the girl any more than she already had been. "Does anything hurt? Did the hooves strike you?"

"I'm not sure. It's all a blur, and I ache all over." India moved her chin up and down, then rolled onto her back and twitched her shoulders. When she tried to straighten her legs, her face contorted. "Oh!"

"What is it?" Phoebe prodded, her gaze sweeping the girl from head to toe.

"My leg. My left one." She attempted to move it again, with the same result. "Oh! That does hurt. It must have twisted in the stirrup as I fell."

Oh dear. "Is it broken, do you think? Can you move it at all? Try again, but slowly."

India did as Phoebe suggested, slowly bending her leg at the knee. It moved as it should, and Phoebe saw no painful angles in the joint or—infinitely worse—bones poking out beneath the leg of her breeches.

"I think it's my ankle," the girl said, and gasped. "Yes, I'm quite sure it's my ankle. Help me to sit up."

Owen placed a hand on her forearm. "Perhaps you shouldn't." He glanced up at Theo. "Can a motorcar be brought out here? If not, a carriage?"

"Of course. I'll ride back to the house and arrange it." Theo loped back to his horse and swung up into the saddle. Within moments, he disappeared into the woods.

"Is she all right?" Suzette walked her horse a few yards closer. "No harm done, I hope."

Phoebe clenched her teeth against what she would have liked to say to the woman. Instead, she helped India sit up, the girl grimacing in pain but not uttering a complaint.

Suzette took her feet from the stirrups and awkwardly dismounted. With a tentative smile, she approached Phoebe and the others. "I do not know what happened. One moment I was following Lord Allerton around the wall, and the next my horse swung about and took off to follow yours. There was nothing I could do."

India's eyes narrowed as she glared up at her fellow mannequin. Phoebe supported her sitting position with an arm around her back, and she felt an angry tension spread down India's spine. "Liar. You did that on purpose, don't say you didn't. What were you trying to do, kill me?"

CHAPTER 4

"I'm telling you it was no accident. She did it on purpose. No one is taking it seriously, but you believe me, don't you, Eva?" India Vale spoke like a plaintive child as Eva helped her out of her riding attire and into a comfortable, soft wool dress. The forest-green color brought out flecks of green in the girl's eyes Eva hadn't noticed before. She helped India onto her bed and settled her against the pillows before setting about rewrapping her injured leg the way the doctor had shown her, snugly but not too tight. She slipped a cushion beneath to keep it raised. A pair of crutches leaned against the other side of the bed near the headboard. She slipped another pillow beneath India's wrist, apparently also injured in the fall.

"I wasn't there," Eva replied calmly. "I didn't see what happened."

"Everyone thinks I'm being dramatic. Lady Allerton, Mademoiselle Chanel, the earl. Even the doctor thinks I'm being contrary because of the pain. As if a sprained ankle and sore wrist could affect my eyesight." With her good hand, India tugged at the cashmere wrap Eva draped around her shoulders.

"I don't at all think you're being dramatic. But you did have quite a shock, and . . ."

"I glanced back an instant before we reached the wall. Suzette was driving that horse on like a madwoman. She wanted me to fall. She's hated me ever since meeting me in London, and all the more so when Mademoiselle Chanel decided she wanted me to model for her."

Eva perched on the mattress facing her. "But does it make sense that Suzette would do something so reckless, when she herself might have broken her neck?"

India clasped Eva's hand. "I didn't say it was an intelligent thing to do, but there was a sick kind of logic to it. She saw her chance and she took it. And it ended up exactly how she wanted it to."

"With you hurt?"

"With me unable to pose for photographs." India leaned back against the pillows, an all-knowing look on her face. "She's jealous, pure and simple."

Eva wanted to persuade her otherwise, but she couldn't erase the sight of Suzette watching India with the photographer yesterday from her mind. In that moment, Eva had glimpsed something close to hatred. Yes, she believed Suzette had been enraged and jealous, but after the way she had been cast aside by Mademoiselle Chanel, who could blame her?

But deliberately causing a riding accident where both humans and horses might have been seriously injured? The two young women were engaged in modeling—nothing more important than that.

Eva's thoughts broke off sharply. Modeling—what could such employment mean to a woman? Though it wasn't something she would aspire to, she thought of some of the other women she knew—Dora, the scullery maid at home, or Connie, the cook's assistant. Or Remie, Mademoiselle

Chanel's personal maid, who skittered about as though fearing a reprimand at every turn. What wouldn't they give to leave their drudgery behind and lead a glamorous life wearing the height of haute couture and being the center of attention? Where would either Suzette or India be without such employment?

Knowing very little about Suzette, she couldn't venture a guess, but she knew for a fact India hailed from a well-to-do family. Though not of the aristocracy, her father had amassed a small fortune in the lucrative world of horse breeding, and his daughter would not be entering into service or any other onerous occupation anytime soon.

Which, now that she thought of it, probably explained the girl's carefree attitude toward yesterday's photo session, why she was so natural in front of the camera. She had little to lose, whereas for Suzette, modeling could mean the difference between maintaining an opulent lifestyle and scavenging for food.

"I could demand to speak with the village constable, you know," India persisted, her plump lips gathering in a pout.

"Yes, that would be your right," Eva agreed, "but I'm afraid you might meet with the same conclusion from him, that this was no more than an unfortunate accident."

India sighed. "Yes, I imagine you're right. Please do me one favor, Eva. Keep that woman away from me."

"I'll do my best. Would you like to telephone your parents? Perhaps arrange to go home?"

India started so suddenly, her swollen ankle fell off the cushion. "Ow! Uh, that is, no. I-I don't wish to worry my parents. There's no need. Perhaps a day or two's rest will set me to rights and I might even be able to pose for a few photographs before everyone packs up and leaves."

"All right, then." Eva studied the girl another moment.

Had she imagined her sudden agitation at the mention of her parents? Hmm . . . Gently she slid India's leg back onto the cushion, and then cupped her hands around the porcelain teapot on the bedside table. "This has grown cold. I'll just pop down to brew another and bring up something to eat as well."

"Thank you, Eva." India allowed herself to sink deeper into her pillows. "Thank goodness for you. I feel as though I have at least one true friend here."

Eva smiled and brushed strands of India's coppery hair back from her face. "I won't be long."

Later, Eva told Lady Phoebe about her conversation with India. They were in Lady Phoebe's bedroom, preparing for dinner. "She absolutely believes Suzette acted deliberately."

"She may be right." Lady Phoebe sat at the dressing table while Eva slid a pair of swan-shaped combs into her hair. "Theo was leading Suzette around to a gate so she wouldn't have to risk jumping the wall, but she broke away from him and took after India like a blazing star. It all happened so fast, but to me it looked as though Suzette was trying to prove something. As if she were both the better mannequin and the better rider, although to be honest, she was not at all competent in the saddle. How she didn't kill herself I'll never know."

Eva took this in as she lifted an atomizer from the dressing table and handed it to Lady Phoebe. "India believes Suzette saw her chance and took it, as she put it."

"That's how it appeared to me, as well." Lady Phoebe squeezed the rubber bulb and spritzed a tiny amount of perfume on her neck and each wrist. "She wanted to catch up to India. As to why, I can't say. I don't know what was in the woman's mind at the time."

"I'm glad it wasn't any worse than it is."

Lady Phoebe agreed.

Eva opened the jewelry cask they had brought from home. Tonight, Lady Phoebe wore a sapphire gown with an overlay of silver tulle. "The marcasite earrings and bracelet?"

"Yes, perfect, although Coco will be sure to find some fault." Although her mouth slanted sardonically, she had made the comment in an offhand way, almost absently. A knock at the door sounded. "Yes, come in."

Lord Owen Seabright stuck his head in the doorway. "Ready to go down?"

Wherever Lady Phoebe's musings had taken her, she instantly returned to the present. "I am, indeed." With a smile that lit her eyes and sent a glow to her cheeks, she came to her feet. "Thank you, Eva. I'll see you after."

"Ah, *mon Dieu*, never have I been so frightened." Suzette Villiers acted as though she were holding court at the lengthy dining room table. Seated at Theo's left, she had regaled them with the morning's ordeal more than once, changing the wording slightly each time, adding new adjectives to emphasize how frightening it had been for her, and insisting the horse had acted of its own free will.

Not according to India Vale, it hadn't. And not according to Phoebe either. She had watched, and so had Owen. He sat opposite and a seat down from her, but their diagonal glances brimmed with incredulity. At the very least, Suzette should have offered an apology and then held her tongue, but she seemed determined to convince everyone she hadn't been at fault. Except that the more she nattered on, the more foolish she sounded. Multiple glasses of wine didn't help.

Julia kept pinching her lips together, as though trying to hold back words she would have liked to utter, while Theo's brow pulled low over his simmering gaze.

"Chessy, you are a horseman." Suzette appealed to the earl. She added emphasis to the end of his name: Chess-ee, giving it a French flair. "Surely you can understand how such things happen."

He flicked a glance across the table at her, grunted, and returned with gusto to his baked fillet of sole. Phoebe couldn't help noticing how little he had contributed to the conversation once the food arrived.

"No more riding for you, my dear," Julia said from the other end of the table. She issued the admonition as though it were nothing more than an expression of concern, but Phoebe heard the determination in her voice. After all, it had been *her* horse that might have been injured. "We mustn't take any more chances with Coco's top mannequin."

"Ha." Seated to Julia's right, Coco grimaced, then smoothed her features. "No, we must not take chances with the *only* mannequin left to us. For now," she added in an undertone. She turned to Julia and swept her with an appreciative glance. "Have *you* ever modeled?"

"Me?" Julia pressed a hand to her bosom. "Hardly. I . . ."

"The granddaughters of earls don't model," Owen explained as a footman offered him a serving of glazed pheasant, "not generally speaking, anyway. Nor do the wives of marquesses." He cast a wink down the table at Theo, who appeared to be half choking on a morsel of food, but Phoebe could see he was trying not to laugh. As far as her enamored husband was concerned Julia may do as she liked, marchioness or no.

"By heaven, they don't." Chessy lifted his wineglass. Before he drank, he gave a little shudder. "Can you *imagine* the talk amongst the old guard, not the least of which would be your own grandmother, Julia. No, no, you model at great risk to your health."

"*Mais non*, that is nonsense." Coco sent an appeal to everyone around the table, as though expecting them all to rise up to defend Julia's right to work as a mannequin. When no one did, she refocused the full force of her persuasive powers on Julia. "You are beautiful, my dear, and you have the figure for it. My clothes would—*non*, they *do*—drape on you just as they should. It is perfection." Next, she petitioned Françoise, seated on her other side and looking sophisticated in an icy-gray silk tunic that fell to her thighs over extra-wide trousers in the same fabric.

"My dear Lady Allerton," the older Frenchwoman said in her cultured English, "you would be the talk of the spring fashion season. You must give it serious consideration."

Julia blushed prettily, as only Julia could, and gave a modest nod. "Thank you, both of you. What lovely compliments you pay me. But . . . oh, I don't know. People always think I'm much more outgoing than I really am. I believe I'd be too shy in front of the camera."

Phoebe frowned and resisted the urge to snort. Julia, shy in front of the camera? She certainly never had been before.

"Nonsense," Coco repeated, more forcefully this time, and Phoebe could see Julia beginning to warm to the subject.

She meant to gauge Theo's reaction to all of this, but instead her gaze landed on Suzette, who had signaled the footman for another glass of wine. Phoebe recalled what Eva had told her about Suzette's expression while watching India with the photographer yesterday. The anger, the loathing. India, confined tonight to her room to nurse her injured ankle and wrist, might very well have lost her life today because of Suzette's . . . what? Ill judgment? Poor riding skills? Or conscious decision to have India out of the way?

The mannequin was staring at Julia the same way now—as if she'd like to make Julia disappear. Phoebe sought Julia's eye, and when she caught it, she shook her head very slightly, but enough that Julia should detect it. She glared a warning with her eyes as well.

Julia only gathered her eyebrows in puzzlement, then shrugged her habitual one-shouldered shrug and laughed at something Coco said to her. Another glance in the opposite direction, this time toward Owen, confirmed that he shared Phoebe's concerns. Chessy, oblivious, had returned to his meal with enthusiasm. Coco continued heaping praise on Julia, appealing in all the right ways to Julia's ego.

"I know." Coco clapped her hands. "We will consult with Narcisse tomorrow. He knows when the camera will adore a face and figure and when it will not. We will let him decide. And if he agrees with me, we will let Claudette and Marcelle work their magic on Julia."

Ah, yes, the three "working members" of Coco's entourage were not present at the table, but instead taking their meal belowstairs. Phoebe gave an inner shrug. They were probably enjoying themselves a good deal more than they would be here, under the critical eye of their employer.

Coco and Françoise continued their persuasive arguments, making Julia titter with amusement one moment and shake her head the next. Phoebe soon found herself distracted by an odd sound outside the dining room. In the next moment the door swung abruptly open, so hard it hit the wall behind it. The sconces trembled, casting wobbly shadows over the table. The crystal tinkled. India stood in the doorway, wrapped in a dressing gown and supported by crutches.

"I hear what's going on in here," she said with an accusing jerk of her chin. "Lady Allerton, I wouldn't listen to Mademoiselle Chanel if I were you. It will only put you in danger."

"*Ma chère fille*, what *are* you saying?" Coco sounded genuinely taken aback. She put down her fork, placed her napkin beside it, and came to her feet. "What dangers could you be speaking of? Are you accusing me of something?"

"No, Mademoiselle, not you. *Her*." Leaning one crutch against her side, India raised her arm, the wrist wrapped in a bandage, and pointed at Suzette.

The other mannequin blushed brighter than the roasted beets on their plates. "*C'est absurde. C'était un accident.*" She shook her head, realizing, apparently, that she had slipped into French. She placed her hands on the table as if to steady herself. The words came haltingly and slurred. "I . . . told you . . . how s-s-s-sorry I am."

"Let's all calm down." Phoebe came to her feet and hurried around the table to the young Englishwoman. "I thought Eva was with you. Please, let me help you back upstairs."

"Eva thought I was going to sleep and went belowstairs for her dinner." India pulled away as best she could without toppling over backward. "And I don't wish to go back upstairs. I won't be shut away and silenced. She tried to kill me today. You all saw it"—she swept her bandaged hand to include Theo and Owen—"and yet you allow her to go on as if nothing happened. To sit at this table and dine on fine food and be ever so amusing. Fools. She's dangerous, and if you've any sense, Lord and Lady Allerton, you'll send her packing this very night."

"Please, India, come with me," Phoebe persisted quietly. She put an arm around the girl. It was then she smelled the brandy on India's breath. How would she have gotten it? Eva certainly wouldn't have brought it to her, especially since the doctor had given India medication for the pain.

The girl refused to move, her gaze riveted on Suzette. "You're going to be sorry about this. *Very* sorry."

After that, Phoebe managed to persuade India to return to her room. She helped her into bed and made her promise to stay put. "Don't make me have to post a guard at your door.

That made India smile, though reluctantly. "You must think me mad."

"I think you're very angry about this morning, and you have a right to be. I saw what happened."

"Then you believe Suzette tried to hurt me."

Phoebe drew a breath as she considered. "Truly, I don't know if it was intentional or not. I agree she had no business being on a horse, even less so riding in an open meadow, and her recklessness could have resulted in serious injuries to you, her, and the horses."

India skewed her mouth, then nodded, apparently satisfied with that. She lay back on the pillows, her long russet braid snaking beside her head.

"Shall I ask Eva to keep you company?"

"No, let her have her evening. I promise I'll be good . . . for now."

Phoebe wished her good night and left to rejoin the others.

Later, a pounding at her bedroom door snapped her out of a deep sleep.

"Phoebe, Phoebe, are you awake?" The door opened and Owen bolted inside. That was all it took for Phoebe to comprehend the urgency of the situation, for Owen promised not to do anything that might compromise her in her grandparents' eyes.

"What is it? What's happened?" She was halfway out of bed and reaching for her wrapper when he stretched out his hand to her.

"Hurry. We've got to get out. There's a fire."

CHAPTER 5

Dread spiraled through Phoebe. "A fire—good heavens, Charles!"

"Julia's got him," Owen was quick to reassure her. "They're already outside, along with his nurse and Hetta. Theo is waking the others."

"Eva."

"The night footman has raised the alert among the staff. She's probably already outside. Come now. We've got to go."

She didn't argue further. Outside in the passage, the sharp scent of smoke burned her nose and scraped at her throat until she coughed. The flames must be close, in one of the bedrooms. Owen kept tight hold of her hand and pulled her quickly along. When she reached the top of the stairs, she saw Coco and Françoise hurrying out of the hall through the front door.

"Go now, Phoebe. Don't stop until you reach the lawn."

But she did stop, unable to move. "What about you?"

"I have to help Theo and make sure everyone gets out. Don't worry about me, I'll be fine. I'll join you before long."

All the guests and a good number of the female staff had gathered along the front drive; others, she was told, had exited through the servants' courtyard from belowstairs. The footmen remained inside, armed with buckets and blankets to fight the fire. Here, in the countryside, it would take far too long to summon the fire brigade.

Eva came running over the moment Phoebe stepped outside. They embraced quickly and then began seeing to the others. Chessy had carried India down the staircase and outside. In only her nightgown, she shivered against the night chill.

The servants had brought lanterns outside and spaced them at intervals on the lawn. A maid went from group to group handing out blankets. Phoebe procured one for India. She scanned the house, searching for the glow of flames. She saw Hetta huddled with baby Charles and his nurse while Julia circulated to check on people. The photographer, clothing mistress, and makeup artist congregated near the hundred-year-old oak beside the drive; Coco and Françoise stood with an arm around the other. All the guests seemed accounted for . . .

No—someone was missing. The thought no sooner slammed through Phoebe's mind than she caught sight of Owen and Theo coming down the front steps. Both men looked grim, their mouths set and their features strained. Theo carried someone in his arms. A nightgown trailed nearly to the ground; arms and legs dangled. The head hung backward over Theo's arm, and a dark braid swung back and forth like a pendulum.

"Who is it?" Eva pressed her fingertips to her lips.

"I'm not sure . . . But I think it must be . . ." Phoebe strained to see through the darkness, but she already knew. At that moment, a scream broke the late-night sibilance of crickets and anxious whispers. It was Coco, and she screamed again.

*   *   *

Ripples of hysteria spread across the front lawn. Another woman screamed, while others burst into tears. Eva couldn't breathe, and she found herself clutching Lady Phoebe's hand, the two of them pressed side by side.

Lord Owen held up his hands. "Please, everyone." But he left off there and offered no reassurances.

Lord Allerton walked past him, carrying the woman down to the lawn. Even in the dark Eva could see the ravages of his war injuries pulling his face tight, stretching the skin and tugging at his mouth. He gently laid the woman on her back. He took the time to straighten her arms and legs and drape the braid over one shoulder.

Mademoiselle Chanel ran across the lawn, her wrapper billowing out behind her and her house shoes making slapping noises against the damp grass. Her assistant, Françoise Deschamps, hurried after her. Meanwhile, the other two women from Maison Chanel—the clothing mistress and the young makeup artist—remained frozen where they were.

Mademoiselle Chanel neared the prone woman and stopped short, her hands pressed to her mouth. She stared down in horror. When no one seemed to know what to do, Eva's legs took her the several yards to where the woman lay.

"Eva, wait." Lady Phoebe had reached out as if to stop her, but then followed.

Kneeling, Eva determined the woman was indeed lifeless, not simply unconscious, for the veil of death had already leached her beautiful face of color. "Suzette Villiers," she whispered. Leaning, she grasped each of Suzette's hands and placed them, one on top of the other, over the woman's torso.

"*Mon Dieu . . . mon Dieu!*" Narcisse, the photographer, still fully dressed, ran up behind Mademoiselle, hesitated, then pushed his way past. Marcelle and Claudette weren't far behind him, but they didn't follow him any closer. They watched with wide, glazed eyes as Narcisse stood over Suzette's body, rocking to and fro as if the world beneath his feet kept shifting. Then he fell to his knees and placed his hand over Suzette's. His head sank between his shoulders. Reverently he lifted her hand to his lips, and then placed it against his heart. His actions astounded Eva, as only the day before he had treated Suzette as though she were of little importance to him or to Maison Chanel.

"Oh!" The cry came from Marcelle, who whirled about and hurried away. Claudette watched her go but didn't follow.

"There are no burns." Lady Phoebe knelt beside Eva. "No scorch marks on her nightgown." She started to reach out, then snatched her hand back and gazed up at Owen Seabright. "I don't understand . . . If the fire didn't . . ."

He breathed out, closed his eyes, and pinched the bridge of his nose. Before he could answer, Lord Chesterhaven appeared at his side. "What happened? Who . . . ?" Chessy's gaze fell to Suzette's lifeless form, and his puzzled features rearranged themselves into a grimace of shock and dismay. "My God. Suzette. How did this happen? Was the fire in her bedroom?"

"There was no fire," Lord Allerton replied, his voice deepened with fatigue.

"How could that be?" Lady Allerton carried her son once more, the baby gurgling and clapping his hands as if this were all a great escapade, and for him, being out of bed at this time of night surely constituted an adventure. Eva glimpsed Hetta's concerned face looming over Lady Julia's shoulder. Hetta nodded when Lady Julia continued, "We all smelled the smoke."

"Yes, smoke." Lord Owen's eyes blazed with a raw emotion. "The flue in her fireplace was closed. It appears Miss Villiers died of smoke inhalation."

"What?" Lady Allerton gasped the word as the shock of this news jolted Eva. "That's not possible. No one in this household would light a fire without first checking that the flue was open. No one." She turned to her husband. "Theo, what do you know about this?"

He ran a hand through his hair and stared at the ground before raising a sorrowful gaze to his wife. "It must have fallen shut."

"Flues don't simply fall shut," his wife snapped.

"My lady, they can." Eva pushed to her feet. She had heard of it before, although the incident had involved a ramshackle cottage and not a grand house like Allerton Place. Still. She spoke quietly, so as not to be overheard by the guests. "If the works have rusted, the hinges can snap and the damper can fall closed."

"But these things are inspected." Lady Allerton looked crestfallen. "Theo, haven't the fireplaces been inspected?"

"Yes, my love, they have. But not in the past year or so. I . . . I don't know when they were last looked at."

"Whyever not?"

Eva knew the answer. Until the marriage of the present Lord and Lady Allerton—until she had brought her money to Allerton Place—there had been no spare cash for things like inspections. It had been all Theo Leighton could do to hang on to his family's ancestral home.

"Julia." Lady Phoebe went to her sister. "It doesn't help to speculate. There needs to be an inspection done as soon as possible."

"Of course there does," Lady Allerton retorted as if her sister were an idiot for even mentioning it. "First thing in the morning. Theo, you'll arrange it."

"Of course, my love."

"What—what do we do with . . ." Mademoiselle Chanel had regained the greater portion of her composure. Though as she pointed down at the body, her fingers trembled.

"We'll have her brought inside. Mrs. Bristol will know what to do," Lady Allerton said. "I'll have tea laid out in the dining room for our guests." To her husband, she added, "You see to Suzette." Then, her face softened. Holding baby Charles on her hip with one arm, she laid her free hand on her husband's shoulder. Not unkindly, she said, "Please." She started away, but stopped and turned back. "And someone must help India inside."

That job fell to Eva, who first ran upstairs and found the girl's crutches, as she adamantly refused to be carried again. Later, belowstairs, the servants were no more ready to return to their beds than the people above. The cook brought out cold meats, cheese, and bread to the servants' hall, and the staff gathered around the table. The housekeeper, Mrs. Bristol; the butler, Mr. Tewes; and the head maid were still upstairs, attending to Miss Villiers. The rest of the Maison Chanel employees, who typically took their meals here, had been invited up to the dining room with the others.

Hetta sat down beside Eva at the table. Her braids, usually wrapped headband style around her head, hung down her back. A flannel nightgown and wrapper encased her stout figure. "Horrible. So very horrible."

"Yes, Hetta, it is. I'm only glad there weren't more people hurt or . . ." Eva left off. That there hadn't been more fatalities didn't take away from the tragedy of Suzette Villiers's death. That lovely young woman, with so much of the world open to her. Whatever jealousies she had harbored, however ill-advised her actions yesterday had been, she hadn't deserved to have her life so abruptly cut short. And in such a manner, something that could easily have been avoided.

Poor Lord Allerton. He'd have to live with the guilt of this for the rest of his life. For, in the end, everything that happened at Allerton Place was his responsibility. And to have foregone the proper house inspections . . .

"Bobby! You're back. Sit down, old man, have something." This came from one of the footmen sitting across from Eva. She twisted round to see another young man hovering in the doorway. It was the first footman, though he wore pajamas and a dressing gown rather than livery. He leaned against the jamb as though his strength had left him all in a rush, his arms hugging his middle, his head down, shoulders bunched, looking . . .

Utterly crushed. Eva's heart went out to him as she realized he must have laid the fires this evening. Good heavens, was he being held responsible?

"Have they given you the sack?" one of the maids asked.

He shook his head. "Not yet. I guess we'll see what the inspector says in the morning." He shuffled into the room. One of his fellow footmen pulled out a chair for him, and Bobby collapsed into it. "I don't understand what could have happened. That flue was open when I lit the fire. I opened it myself. And I *always* double-check."

"Of course you do, mate," another said. "We all do."

"Maybe the lady closed it herself," the cook's assistant suggested.

"Why would she do a foolish thing like that?" someone else asked.

"Maybe she brushed up against the chain or something," the assistant mused, "and it came loose."

"A flue chain shouldn't come loose from its hook so easily," Eva said. The chimneys at Foxwood Hall, and indeed many manor houses, had flues at the top of the chimney, beneath the cap, rather than just inside the hearth. Closing the flue off at the top of the stack prevented animals from crawling in. The damper was opened and closed by a chain beside the hearth. When the damper was open, the chain sat secured on a hook. When the damper was closed, the chain simply hung loose. "Unless the hook was broken?"

"I don't know," Bobby said, sounding beyond weary. "It wasn't when I lit the fire. I secured the chain on the hook and gave it a tug to make sure. I always do."

"Then the mechanism nearer the damper itself must have broken." Something a simple inspection would have caught, Eva acknowledged.

The cook's assistant, who reminded Eva of Dora, the rather flighty scullery maid at home, hugged her arms around herself. "Maybe someone pulled the chain loose later."

"What on earth are you getting at, Mabel?" Mrs. Bristol strode into the room, with Mr. Tewes following in her wake. The servants around the table came to their feet, as did Eva, a sign of respect for the highest-ranking members of the household staff.

Mr. Tewes motioned with his hands for them to resume their seats. "Have you all been speculating? You know the rules about that."

That, too, Eva understood. Gossiping and spreading rumors were strictly forbidden among the servants at Foxwood Hall, which of course didn't mean such talk didn't take place. Just not in front of the butler or housekeeper.

Mabel sat up straighter. "I'm just saying. If the flue was open, it had to have got closed *some* way or other. And the makeup girl . . . what's her name?"

Eva well knew she meant Marcelle, but she wasn't about to supply a name and add to the conjecture.

"Well, anyway . . ." Mabel went on. "I heard her and the other lady, the one who takes care of all the clothes, talking about how no one really liked the head mannequin. They were saying she's mean and stuck-up. And that's exactly who's lying dead upstairs this very moment, the head mannequin."

"That will be quite enough, Mabel," Mrs. Bristol admonished as she took her seat near the butler at the head of the table. "Perhaps tomorrow we'll know more. For now, eat up, and then everyone back to bed."

Eva didn't think she or any of them would get much sleep that night. The damage had already been done, the seed planted, and by morning, she predicted, belowstairs would be buzzing with talk of suspects and motives.

Phoebe backed farther down the drive, looking up at the roofline and raising a hand to shield her eyes from the morning sun. Owen strolled beside her, his hands clasped behind his back. He faced forward, as if he had no interest in the inspection taking place high above them.

"Unless you can read lips," he said, "and at great distances, you're not going to learn much until the inspector is finished."

"It's taking forever."

"Not really. He's only gone up a few minutes ago. And there is more than one chimney that needs inspecting."

Phoebe sighed and turned to face the direction in which they were walking. "Eva said one of the servants suggested Suzette had enemies at Maison Chanel."

"I would imagine envy runs high at a fashion house, especially one presided over by our charming Miss Chanel."

Phoebe nodded at the truth of that. "Still, her implication was that one of the other employees murdered Suzette. To resent someone enough to commit murder . . . Workplace sentiments hardly seem enough to warrant that."

"That's not what you thought at Crown Lily Potteries, when you believed one designer murdered another out of professional jealousy."

"Yes, well, I've learned a thing or two since then, haven't I?" She craned her neck to glance back up at the roof. Another man, an assistant she assumed, had made his way along the slant of the eaves to join the inspector. She spotted Theo higher up, where the roof flattened at its center, protected by a stone balustrade. "It's a quandary, on the one hand hoping this was an accident and not a case of murder, yet not wanting it to be Theo's fault, either. Poor Theo. Poor Julia."

"Poor Miss Villiers."

Phoebe shuddered. Owen's arm slipped around her waist and he drew her closer.

"I'm sorry. That sounded unfeeling of me," she whispered.

He bent his cheek to her hair, then kissed the top of her head. "I don't want it to be Theo's fault either. He and Julia have been through so much to get to this point. They deserve to be happy. And Charles certainly doesn't deserve to grow up in a home shadowed by death, accidental or otherwise."

"I'm afraid it's too late to avoid that."

A *halloo* from the house echoed down the drive, and they stopped again and turned. Theo, still on the roof, was signaling to them. Phoebe and Owen started back.

Inside, they heard voices and the sounds of dishes and cutlery coming from the dining room. Most of the others hadn't yet arisen when Phoebe and Owen had eaten, but they were obviously up now. A lively mixture of French and English spilled from the doorway. Far too lively considering one of their number had died the previous night. High-pitched laughter floated above the other voices— laughter Phoebe recognized as Coco's.

"Do you hear her?" she murmured to Owen.

He made a grinding sound in his throat. "She seems to be enjoying her morning well enough."

"She acted as though she was devastated last night, but her grief was certainly short-lived."

At the clatter of footsteps on the marble flooring, they turned to see Julia approaching.

"Theo just called down on the attic speaking tube," she said briskly. "They'll be down in a moment, he and the inspector. Care to join us in Theo's office?" Though the invitation was cordial enough, Julia's voice was grim. Phoebe studied her sister's features. Usually so vibrant and fresh-looking, as if she slept like a baby every night, this morning a pallor tinged her complexion and half-moon smudges cradled her eyes.

"Yes," Phoebe said, covering her surprise at the invitation. "If you want us there, Julia."

"I do. I'm not sure I can . . ." She shivered and shook her head. "I don't think I can deal with this alone." More quietly, she added, "I'm glad you're here, Phoebe." She smiled up at Owen. "I'm glad you're both here."

They filed into Theo's office and waited in tense silence. Some minutes passed, ticked away irksomely by the clock on Theo's desk. Then, without preamble, Theo and another man strode into the room. Theo stopped short, his gaze landing first on Owen, and then Phoebe, sitting side by side on the leather sofa.

"Please," Julia said without expression. She sat in Theo's wood-framed leather chair behind the desk and made no move to vacate her seat. "I want them here."

Theo nodded once and shut the door. He and the other man remained standing. "Tell my wife what you told me," he said to the inspector.

"My lady." Holding his hat in his hands, the man gave a deferential bob of his head. "The chimneys and the dampers are all sound. Nothing had come loose. If the flue was closed, it is likely because it was already closed when the fire was lit."

"Or closed by someone after the fact." Phoebe reached for Owen's hand, finding confidence in the firmness of his return grip.

"No, that can't be." Julia surged to her feet. "There has to be something wrong. Are you sure you did a thorough check?"

"Quite sure, my lady," the inspector said. He gave an apologetic shake of his head. "My assistant and I took special care to be certain of our conclusions. There is no doubt. The flue did not close because of a mechanical failure."

Julia stood silently for several moments. Turning, she stared out the window at a sweep of front lawn, the sunlight silhouetting her form. Phoebe watched her shoulders rise and fall, and then she swung around again. "Then Robert must be sacked."

"Julia—" Theo began, but she cut him off.

"No, he must go immediately. We can't have that kind of incompetence in this house. A woman is dead, Theo."

He stared back at her, then put his hand on the inspector's shoulder and ushered him from the office. They spoke a few words. Then Theo turned back into the room and shut the door. "The police must be called. There must be an investigation."

"For what?" Julia demanded. "A footman who can't tell the difference between a flue that's open and one that's closed? Again, Theo, a woman *died* . . ."

Phoebe rose from the sofa. "Julia, please. Theo's right. We can't jump to conclusions. Robert's life hangs in the balance as well. We don't want to accuse him without having all the facts."

"What facts?" Julia gave a humorless laugh. "A fire was set in a hearth with no ventilation. The room filled with smoke, and Suzette Villiers died."

"Julia." Theo's sharp tone made them all flinch. "I'm sending for the police and there's an end to it."

Their gazes locked for several seconds. The tension wrapped around Phoebe, holding her immobile while a silent skirmish took place between the pair. Her features set, her jaw clenched, Julia came around the desk. Her nose was pinched as she regarded her husband. "Do as you must, but I won't be a party to it."

Theo's brows gathered in pained mystification. "You'd rather condemn a young man without being certain?"

Julia's features crumpled. In the next instant, she threw the door open and ran from the room.

CHAPTER 6

After putting away Lady Phoebe's laundered riding clothes, Eva took a moment to glance out the window at the gardens below. With Mademoiselle's photography project having been halted, tranquility and order had been restored. Eva wondered for how long. Would the group from Maison Chanel pack up and hurry off to their next destination?

She was about to turn away when motion caught her eye. A flash of blond, the flurry of blue silk. Was that ... Eva pressed closer to the window. Lady Allerton had gone running down from the terrace and showed no signs of slowing. She veered onto a footpath as if choosing her direction at random. As if it didn't matter. Lady Allerton never did anything without good reason, each part of her day always meticulously planned out.

Something new had happened to upset her.

Eva didn't waste another moment, but made her way down the back staircase, through the servants' domains, and outside. A stone flight of steps brought her up to the sculpted hedges that separated the kitchen gardens and greenhouses from the formal gardens. She didn't hesitate in pushing her way through the gate. Only then did she stop. Where had Lady Allerton gone?

Perhaps a few dozen yards beyond the foot of the gardens stood a folly, much larger than the one at Foxwood Hall, though in greater disrepair—and not because the Grecian structure had been designed to look like a ruin. Eva set off in that direction, merely following a hunch but hoping she was right.

Sobs reached her halfway across the expanse of lawn between the gardens and the folly. She sped her steps, then slowed, suddenly realizing Lady Allerton would be alarmed if Eva suddenly burst in upon her. This folly, she now saw, had an inner room, its glass windows concealed by stone latticework and carefully placed foliage. Eva walked up the steps beneath the portico.

"My lady? Are you here?"

"Go away." The words were muffled, but Eva heard the tightness of Lady Allerton's throat.

"My lady, it's Eva. Please let me come in."

"Oh, Eva . . ."

Several second passed. Low sobs emanated from the folly. Eva heard her effort to stifle them. She went to the door, nearly twice her height and covered in bronze filigree. Turning the handle, she gently pulled the door open a few inches. "My lady."

Lady Allerton sat in a garden chair before a wrought-iron table. Her face was turned away from Eva, cradled in her hands, one of which held a handkerchief. Eva went to her and crouched beside her chair.

"My lady, what is it?"

"Oh, Eva," she repeated as if her heart had broken. Apprehension clutched at Eva's heart. Had she argued with her husband? Lady Allerton's next words only heightened Eva's fears for her. "My marriage is over."

"I can't believe that." At least, she certainly didn't wish to. "Why would you say such a thing?"

"Because I'm cursed."

This is not what Eva expected to hear. She reached for Lady Allerton's free hand and moved it away from her face. "There's no such thing."

"There is, Eva. I'm cursed. I'm being punished for being a bad person."

"You're not a bad person, my lady. Far from it. You're a wonderful mother, a loving granddaughter, a good sister . . ."

Lady Allerton shook her head at all of it. "No, I'm not. I've been a terrible sister, and a selfish granddaughter, and . . ." Here she stopped, her lips compressing. She mopped at her tears with the handkerchief. "There isn't anything I wouldn't do for Charles. I love being with him, watching him grow and learn. Perhaps there, I haven't been *so* horrid."

"You're not horrid at all." Eva injected persuasive force into her voice. "Your family loves you. And so does your husband. I've seen how he looks at you. My lady, he's utterly smitten."

"Perhaps, but . . ." Her head went down, the crimped curls falling forward over her face like a curtain. "I wed Gilbert Townsend when I shouldn't have. I had no right marrying him, but I did it for selfish reasons and look what happened. Dead, on the first night of our marriage. And now . . . now *this*."

"Lord Allerton is very much alive, my lady."

"But Suzette Villiers is dead, and there was nothing wrong with the flue. Theo is bringing the police in to investigate."

"That's a good thing, isn't it? To get to the bottom of how that poor thing died?"

Lady Allerton snatched her hand from Eva's and came to her feet. "Don't you see? Gil was murdered. Now Suzette might have been murdered right here in this house. It's a sign, Eva. A sign I should never have married Theo. A sign our marriage will soon be over."

"I don't believe that for a minute." Eva rose to her feet as well. "This case is very different. For one thing, you have no connection to the deceased other than that she died here. And you're certainly not to blame for her being at Allerton Place. You invited Mademoiselle Chanel, and she invited the others. Without your permission or knowledge, I might add." Eva tried to keep the indignation from her voice, but with only marginal success.

"Mademoiselle Chanel," Lady Allerton repeated.

"Yes. Not that she is to blame either, but—"

"What am I thinking? I'm neglecting my duties as a hostess. I should be with the others. Coco must be distraught. Suzette had worked with her for several years now. They were close."

Were they? Mademoiselle Chanel hadn't treated Suzette like a valued employee, much less a close friend, when she decided to replace her with the much younger India Vale.

But she kept this to herself as Lady Allerton dried her tears, blew her nose, and squared her shoulders. Within moments, the resilient, determined Julia Renshaw had returned, and Eva had no doubt that by the time she reached the house, the redness would have vanished from her eyes and her skin would once more glow with its usual vigor.

They walked together partway across the gardens, then parted as Eva returned to the servants' yard and Lady Allerton mounted the steps to the terrace. At the gate, Eva cast a glance over her shoulder. Lady Julia nearly stumbled on a step, her ankle turning. She prevented herself from falling by gripping the railing, but in that moment the vulnerability returned. Lady Allerton's head went down, and Eva watched her effort to collect herself. Then, with a visible breath, she released the railing and continued up the steps and into the house.

Phoebe hurried down from the nursery, where she had stolen some playtime with Charles, to meet Owen in the first-floor sitting room set aside for guests. They'd both noticed no one else seemed to use it and thought they might seize some time alone together. She couldn't help feeling her grandmother's disapproving eyes on her back as she turned the knob and stepped inside, even though there was nothing improper about doing so. The room was furnished in tans and greens, the upholstered chairs quite upright, the settee just large enough to seat two and not terribly comfortable, and the pair of French doors with their sheer draperies, leading out to a small balcony, were sure to give anyone looking up from the grounds a generous view of the room, provided the lights were on.

He arrived a few minutes later. "Sorry to keep you."

"Not at all. I've only been here—"

In three strides he'd crossed the room, gathered her in his arms, and pressed his lips to hers. So much for nothing improper going on here. And yet, even acknowledging they might be seen from below, she didn't push him away, but melted against him and lost herself to the sensation of his mouth on hers.

It went on for some moments, and when they finally came up for air, he pulled back smiling. "Em, yes. Sorry. Couldn't help myself."

She compressed her moistened lips and pressed her fingertips to them. "I suppose we should step away from the doors."

"I suppose that would be wise."

Hand in hand they went to the settee. Before she managed to lower herself onto the velvet cushion, he was at it again—or rather, *they* were, for she was as culpable as he.

His breath grazed her cheek. "How are you holding up?"

And just like that, they returned to the reality of what had happened the night before.

"I'm all right. Julia isn't, though. Eva hinted that I should be extra kind to her, which means she's terribly upset."

He held her hand once they'd settled side by side. "Did Eva tell you what about, exactly? Julia usually takes everything in stride. Even things like this."

"Eva would never betray a confidence, but the fact she said anything at all proves she is exceedingly worried about Julia. I'm assuming it's more than Suzette Villiers having died last night. That's bad enough, of course, but as you said, Julia takes everything in stride. But not this, apparently."

"Perhaps she's afraid there will be legal consequences."

Phoebe started. "Legal consequences? For Julia and Theo? What do you mean?"

"Suzette's family, if she has one, might decide to sue." His brow furrowed. "I know the inspector said the damper wasn't faulty, but a clever solicitor could still claim liability."

"Good heavens. That would be awful. And quite unfair."

"The law isn't always fair, especially when money is involved."

"Then we have to do something. We can't let Julia and Theo take the blame when—"

"Oh, no you don't." He cut her words short with another firm press of his mouth, and then he spoke against her lips. "Forget it, for the time being at least." He drew back to look her squarely in the eyes. "Phoebe, we haven't seen each other for weeks. Forget everything else for the next several minutes and simply *be* with me."

"Yes . . . I'm sorry . . . I . . ."

"Yes, I know how your mind works." His arms went around her again and he held her tightly to him. "If there's a quandary to be solved, you must solve it. But Allerton Place is Theo's and he knows how to protect it. Let him worry about matters, for now. You'll find he's rather astute." Between each word his lips danced across her cheek, to her chin, and down her neck to where the collar of her frock exposed the little dip at the base of her throat. "Perhaps you'll discover you don't always have to save everyone."

"But—"

"Uh-uh. Shhh."

They spoke no more on the matter—on any matter, for the next, oh, Phoebe didn't know how long. Didn't care. And she realized yes, they *had* been apart for too long this last time and the separations were becoming irksome. He in Yorkshire, she in the Cotswolds. It was too far for casual visits and yet . . .

That thought and others like it drifted away until she was conscious only of him—the feel of his lips and his hands, the fresh, outdoorsy scents she had come to think of as essentially his, and the warmth of his cheek against hers. That melting sensation returned, and while a voice inside her said the proper thing to do would be to sit up, move away, even stand, she did none of those things.

At least, not until a soft knock at the partially open door brought them once more to their senses. Owen had left the door an inch or two ajar—ostensibly to lend an air of respectability to their being alone in the room together, but given the positioning of the settee, they would see the door opening before anyone coming in would see them. By the time Theo entered the room, they had sat up, moved apart, with the necessary instant to smooth their rumpled clothing.

Not that Phoebe's frock had become all that rumpled, mind you.

"Sorry to interrupt," Theo said in lieu of a greeting. It was on Phoebe's tongue to insist he wasn't interrupting anything, but he continued, "Owen, if you wouldn't mind, I could use your help when the police arrive. Which should be at any moment."

Owen came to his feet before Theo had finished speaking. "Of course. You telephoned for them, I gather."

"Julia still isn't having it. She's insisting it was all a horrible accident. She even wants me to sack poor Robert." Theo shook his head, his expression bleak. "There is no good answer to any of this, but I won't dismiss a man from his place of work without being certain there's good reason."

"Bravo, Theo." Phoebe rose and went to him, and laid her hand on his forearm.

He searched her features. "This isn't like Julia, this stubborn insistence." He broke off with an ironic twist of his mouth. "No, it *is* like her, as you well know. But not in matters like this. Not when lives are involved. Phoebe, do you understand it?"

"I wish I did, but no. All I can say is she'll come around. She always does." Phoebe believed that with all her heart. In all the years since Papa's death, Julia had by turns retreated into herself, lashed out, gone off without telling anyone where she was going, and half a dozen other abrupt actions that had left the family scratching their heads. Her relationship with Phoebe had often been contentious. But in the end, she had always remembered where her loyalties lay—with her family—and she had never once let them down.

She didn't need to say all that, though. Theo already knew. His single nod revealed that he did.

"You'll come down, then?" he asked Owen. When Owen said he would, Theo left them alone.

Owen took Phoebe's hands in his. "I've never been so utterly annoyed and yet so relieved at the same time. If he hadn't come in when he did . . ."

"Who knows how long before we might have lost our heads entirely," she finished for him. She tried to bite back a smile, but however improper their actions had been, she couldn't regret a single bit of it. And they hadn't actually lost their heads, had they? "Kiss me one more time and then go and help your friend."

Eva was just pushing through the service doorway, on her way to Lady Phoebe's room with fresh flowers for the vase on her bureau, when Lady Phoebe herself stepped out of the upstairs sitting room a little way down the corridor. Lord Owen was right behind her. They looked . . .

Positively giddy. Perhaps not to the undiscerning eye, but after all these years in the Renshaws' employ, Eva had developed nothing so much as a discerning eye when it came to her ladies. The pair obviously didn't see her, for they turned to each other, embraced, and . . .

Goodness. Eva dropped her gaze and hurried the last few steps into Lady Phoebe's room. There she stopped and looked about her, for several moments forgetting why she was even there. Then she noticed the long-stemmed bouquet in her hands. She had selected each bloom from the hothouse herself.

"Oh yes." Taking the vase, she brought it and the flowers into the bathroom, filled the vase halfway with water and arranged the bouquet of roses, peonies, and hollyhocks.

"That's lovely." Lady Phoebe had come in and stood by

the fireplace. Though no fire glowed in the hearth, she appeared flushed as if standing in the heat of the flames. "Thank you, Eva."

"You're very welcome. What else can I do for you?"

"Nothing now." She gazed down at the finely embroidered fire screen. Was she purposely turning away? "The police are here, or will be shortly. Did you know?"

"I didn't. Did Lord Allerton send for them?"

"Yes, despite Julia's objections." She peeked at Eva over her shoulder. "Honestly, I don't know what's gotten into her."

"Be patient," Eva said, understanding but unable to reveal the details that had been entrusted to her. She brought the vase of flowers to the bureau, turning it this way and that after setting it down to find the best angle. She did a little more rearranging. "What have you been up to this morning?"

"This morning?"

Eva could have bitten her tongue. Why had she asked? She had a good notion of what Lady Phoebe had been doing and with whom, but she had no right to pry. Why should it bother her? Lady Phoebe would be hard-pressed to find a better man than Owen Seabright. Eva had long approved of the match. But seeing them together as they had been only minutes ago, so entirely immersed in each other as to be unaware of their surroundings and who might be watching . . . She had felt like a trespasser. She had suddenly felt so . . . unnecessary.

She shook the thought away and, to change the subject, asked, "Is there any more riding planned for the near future?"

Her lady visibly relaxed at that question. "No, but I'm thinking of asking Julia or Theo if I might take a horse out later this afternoon. It depends on what the police have to say. I might want to be on hand for Julia."

"She might need you," Eva affirmed. To herself she added that Lady Julia might not simply need Phoebe today, but always. If Lady Phoebe were to marry Owen Seabright, wouldn't she leave home and live with him in Yorkshire? How far away that was! And would she take Eva with her? Eva had been at Foxwood Hall all through the war years and even before. Initially, she had tended all three Renshaw sisters. More recently, Lady Julia had Hetta, but Eva still looked after Phoebe and Amelia. If Eva went away with Phoebe, who would be there for Amelia? A stranger?

And what about Eva's parents? She would be leaving them, too, and the farm she had grown up on just outside the village of Little Barlow. How often would she see them?

Then there was Miles. Constable Miles Brannock, with whom she had been stepping out these past couple of years; with whom she could envision an eventual future. Not right away, not while her ladies still needed her, nor while Miles worked his way up in rank within the police force, for a man could hardly support a family on a constable's wages. But someday, when the right circumstances presented themselves . . .

Eva could stay in Little Barlow. She knew that. If she appealed to Lord Wroxly, he would see that she stayed on at Foxwood Hall with Amelia. But then Lady Phoebe would be on her own, with a new lady's maid who didn't know her—didn't understand her determined ways, her courage, her intelligence . . . and yes, her fears. The very idea filled Eva with a great, welling sadness . . .

"Eva, are you all right?" Lady Phoebe came closer, reaching out her hand to touch her fingertips to Eva's cheek. "You're not coming down with something, are you?"

"No, I'm fine. I'm sorry, I was lost in thought for a moment. Thinking about poor Robert, I suppose," she fibbed, although it wasn't so very untrue because she *had* been worried about the poor footman, called Bobby by everyone belowstairs, for most of the morning. She returned to the bureau, opened the top drawer, and began rearranging stockings and underthings that were neatly folded and perfectly arranged in the first place.

"Eva." Lady Phoebe placed a hand on Eva's arm to still her. "I can't help but think something else is wrong." She hesitated a moment before letting her hand fall to her side. An awkward silence fell between them, something that rarely, if ever, happened. Not between the two of them.

Eva simply couldn't shake the sensation that life was about to change—was already changing, and that the closeness she had always shared with the young woman beside her would soon end. Lady Phoebe would naturally transfer her trust and her confidences to the man she loved, and while Eva might continue to be her maid and her friend, it wouldn't be the same.

She couldn't say any of this. It wouldn't be right; wouldn't be fair. Lady Phoebe deserved a life of her own, especially after these past years of having to be strong for her family—but not always appreciated for it.

Eva carefully avoided Lady Phoebe's gaze. "I'm unsettled, is all." That much was true.

Lady Phoebe scrutinized her face, while Eva tried to smooth away the evidence of her misgivings. To no avail, apparently. "Oh. I think I see. You must have just been coming up when . . . I thought I heard . . ." Another awkward, painful pause held them both motionless. "Eva, I—"

"No, don't be silly. It's quite all right. I should go back down and see if . . . if there's something Mademoiselle Chanel wants doing so Hetta and Remie aren't run ragged. Unless you need me?"

"Not at the moment, thanks. I suddenly feel the need to go down and hear what the police are saying. I stayed behind just now because Owen would prefer . . ." She shook her head and didn't finish. Eva could guess what Owen would prefer—that Phoebe not involve herself in another potentially dangerous situation. But if he believed he could contain her curiosity, her courage, or her need to do for others . . . well . . .

She gave an inner sigh and started on her way downstairs.

CHAPTER 7

Phoebe hadn't far to go after leaving her room, as low male voices led her the short distance to Suzette's bedroom. She peeked into the open doorway.

Near the fireplace, a constable in uniform held the chain that worked the flue. He tugged a couple of times and slipped one of the links onto the hook that held the flue open. A portion of the chain dangled from the hook and he gave it a jiggle. He tapped the contrivance with his fingertips, first gently, then more firmly. A second policeman took notes. Owen and Theo looked on.

"Well," Theo finally prompted. "What do you think?"

The first officer, a barrel-chested man with a balding pate, shrugged. "Must have been an accident."

"Why do you say that?" Phoebe went into the room. Owen blew out a breath at the sight of her, while Theo appeared to take her entrance in stride. She gestured at the hook and chain. "It doesn't look as though you've knocked the chain loose simply by swatting at it."

"Phoebe," Owen murmured, but she paid him no mind as she waited for the constable to reply.

"As I was about to tell Lord Allerton, the arrangement's

old and flimsy. Look here." He unhooked the chain and held it out for them to see. "This here link is partially open. If that's the link that sat in the hook that night, it easily could have slipped off."

Phoebe moved closer and took the chain from his hand. As he'd indicated, one link wasn't quite closed, but the gap between the two ends was minuscule and wouldn't likely have made a difference.

"We've been through the room," the man went on, "and there's no sign of anything out of order. No indication anyone but Miss Villiers had been in here that night."

"What would you expect to find?" Phoebe asked him bluntly. "Anyone could have come into the room—the door wouldn't have been locked would it, since Mademoiselle Villiers basically passed out as soon as she was put to bed. That also means she would not have been awake to knock the chain loose herself. So how could this have been an accident?"

Both constables wrinkled their noses. The one doing the talking angled a glance at Theo, who only shrugged and waited for the answer. The man sighed. "If the footman who lit the fire didn't secure the hook properly, the tension from the damper might simply have tugged the link off the hook in time."

"But the chimney inspector said everything looked sound to him."

"Phoebe," Owen murmured again. "Please."

She pivoted to face him. "It's not fair to blame a footman out of hand. Especially when there are so many people in this house, more than one of whom might have held a grudge against Suzette."

"If you're accusing India," Theo started, but Phoebe interrupted.

"I'm not specifically blaming anyone. I'm only saying the matter needs further looking into."

"Did I hear correctly? The chain wasn't secured properly?" Julia stood in the doorway as she asked her question, and then stepped inside.

"We aren't sure yet," Phoebe replied, but the constable cut her off.

"It does appear that way, my lady. Despite what this young woman has to say . . ." He trailed off with a frown in Phoebe's direction.

"My sister often has her own way of looking at things," Julia said peevishly. "What's important are the conclusions you've drawn, Constable."

"We've found nothing to say it was anything other than an accident, perhaps preventable if the person who lit the fire had taken better care to hook the chain properly."

Julia nodded. "That's what I thought."

"Perhaps a detective should be called in," Phoebe suggested.

Julia ignored her. "Thank you both for coming. You've set our minds at rest and now we know what action to take."

She saw the officers down to the hall herself, leaving Theo, Owen, and Phoebe alone in the room. "What does she mean, action to take?" Phoebe fisted her hands on her hips. "What is she planning to do?"

"Sack Robert, as she said earlier," Theo supplied. He pulled at his chin and shook his head.

"Rotten for Robert," Owen commiserated. "Is there nothing you can do?"

Theo looked up at that, his eyes meeting Owen's directly. "There is. I won't let him be dismissed. I don't know if Phoebe's right or not, but the constable did say this was an unfortunate accident. I won't see a young man tossed out because of an accident. The inspector never mentioned the broken link in the chain, though he should have."

"It isn't broken." Phoebe lifted the dangling chain and held it aloft. "It's slightly separated, nothing more. Even if this particular link did sit on the hook, how on earth could it have opened enough to come loose, and then closed itself back up again, except for this sliver of a gap?"

Owen lifted the chain from her palm and peered at it closely. "She does have a point." When Phoebe reacted to that with an I-told-you-as-much lift of her brows, he dropped the chain. It swung and scraped against the woodwork of the hearth. "That doesn't mean you need to involve yourself."

"It certainly does not." Julia was back and moved through the doorway with an imperious lift of her chin. "You're not to interfere, Phoebe. Need I remind you again that this is my home, mine and Theo's. We will run it as we see fit. Theo, as I've said before, Robert must go. Immediately. There's no longer any question."

"No." The word burst from Phoebe's lips.

"Phoebe, you needn't be here." Julia pointed the way to the door.

With a rising sense of misery, Phoebe silently appealed to Theo, who in turn stared hard at Julia as if seeing her for the first time. So many emotions filled his eyes. That he adored his wife could never be questioned, for the blaze of love was plain to see, as was the depth of his respect for her. But his nostrils flared and his mouth flattened. "No, Julia. I will not dismiss Robert. And neither will I dismiss Phoebe's suspicions."

Julia's lips parted but no sound came out. Her hand went to the base of her throat. Phoebe had never seen her sister speechless. The air between her and Theo felt charged and ready to spark. Phoebe's gaze darted to Owen, and he nodded ever so slightly. Together they slipped from the room and hurried down the stairs, putting as much distance as possible between themselves and the storm about to break.

Later, Eva found Robert in the boot room, perched on a stool and half-heartedly rubbing polish into a pair of Hessian-style riding boots—Lord Allerton's by the looks of them. Each circular swipe of the cloth seemed to be an afterthought, the young man's gaze pinned somewhere on the wall beside the door. He didn't even look over at the sound of Eva stopping in the doorway.

"Bobby? Are you all right?"

The cloth went still. "Hello, Miss Huntford. Can I do something for you?"

"No, Bobby. I only wanted to tell you not to pack your bags too quickly." She offered him a warm smile. "You might not be going anywhere." Indeed, Lady Phoebe had found her earlier and told her how Lord Allerton was determined not to make any rash decisions without further investigation.

"We'll see, Miss Huntford, though I appreciate the sentiment."

Eva crossed the threshold. "No, it's true. I can't tell you exactly what I heard, but you're not to lose heart. For what it's worth, I don't believe you had anything to do with that flue being closed."

He stared down at the boot in his lap, before carefully placing it and the rag on the table beside the boot's mate and the open can of polish. "Miss Huntford, I truly thank you for that. I don't know what happened, but I'm certain all was as it should have been when I lit the fire and left that room."

Eva went to stand across the table from him. "Exactly what did happen that night? From the very beginning. How many fires did you light up on the first floor?"

He eyed her warily, his head turning slightly to one side. "Why is it important to you?"

"A good question," she admitted with a nod. "If you promise not to spread it about, I'm very interested in learning the facts of how Miss Villiers died. And I certainly don't want to see an innocent person blamed, whether it's believed to be an accident or otherwise."

He didn't look quite satisfied by this explanation and continued studying her through narrowed eyes. Whatever thoughts passed through his mind, however, he obviously concluded that answering her question couldn't hurt his situation. "Only two," he replied, holding up his index and middle fingers. "One in Mademoiselle Chanel's room, and the other in Miss Villiers's. The others all said the night was mild enough they didn't need a fire."

"All right, so which fire did you light first?"

"The one in Mademoiselle Chanel's room. Her maid watched me the whole time. Practically stood over my shoulder as I placed the logs and kindling and set it alight. Said I'd better make sure the fire wouldn't smoke, and I told her I knew what I was doing. Which I do. And before I did any of that, I opened the flue and secured the chain." He said this last with emphasis.

"And before you left the room, you had the fire going?"

"I did, but low. I always build them so they don't flame high until they're poked a bit."

"The same in Miss Villiers's room?"

"Of course the same." His voice rose with a steely edge of anger. He compressed his lips. "Sorry, Miss Huntford. Don't mean to holler at you. But yes, I always follow the same exact steps. Mr. Tewes taught me himself when I became a footman."

Eva frowned at that. "Forgive me for asking, but aren't you first footman?" When he nodded, she asked, "Why is the first footman given the task of lighting fires at all? Why not the second footman, or one of the maids for that matter?"

"Normally, they do, but when we've important guests, Lady Allerton likes for only the footmen to do it. She doesn't like the maids to be seen, says footmen present a more distinguished image. That night was my turn."

"I see. So then, when you left Miss Villiers's room, her fire was burning low, the flue was open, and there was no smoke coming from the hearth?"

"That's right."

"Miss Villiers hasn't a personal maid, and she was rather incapacitated when she was brought up to bed. Who would have been expected to poke her fire to life? You?"

"Crikey, Miss Huntford, no! I'd never enter a lady's room while she was in it. Not for any reason. Not even if she asked me." A wash of red stained his face.

"I believe you. So . . ." She trailed off, thinking. And then hit on the answer. "Remie."

"What?"

"Not a what, Bobby, a who. If Miss Villiers couldn't do for herself that night and I wasn't asked to help, it must have been Mademoiselle's maid who helped her to bed and, perhaps, poked the flames in the hearth to life." Of course, that didn't mean Remie had been negligent or malicious. The flue might have been functioning properly when Remie left the room. Someone else might have entered later . . .

"*Ahem.*" Mr. Tewes, dressed in his formal daytime attire of black morning coat, cravat, and gray striped trousers, announced his arrival with a discreet clearing of his throat. He came in, looking none too pleased about his current errand. "Bobby, we need to speak."

The footman drew a breath. "Here it comes."

Eva's heart lodged in her throat. Had Lady Phoebe been

wrong about Lord Allerton putting his foot down on the matter? "Please, he isn't being sacked?"

"No, he's not. But perhaps you should leave us, Miss Huntford."

"No, Mr. Tewes, Miss Huntford can stay." Bobby gave a grim chuckle. "I feel she's my one true ally here."

"No, not your only ally," the older man said. "I don't believe you were at fault, either. Not for a moment."

"But Lady Allerton does." Bobby's chin went down.

"*Lord* Allerton does not," the butler informed him with no small measure of doggedness. Then he sighed. "But because his wife is so adamant you're to blame, for now— and I emphasize *for now*—you'll being bumped down to third footman. Jonathan will be acting first footman until the matter is cleared up."

"Oh, but that's not fair," Eva blurted before she thought better of it. "Bobby's being punished without proof he's done anything wrong."

"That may be," Mr. Tewes said, the regret plain in his voice, "but these are Lord Allerton's orders. Oh, and . . ." Here he sighed again. "I'm afraid your pay will reflect the fact."

"I figured as much," the young footman murmured. He clamped his lips and swallowed.

Eva wanted to cry for him. He might have a family— parents, brothers and sisters—who were dependent on the money he sent home. That was the case for so many servants, including some Eva worked with at Foxwood Hall. Or he might be saving, putting away every penny he could so someday he might change his life by moving away and taking up a new profession. It would take him far longer to do so on a third footman's salary.

"Well, then." Mr. Tewes drew himself up. "I'm sorry, and that's a fact. However, we must get on with things, mustn't we?"

Bobby nodded. "Yes, sir, Mr. Tewes."

"There's a good lad. Chin up. This matter will right it-self in time." With that he turned on his heel and went about his business.

"I'm so sorry, Bobby," was all Eva could think to say. Small consolation, that.

"It's all right, Miss Huntford. At least I'm not out on my ear." He glanced down at the pair of boots on the table, placed one in his lap, and took up the rag again.

Eva resisted the urge to smooth his hair, as she might have done with her brother years ago before the war had taken him. She smiled at the memory of how those tender gestures used to make Danny toss his head, swat her hand away, and demand she stop babying him. She guessed Bobby wouldn't take to such overtures with any better grace than Danny, so she left him to his work and went to tell Lady Phoebe about this latest development.

Though the sky had turned overcast, Phoebe shaded her eyes from the glare of the photographer's lighting equip-ment. Coco had insisted on proceeding with the pho-tographs today. As if nothing had happened. As if one of the two mannequins who should be modeling this clothing hadn't met a tragic death.

Coco had persuaded India to leave not only her bed but the house as well. Now they were in the gardens, near the fountain with its cherubs and satyrs, preparing for the next round of pictures. India currently wore a military-inspired ensemble, but with a figure-skimming looseness rather than restrictive tailoring.

India leaned on her crutches near the fountain while Coco and Narcisse argued about the artistic goal of the photos about to be taken. Coco disagreed not only with the photographer's choice of location within the gardens but the harsh light and subsequent shadows thrown onto the carved marble by the reflectors and bounce boards Narcisse used to direct and intensify the sun's natural light. Though the pair quarreled in French, Phoebe caught the gist.

"Will you not trust me for once? I know what I am doing."

"The results are going to be too severe. Too unforgiving. Look at her." Coco gestured at India, who seemed not to be following the debate but rather was admiring the nearby flower beds and the trees tinged with early autumn gold. "She is a child. She is everything that is soft and new. These cold marble carvings and your harsh lighting might have worked for Suzette, but not for this one."

Narcisse grimaced at the mention of Suzette. He turned partly away, hands on his hips. "We should not even be doing this. Not yet. She died only a night ago. *A night ago*, Mademoiselle! This is wrong."

"It is not wrong. Would she want us to mope?"

"Perhaps."

"Who pays your wages?"

He pushed a breath between his teeth. "You."

"Yes. And I must have these photos before it is too late to attract enough interest to open a show in London. I am sorry, but we must continue. Now, about the reflectors. If you would simply take them away and shoot with natural light—"

"You wish to show your fashions in London? Then you need photos that captivate and spark the imagination, not bore people to death. You want to create a story, a mood. A world other women will want to inhabit."

"And this fusty old fountain will do that? How?"

Narcisse shook his head, his youthfully handsome features tight with frustration. "I cannot tell you exactly how. I can only show you. Later, when I develop the film."

Coco glared at him, her arms crossed, one corner of

her lip caught in her teeth. Then she beckoned India over. She came with tentative, one-footed steps aided by her crutches.

"Yes, Mademoiselle?"

"Do as he tells you." She threw up her hands as if in surrender. "And let us both hope he makes something of today, so we will not have to start all over tomorrow."

"All right, Mademoiselle," India said brightly, apparently unperturbed by the past several minutes. She giggled. "I just hope I don't fall on my face."

"If you do," Narcisse said in English as he approached her, "I shall take brilliant shots of you on the ground." He used his fingertips to pull strands of coppery hair loose from the chignon at her nape, studied her, and freed a few more to float around her face. "All right, come."

He guided India into the position and pose he wanted, and then moved his reflectors around her to capture the weak sunlight just so. The scene burst to life in a dramatic display of light and shadow, with India's features pale yet vividly striking against the backdrop of the fountain and the foliage behind it. Narcisse had been right, Phoebe decided, although as he had said, the proof would be in the developed photos.

Coco drifted over to where Phoebe looked on. "Did you understand any of that?"

"Enough. I think you're right to trust your photographer." The lighting wasn't all he had been right about. It *was* wrong of them to return to work so soon after Suzette's death. Disrespectful. But just as Julia tended to get what she wanted, so did this woman. Except, Narcisse had managed to convince her to try today's shoot his way. Good for him.

And good for Phoebe. For the next few minutes, at least, she seemed to have Coco all to herself. Even Julia hadn't come out to watch yet, though Phoebe expected her any moment. Would Coco again try to persuade her to pose?

"I didn't think India would be able to pose for photos this soon," Phoebe commented as she and Coco watched Narcisse help India lean carefully against the fountain before taking her crutches away. The girl laughed nervously but kept her balance.

"She is special, this one. Born to be part of the fashion world."

"Like Suzette?" Phoebe watched Coco's features, noting the slight pinkening of her cheeks at mention of the deceased mannequin. "Even *I've* seen her face in the magazines, and as you and my sister have pointed out, I don't take much interest in fashion."

Did she expect Coco to apologize or contradict her? The woman only said, "Yes, Suzette had talent, but lately . . ."

Phoebe waited. When Coco didn't say more, she prompted, "Had her interest waned lately?"

"Not her interest. She loved the attention. Craved it. Always. But she had begun to lose her appeal somehow. Lost that quality, the spark, that made her special. Made her stand out in a room full of other beautiful women. It was not her age. Nothing physical. She simply did not sparkle anymore." Coco shrugged and watched Narcisse turn India in profile to the camera. "This one—she is just coming into her own. She does not yet know her own potential, and that is when a mannequin is at her best."

"Her ego won't get in the way, you mean."

"*Oui*, I suppose that *is* what I mean."

"I'm sure their backgrounds are very different. Where was Suzette from?"

"The north somewhere. Some little village." She frowned in thought. "Perhaps she said in the Lorraine region."

Perhaps? The answer surprised Phoebe in its vagueness. The two women had worked together for several years. Did they never discuss their past lives?

She kept those questions to herself and assumed a neutral expression. "The north of France saw the worst fighting during the war, I understand."

"*Oui.* I stayed in Paris, so I did not see it myself. We had our hardships in the city, to be sure, especially in the beginning, but within a year or so, order prevailed. Women filled the workforce—as here, *oui?*"

"Yes, that's right."

"And little by little, the shops and cafés and theaters reopened."

"Suzette must have spoken of her struggles, though."

"Not much."

How reticent the woman was being about her former favorite. How easily she dismissed Phoebe's questions about her. But Phoebe wasn't ready to give up. "How did you find each other?"

She didn't imagine Coco's sigh of impatience, however quiet it was. "In the third year of the war, Suzette came to Paris. I discovered her at a tiny theater on the Left Bank. I don't even remember the play. Ah, she had no voice for drama, or for song, but her face. Such classical perfection, *non?*"

"She was beautiful, yes."

"Beauty—eh." She swiped a hand at the air. "Anyone can be beautiful. It is how one carries oneself, how one uses the facial expressions to convey emotion—this is what makes the difference between mediocrity and true talent."

"I see. Do you think something in Suzette's background, from her past, could have inspired her talent?"

"It is possible." The woman gave a quick lift of her bold

eyebrows before shrugging in dismissal. "But not likely. One is either born with it, or not. Besides, as I said, she did not speak much of her home, and I did not ask." Another shrug. "And now I must pay closer attention to what my photographer is doing."

"You still don't trust him completely, do you?" It was an observation, not a question.

"I trust no one completely when it comes to my business. That is the secret of my success."

Phoebe watched the designer walk over to the photographer, and then approach the mannequin. They spoke some words that made all three laugh. But did the two of them, India and Narcisse, understand they would never have Coco Chanel's full confidence, or her compassion? She knew so little of Suzette beyond the surface details of the young woman's life. Had she never thought to delve deeper, to learn what forces had forged Suzette's spirit? No, she apparently had been happy to accept Suzette on face value—especially considering the value Suzette had brought to Maison Chanel's profits.

Phoebe believed Narcisse could take care of himself. Something in his bearing spoke of worldliness and perseverance. But Phoebe worried for India. The girl was young and couldn't have much knowledge of the world yet. Presently, she basked in the attention shown her by Coco and Narcisse. How long before they turned their backs on her?

"Hello, Remie." Eva pushed the door to Mademoiselle's room more fully open and ignored the look of irritation on the other lady's maid's face. "Can I help you with that?"

Remie stood at the side of the canopied bed, in the middle of changing the linens. An odd time to be doing it. "*Merci, mais non.*"

Eva didn't take the refusal as a hint to leave and ventured farther into the room. "Do you always wait until midday to freshen Mademoiselle's room?"

"Mademoiselle . . . how do you say? . . . *rested* after *le petit déjeuner.*"

"And she has you change her sheets?" Eva couldn't keep the surprise from her voice. She did know of employers so exacting as to make their servants change the bedlinens more than once a day, but such individuals tended to be rather high up on the nobility ladder and had brought such idiosyncrasies with them from the Victorian age. But even the Earl and Countess of Wroxly didn't insist their servants perform unnecessary tasks. And Ladies Julia, Phoebe, and Amelia would certainly never expect such a thing.

Mademoiselle certainly thought highly of herself, didn't she?

"Let me give you a hand." Again ignoring the reluctant look on the other woman's face, Eva went to the opposite side of the bed and took hold of the edge of the top sheet. They snapped it briskly between them and let it float to the mattress with creaseless precision.

"Remie," Eva said in faltering French as they took up the pillows to change the cases, "did you help Mademoiselle Villiers to bed the night before last night?"

The woman froze and then replied in French with a question of her own. "*Pourquoi?*" *Why?*

"Because, as I'm sure you've heard, one of the footmen is being accused of lighting the fire without opening the flue. But if you helped Mademoiselle to bed, you would have seen or smelled smoke at the time. Unless there wasn't any."

"There was no smoke." She slid a pillow into its satin case.

"Then Robert couldn't have left the flue closed. He lit the fire before Mademoiselle came up to bed. It must have fallen closed afterward." Or was purposely closed by someone. "Did the police talk to you about it?"

"*Oui.*"

Remie turned her back on Eva to continue changing the pillowcases, and Eva surmised she had gotten all the information she would out of the woman. Remie claimed there had been no smoke in the room when she helped Miss Villiers to bed. Assuming she was telling the truth, a new scenario occurred to Eva. The police believed the gap in one of the links caused the chain to slip from the hook. But perhaps the gap occurred after the fact, when someone purposely tugged the chain loose.

Could Remie have any reason to murder Miss Villiers? True, by all accounts the mannequin had been difficult to work with, but Remie hadn't worked for or with Miss Villiers. It seemed to Eva that her fellow lady's maid had one immediate goal—to keep Mademoiselle happy so Mademoiselle wouldn't turn her temper on Remie. If Remie had wished to kill anyone . . .

Well. Eva bit back a cynical laugh and left the other woman to complete her task. It was time to strike up a conversation with the next person on her list.

CHAPTER 8

Eva found Marcelle, the makeup artist, outside in the garden near the clothing tent. With only one mannequin who needed her skills at present, she sat at her dressing table, chin in her hand, her cases and triptych mirror at the ready. By the fountain, India Vale posed for photos, while Mademoiselle Chanel stood near the photographer and his tripod. She spoke sharply, snippets carried on the breeze, and gestured with her hands, and then went to change the angle of the hat India wore.

Without waiting to be invited, Eva took the chair beside Marcelle's, as though she had come to be made up like a mannequin.

"*Bonjour*, Miss Huntford." Marcelle didn't lift her chin from her palm as she spoke. She looked decidedly glum.

Eva crossed one leg over the other, settling in and implying she had no intention of leaving anytime soon. "How are things going today?"

"The same as any other day," Marcelle intoned. She stared across the way to the fountain, where the photographer was just then helping Miss Vale to perch at the edge of the basin. The mannequin wore a deep blue pleated skirt and matching jumper ensemble, with ivory leather oxfords and an ivory beret. "She is on her third outfit. I am surprised Mademoiselle did not call you to help. Claudette has been getting her changed."

"I see her crutches there leaning against that tree." Eva shaded her eyes as she gazed at the photographer's make-shift outdoor studio. "Then her ankle isn't much better."

"*Non.* But she does not complain. Mademoiselle likes that about her."

"Do you find her easy to work with?"

Marcelle shrugged. "It has only been two days. Everyone is easy at first. They are excited to be the center of the attention. Happy to do as they are told."

"And then?"

Marcelle harrumphed.

"I take it you don't always like working with mannequins."

The girl shrugged. "It depends. But it is my job."

"Your English is quite good," Eva said. She had noted the fact right away. "All of you."

"Mademoiselle insists upon it. It is a condition of employment that we learn fluent English. Besides expanding into this country, she hopes to take Maison Chanel to America someday."

"I see. That's very ambitious."

"*Oui.*"

Eva studied the reticent girl. Like Eva herself, Marcelle wore nearly all black, except for the gray shirtwaist beneath her open cardigan. The outfit appeared to be one of Mademoiselle's signature jersey suits, but not especially tailored to Marcelle's pleasantly rounded figure. The cardigan pulled slightly around her shoulders, and the skirt hugged her thighs. Perhaps a castoff from the previous year's collection? Further, as much as Marcelle showed true talent in making up others, she herself wore no cosmetics. Granted, her lashes were black and thick and had no need of enhancement. So far, the makeup artist had shown very little variation in her daily attire, wearing black and muted tones as if she didn't wish to bring attention to herself. Very much like a lady's maid, who never sought to outshine her employer. Perhaps Marcelle lived by the same rule, except it was the mannequins whom she must never compete with.

She wondered, had Suzette Villiers treated Marcelle with the same disdain many wellborn ladies showed their maids?

"You didn't care for Suzette," Eva ventured.

Marcelle's eyes narrowed as she continued to stare at the group in front of the fountain. She tugged her cardigan closer around her. The day had grown cooler than it had been previously. "We had more in common than you might think," she said at length.

The comment, entirely unexpected, took Eva aback. "Did you? Such as what?"

"We both hailed from the Lorraine region, in the north of France. We both saw much fighting during the war years. We both suffered at the hands of the invading army."

"Goodness. I would think such experiences would forge a strong bond between you."

"*Non.* Suzette liked to pretend it did not happen. That the Germans did not steal our homes and food, that they did not destroy whole villages and the people who lived there."

Eva slid her hand along the tabletop to cover Marcelle's. "I'm sorry. It must have been dreadful."

Marcelle shuddered.

"Did you lose loved ones?"

"*Mon père*," Marcelle whispered. She heaved a tremulous breath. "And later, my sister died of the hunger."

"I'm so terribly sorry. I lost my younger brother, Danny, in the fighting." Eva tightened her hand around Marcelle's, noting how small it was, how delicate the fingers despite the girl's overall plumpness.

Marcelle met Eva's gaze and nodded, her own eyes dark and gleaming with emotion.

How could Marcelle and Eva, perfect strangers, bond over this common experience, but not Marcelle and Suzette, who had shared so much more? Though Eva wished she could simply be this young woman's friend, she knew she must continue to probe. "And Suzette? Had she lost people?"

"As if she would have cared, but *non*. They were spared."

"Why is that?"

Marcelle shrugged. "I do not know. Some were lucky."

"Was she . . . unkind to you?" Eva asked on a hunch.

"No more so than to anyone else." Marcelle drew her gaze away from the activity at the fountain to again meet Eva's gaze. "You wonder then, why I did not care for her. I will tell you. She was a vain, careless, selfish *little* girl. A child in a woman's clothing. She was older than me, yes, but only in years."

"I see. Did the others think so, too?"

"Some. Not all. Beauty blinds those who gaze upon it, does it not, Miss Huntford?" Marcelle made a little sound of disgust. "And some are willing to overlook faults when it is to one's advantage."

Marcelle had turned back to the fountain, and Eva followed her gaze—to the photographer. It suddenly dawned on her that perhaps Marcelle had feelings for Narcisse, a regard that went unreturned. Perhaps Narcisse had turned his attentions on Suzette.

Eva frowned. From what she had observed of Suzette and Narcisse that first day in the gardens, he had been only too eager to replace her with young India. He had rushed Suzette through her photos. And yet . . .

Her thoughts returned to the night before last, to Suzette, laid out on the ground, lifeless, and Narcisse falling to his knees beside her, kissing her hand . . .

"Marcelle"—she prodded the girl's attention back to their conversation—"were Suzette and Narcisse in love?" Had Suzette spurned him, and as a result, enraged him?

Again, Marcelle made a sound of disdain in her throat as she surged to her feet. "Love? Suzette? *Non.* She could not love. To love, one must have a heart, a conscience. She had neither. Nor morals. I pity any man who ever fell into her clutches. Now, if you will excuse me." She hurried down the path and through the gate into the servants' yard.

"Another scone, India?" Phoebe lifted the tiered porcelain tea stand and offered its delicacies to the girl, sitting next to her in the other armchair beside the drawing room hearth. The small table between them held their cups and saucers, while the teapot sat on low table before them. At the far end of the room stood the partially empty racks of clothing, those not used in today's shoots, which had taken up permanent residence there for the duration of Coco's visit.

The others were taking their afternoon tea on the terrace, but India had determined that after the morning's photo shoot she had had enough of the outdoors for the time being. Phoebe had jumped at the chance to spend time alone with her. Owen had begun to offer to join them, but Phoebe had given him an adamant message with a glare and a quick shake of her head.

"These are wonderful." India chose one raspberry and one orange almond scone and plopped them onto her plate. "Better even than our pastry chef's at home, and he's supposed to be one of the best. Mama found him in Monaco just before the war."

"Did she?" Phoebe selected one as well and placed the stand back on the sofa table. "Do your parents travel often?"

"Lots before the war. They left me home with my governess, of course." India spoke around the crumbs in her mouth. "I didn't mind. I got to spend my days riding and helping Mr. Sampson—that's our head groom—and honestly, Dodgers—that was my governess, although her name was actually Miss Dodson—was bags of fun when she wasn't making me study. Oh, my, this lemon curd!"

"And now that the war is over? Are your parents traveling again?" Phoebe wondered whether they even knew their daughter was here.

"Mm," she replied with a nod, "they're getting back to their wandering. And once again, I don't mind. Gives me more freedom."

"To do things like modeling." Phoebe lifted her teacup for a sip. "Do they know?"

"I wouldn't think so. Leastwise, I haven't mentioned it. Don't think they'd much care, though."

"It's exciting, isn't it?" Phoebe pretended to consider. "Or is it? Perhaps after the first few shots it begins to feel rather all the same?"

"Oh no!" India washed down her latest bite with a swallow of tea. "It's jolly exciting. I adore wearing Mademoiselle's styles. I predict she'll be huge in England someday soon, when people have money again. Do you think she'll let me take anything home, when we're all finished?"

"I couldn't say, really." Phoebe couldn't help smiling at the girl's enthusiasm. She sobered quickly enough. Of everyone here, India had been the most hostile toward Suzette, and had the most reason to wish ill on her. The question was, how ill? "It's a shame you and Suzette had such a falling-out before she could help you with your modeling. Or were you at odds beforehand?"

"Not at all, at least not on my side." India set her now-empty plate aside. "It was so exciting meeting everyone in London. It was at dinner one night at Simpson's in the Strand—do you know it?"

"I've dined there a time or two, yes."

"I was there with my cousin, and Mademoiselle, Chessy, and Suzette came in. Chessy and I are well acquainted, you see, because he's such a good customer of Papa's. Horses, you know."

"Yes, I know."

"Yes, well, Chessy introduced me to Mademoiselle and Suzette. I was a little surprised, considering he'd always treated me like Papa's little girl, but suddenly he acted as though he and I were great chums. I was delighted to meet Mademoiselle. I've seen her fashions in Mama's magazines."

"And she was obviously delighted to meet you," Phoebe commented, "since she invited you down here to model."

India went quiet a moment. "I believe that was exactly the moment Suzette took a dislike to me. Which only grew once we arrived here and Mademoiselle decided I would be the focus of the shoots. As if I were to blame for that."

"She took her frustration out on you," Phoebe observed. "And that in turn made you very angry."

"Of course it did," India snapped. "She could have killed me."

"Angry enough to wish to get even with her?" Phoebe asked after a pause.

"Yes." India's lack of hesitation, and the steadiness of her reply, shocked Phoebe. She hadn't expected the girl to admit to such a thing. But then India went on. "I wanted to see her in the same pain I felt. And I wanted her tossed out of this house. But the other night, after the scene I caused in the dining room, I went back to my room and stayed there. All night," she added with a significant look at Phoebe. "I know the police said what happened was an accident. But you don't think so, do you?"

"I'm not certain," Phoebe lied, then changed the subject with another question. "You'd been drinking before you came down, hadn't you? You're rather young for that, aren't you?"

"Am I?" India shrugged. "Narcisse brought me a bottle of brandy. He said it would help with the pain in my wrist and ankle. It did help, with the physical pain. But not with the anger. It only made it worse."

"Spirits can do that."

The terrace doors opened, and the others streamed into the drawing room between the racks of clothing, cutting Phoebe's talk with India short. But she'd been left with much to think about. Would India have admitted to the breadth of her anger if she had murdered Suzette? The girl was ingenuous, to be sure, but stupid? Phoebe didn't think so.

Narcisse had apparently come to her room that night, and Phoebe would have liked to know how long he stayed. Did he hand over the bottle and leave, or had he come in and made himself comfortable?

While the others ranged themselves around the drawing room, discussing how they'd like to spend the remaining hours of the afternoon, Phoebe excused herself. She hadn't gone far across the hall before she heard footsteps behind her.

"Phoebe, wait."

She turned as Owen caught up to her. "I'm just going up for a bit."

"Yes, good. Theo has proposed another ride this afternoon. This time you, me, Chessy, and Julia, since neither of them rode that first time."

"Perhaps tomorrow, in the morning."

"Why not now?"

She moved closer to him and gazed over his shoulder into the drawing room. The others seemed engaged in conversation, but one never knew who might be listening. She grasped Owen's sleeve and tugged him into the empty dining room. "I need to speak with Eva. She and I have been asking some questions and—"

"I know you have and I wish you'd stop. It's dangerous, Phoebe."

"If we stop, who will get to the truth of what happened to Suzette? You don't believe that rubbish about the chain magically falling off its hook, do you? It's ridiculous, yet the police seem to have washed their hands of the entire affair. The building inspector said the chimneys and flues are sound. What makes a constable more of an authority on the subject than him? Besides, we're only speaking to people."

His jaw hardened. "That's how it always begins. Then the next thing I know, you're in grave danger. Why do you insist on putting yourself—and your maid—in harm's way?"

"I don't force Eva to do anything. But on the one hand, there may be a killer among Theo's and Julia's guests. On the other, Julia is threatening to sack an innocent footman. He's already been demoted."

"Phoebe." He took her hand in both of his, his fingertips gently grazing over her knuckles. The sensation sent warmth tingling up her arm and melted a portion of her resolve, until he spoke again. "I understand all that. You feel compelled to help and you're good at it. I'll admit that. But my darling, if you are going to be my wife one day, I must insist you learn to be more careful of your safety. I cannot not have you placing yourself in peril."

Cannot have you? Phoebe went very still as Owen's words rang in her ears. Had she heard correctly? She scanned the features she had come to know so well, come to—yes—love, yet in their handsome planes and lines she saw no trace of the *man* she had thought she loved. The Owen who understood her—*truly* understood—and accepted her for the person she was.

She raised an eyebrow at him and gently pulled her hand from his. "Was that your idea of a proposal?"

"I . . . we do have an understanding, don't we?" He reached for her, but she stood her ground. "When I propose, Phoebe, I'll do it properly, not here, skulking in the shadows of an empty room so the others can't hear us."

She nodded, offered a wan smile, and let the matter drop. But her throat tightened and her heart ached. For the first time, she entertained doubts about the answer she would give him when he did finally propose. If she said yes, would he attempt to control her from then on, as so many husbands did? Did he believe he could and should curtail her actions? She had thought she knew him better. She had thought he knew *her* better.

He grinned down at her, obviously certain he had won this round. "So, what about that ride?"

"Fine. I'll go up and change." After all, she thought, while she donned her riding clothes she and Eva could talk.

Eva watched Marcelle disappear through the hedge and heard the gate slam behind her. Well, she certainly hadn't handled questioning the girl as smoothly as she would have liked. Still, she had learned a thing or two. Marcelle's resentments toward Suzette ran deep, and they somehow included Narcisse.

With a sigh Eva stood and was about to follow Marcelle down to the servants' domain when the terrace doors opened and Claudette came out with several outfits draped over her arms. The breeze tossed her cropped hair about. She shifted the outfits to one arm and used her free hand to smooth down her chestnut curls. She spotted Eva and nodded.

"I am glad you are here," she said when she'd descended to the garden level. "These are the outfits Mademoiselle wants photographed this afternoon. Could you help me ready them? As you know, they must be perfect, not a pleat out of place."

Eva smiled, pleased at the prospect. Of all of Mademoiselle's assistants, Claudette often seemed rather elusive. Unlike Narcisse or Marcelle, whose tasks ended once the mannequin no longer needed their skills, Claudette had to keep the clothing in perfect condition, and that included preparing it beforehand as well as seeing to its laundering afterward. That kept her busy throughout most of the day.

"I'd be glad to help." Eva followed her into the tent. While they worked, ironing and slipping the outfits onto hangers, Eva struck up a conversation.

"I'm so very sorry about Suzette. Her loss must be unbearable for you."

"Mmm . . . *Oui*."

That was all? Had poor Suzette not had a friend among them? It seemed she would have to coax information out of Claudette, as she had with Marcelle. "You must have worked closely together these past several years. Were you great friends?" She almost choked on her own question, fully aware of what the answer must be.

"She could be difficult."

"Oh, I'm sorry to hear that. How so?" As Eva waited for the reply, a black silk evening gown with silver beading hung like midnight rain from her two-handed grasp.

Claudette draped a jacket over the ironing board but made no move to lift the iron from its warmer. "May I be frank?"

"Of course you may." Eva hoped she spoke true, because if suspicion *should* fall upon Claudette, she would feel compelled to disclose anything the woman told her.

"Suzette often complained about the condition of the clothing she modeled. She would blame me and try to get me in trouble with Mademoiselle. She could have had me fired on many occasions if Mademoiselle had paid her any mind. Luckily for me, Mademoiselle understood Suzette's whining for what it was."

"How very distressing for you, though."

"Yes, but in the end, Suzette hurt herself. Why else was Mademoiselle eager to replace her with a younger and more agreeable girl? I like this India. She laughs and does as she is told."

"She does seem a good-natured girl." Marcelle had indicated that many mannequins were cooperative—at first. Egos could be devilish things, and Eva hoped India wouldn't fall prey to hers. "Did the others have trouble with Suzette as well?"

"Why do you ask that?" Claudette propped a hand on one slender hip, her sharp expression so like Mademoiselle's that, in that moment, they might have been sisters. "Why do you ask so many questions? Her death was an accident, no?"

"Forgive me for being a busybody," Eva said rather than answer the question. And then she spoke what was, for her, a truth—if not *the* truth. "I suppose I'm trying to learn more about Suzette, because it seems so very sad to me that she died here, so far from home, where so few people knew her."

Claudette's hand dropped to her side. "That is true.

Well, if you would know all, you might wish to ask Narcisse."

"Narcisse?" Eva's eyes widened in curiosity. "Why him?"

"You asked if anyone else had trouble with Suzette. Before we left France, the two had a frightful row."

"What about?"

"I cannot say. We were all at the studio, and they were on the floor above me. I could hear their shouting. Not the words, mind you, but the anger, like thunder rumbling overhead."

CHAPTER 9

Eva tied the cravat around the collar of Lady Phoebe's riding blouse and secured the cameo brooch beneath the knot. "I didn't expect to learn that Marcelle and Suzette grew up in the same area, in Lorraine. The fighting was dreadful there during the war."

"Did they know each other at the time?" Lady Phoebe tugged lightly at her cuffs before Eva helped her on with her riding jacket.

"I'm not sure, but Marcelle told me Suzette hadn't lost any family in that time. Marcelle merely said *some people were spared*. She rather freely admitted to despising Suzette, although their animosity seems to stem from their time working together for Mademoiselle."

"Yet, it could have begun sooner, during or because of the war." Lady Phoebe stood in front of the tall mirror while Eva re-pinned some strands that had fallen loose from her bun.

"Perhaps, but I do believe there was something between Suzette and Narcisse." Eva gathered up Lady Phoebe's boots and gestured for her to sit. "And I believe it caused Marcelle to resent them both. Not only that, but Claudette told me Suzette and Narcisse had a thunderous row right before they all left France."

"Good heavens, a ménage à trois." Phoebe tugged her left boot the rest of the way on. "India despised Suzette as well. Of course, that was no secret, not after dinner that night. What did surprise me, though, was how calmly she admitted to wanting Suzette to suffer for the riding accident she caused. Would a murderer do that?"

"Perhaps she's more clever than we give her credit for." Eva pushed up from her kneeling position on the Persian rug, giving a little puff of breath as she did so. Goodness, such times reminded her that her thirtieth birthday wasn't far off. She must redouble her efforts to remain fit.

"There is that, I suppose," Lady Phoebe mused. "I have trouble thinking of her as anything more than an innocent young girl. But perhaps she's fooling everyone."

"I know of another young lady who, when she was not much older, surprised everyone by helping track down another murderer." Eva winked down at Lady Phoebe, then reached out to help her up off the hassock she had perched on. "I've an idea. India is about Amelia's age. Why not ask your sister if she can find out anything about her? Given India's father's connections among the aristocracy, it's possible one of Amelia's friends knows her fairly well."

"That's a splendid idea." Lady Phoebe pulled a face. "I don't know why I didn't think of it."

Eva grinned. "That's what you have me for."

"So true." Lady Phoebe tapped her forefinger against her chin. "With Amelia in London with the Olivers, she might have access to more of India's acquaintances than if she were home. I'll put in a call this afternoon. In the meantime, Chessy will be riding with us today. Perhaps the opportunity will present itself for us to have a little chat. I keep thinking about his reaction to Suzette's death, and that it could mean they were more than casual acquaintances."

"Goodness, a fourth participant in the possible amours of Suzette Villiers?" This knot grew more intricate by the day.

"By the way," Lady Phoebe said, "India also admitted that Narcisse brought her a bottle of brandy to help with her pain that night."

"Helpful chap, isn't he?" Eva's sardonic tone wasn't lost on Lady Phoebe, who pulled her lips into a half smirk. "With Suzette gone, does he think to replace her with a new mannequin? Or had he already done so when Mademoiselle turned her favor on India?"

"Perhaps he decided to be rid of Suzette so he could pursue greener pastures," Lady Phoebe said darkly. "We need to learn more about this man."

Eva handed Lady Phoebe her riding crop, and then set her cap on her head. Lady Phoebe tucked the strap beneath her chin. "I'm off then."

"Do be careful, not only of the ride but the company you're keeping. If the Earl of Chesterhaven had anything to do with Miss Villiers's death, you don't want to let on you suspect him."

"And you be careful as well with your queries, especially if you find the chance to speak with Narcisse. Good luck, and I'll see you after."

They exited the room together and went their separate ways down the corridor.

The ride had been a good one. All five of them—Julia, Theo, Owen, Chessy, and Phoebe—were equally matched when it came to their prowess in the saddle, and there had been no mishaps. Not even potential mishaps. Phoebe could see that Julia took comfort in that. For the first time since Suzette had been brought out to the lawn, Julia had seemed calm and confident. Her usual self. Riding had always done that for both of them when they were girls. There had been little that a brisk canter along a woodland trail couldn't solve, or at least put in proper perspective.

Even Owen hadn't balked at the prospect of Phoebe jumping the hedgerow. Granted it wasn't a particularly wide or tall hedgerow, and her horse had taken it smoothly, but Phoebe had half expected Owen to cry out for her to stop. She wouldn't have. But she was thankful it hadn't been put to the test.

Her only disappointment during an otherwise glorious afternoon was not being able to catch a private word with Chessy. Which was why, when they arrived back at the stable block and the others made directly for the house, Phoebe stayed behind after Chessy announced his intention of checking on the filly he planned to purchase from Theo.

"I'd love to see her, too," Phoebe eagerly declared, and when Owen asked if he should stay as well, she reminded him that he had promised Theo a game of chess before going up to dress for dinner later.

Without waiting for the groom, Chessy led her through the stables. They were immaculate and impressive with their vaulted ceilings, Belgian block flooring, spacious stalls, and an abundance of polished brass trim. They stopped outside a stall near the end of the row and Chessy made a clucking noise. The horse inside, a thoroughbred with a bright chestnut coat and virtually no markings, turned about and hung her head over the gate.

"Hullo, you." Chessy ran his hand down her neck. He unlatched the gate and stepped inside. The filly's haunches shivered, but she stood patiently, making no attempt to leave the stall. Phoebe followed him in.

"Oh, she *is* lovely," she said wistfully.

"I told you you could have her if you want."

Phoebe sighed. "No, I'm afraid my grandfather isn't ready yet to introduce horses back onto the estate. It was so hard for him when the army took ours. He truly mourned the loss."

"That was a long time ago. More than a half-dozen years." Chessy held her gaze, his own filled with sympathy.

"To a man like my grandfather, it hasn't been long enough. And of course, there are the expenditures in keeping horses." She didn't elaborate, but instead reached up to stroke the filly's glossy coat. "Do you mean to race her?"

"She's of good stock, so yes, in time. She'll need a good deal of training first. Perhaps she'll be ready when she reaches her third year."

He spoke so nonchalantly. Did he realize how many of the old families, like Phoebe's, could no longer afford such endeavors? She knew his family's real estate holdings were vast and covered many parts of Europe and beyond, which in great part had shielded them from the privations caused by the war and resulting economic decline. The Hewitt-Davies family enjoyed almost unheard-of advantages nowadays, and she had no doubt Chessy used his money and rank to obtain whatever it was he wanted.

Phoebe wondered what, precisely, *did* the Earl of Chesterhaven want? Besides a new filly to race, that is.

"How long have you and Coco been acquainted?" she asked him, hoping to sound more like a nosy young socialite than someone investigating a possible murder.

Chessy threw back his head and laughed, startling both Phoebe and the filly. After soothing the latter, he said to Phoebe, "Not long. A few months only. We met in Fontainebleau last summer and renewed our acquaintance this past spring."

"I see." Phoebe tilted her chin at him. "Why the laughter?"

"Sorry. It's just that she's been pushing . . ." He whooshed out a breath. "Look, you and I hail from the same world, the same set of rules. So you'll understand what I'm about to say. Coco would like nothing more than to become the Countess of Chesterhaven." The dry delivery of this pronouncement told Phoebe all she needed to know about Chessy's views on the matter.

Still, to keep him talking, she said, "I take it you're not keen on the idea."

"She's all but insisting I take her to Balestoke, where my family has lived for generations. You and I both know that while I might entertain her there, that's all it could ever be. But how to tell this very determined Frenchwoman that my duty to my family is to marry a titled heiress and continue the noble bloodline?" He gazed fondly at the filly, smoothing his hand down her sleek nose. "You know all about noble bloodlines, don't you, girl?"

"Are those your sentiments, or your family's?"

"One and the same, as well you know."

Phoebe didn't know that she did. Not anymore; not since about halfway through the war when she realized all people bled red and life was too precious not to seize happiness where and when one found it. But perhaps Chessy simply didn't feel for Coco what she felt for him.

Or did she?—a question raised by Chessy's next words.

"It's not me she wants, in any case. She's only ever truly loved one man. Boy Capel. He financed her early endeavors, so even then, her amours weren't strictly pure, so to speak. Died in a car crash, poor chap. Coco's never really gotten over it."

The name was familiar to Phoebe; she remembered reading about the accident in the newspapers just after the war, though at the time there had been no mention of Coco Chanel. And no wonder. Arthur Capel, a shipping tycoon and polo player, had been married with two young daughters. Phoebe did her best to sound naïve. "What *does* she want from you, then?"

"My title and money. What else? Though, in fairness, one can hardly blame her given her background. You'd never guess it, but she grew up penniless, in an orphanage in some wretched and unreachable part of France. Had to claw herself out of poverty, and damned if she didn't make a splendid job of it."

"But it's not enough for her," Phoebe guessed.

"Exactly. She wants more. She wants to be certain poverty can never again touch her. I'm afraid she'll never be satisfied."

Poor Coco. Poor Chessy. Phoebe almost laughed out loud at her thoughts. Perhaps they *did* both deserve a measure of sympathy, but at the same time, they were using each other. If Coco wanted Chessy for his money and connections, he in turn enjoyed her company to satisfy his own pleasure without the inconvenience of a commitment. Phoebe had seen it countless times before.

"And Suzette?" she asked, hoping to catch him off his guard.

His eyebrows twitched. "What about her?"

"Oh, I noticed you seemed to purposely ignore her that night at dinner, and it made me wonder if it was because Coco was there." She tried to imitate one of Julia's careless shrugs. "It just got me thinking, is all."

"That Suzette and I . . . ? Er, no. Good *heavens*, no. Certainly not. The very idea . . ."

Doth he protest too much? "Funny, because apparently she and Narcisse had a terrible row before leaving France. You were with them all then, weren't you?"

"What are you implying?" He rubbed his thumbs across his fingertips in rapid little motions. "That their row had something to do with me?"

"Did it?"

He noticed her gaze straying to his hands and stilled his fingers. "Never mind about either of them. Suzette is gone and Coco will land on her feet. She aways does." He turned to face her fully, with a subtle step that put him between her and the stall door. "My family would never object to a girl like you, Phoebe."

She tried to back away from him, but the horse blocked her retreat. "Well, there is certainly no shortage of marriageable heiresses in England, is there? I'm sure you'll find one to your liking."

"You're a coy one, aren't you?" He smiled, bringing attention to the lines bracketing his eyes and mouth and the fact that he must be a good twenty years older than her.

"Hardly."

"Come. There had to be a reason you stayed behind with me."

"Yes, the filly." Whose shoulder now pressed up against her back.

"You and I, Phoebe. We could be the toast of society."

"No, we could not," she firmly contradicted him.

"Oh, now don't tell me you're spoken for. I've heard no announcements about you and Owen Seabright, and I don't believe there ever will be. He's having fun at your expense, my darling." He seized her hand and held it tightly.

"What is or is not between Owen and me is none of your concern."

"If he was going to ask you, he'd have done it by now. Don't you see?" He tried to tug her closer. Phoebe dug in her heels, half wishing the horse would take a bite out of the man's arm. "He's all wrong for you anyway."

His gall astonished her. "Is that so? And you know this . . . how?"

"He's in trade. His wretched woolen mills will always be more important to him than you or any woman. And do you know that, because of it, he's become the laughing-stock of all the gentlemen's clubs. He doesn't dare show his face at The Rag or Brooks's these days."

"No, why would he? He's rarely in London. And perhaps he simply doesn't care for the futility of sitting around in wing chairs, drinking port and gossiping like an old hen."

Chessy let out a roar of laughter. "I do like a woman with spirit, and I'm always up for a challenge. If you don't believe I'm right for you now, Phoebe, you soon will."

He tugged on her hand, propelling her toward him with a lurch. At the same time, his free hand wrapped around her nape, effectively trapping her. His head dipped, and his mouth drew near.

She shoved at his chest. "Chessy, stop it. Chessy! *Lord Chesterhaven*, you will *stop* this at once! You're behaving like a spoiled little boy."

"A boy? Dash it, you're wrong there. I'm very much a man. Let me show you . . ."

No thought went into the curling of her hand or the up-ward swing of her arm. Her blow landed squarely beneath his chin, snapping his head—and those seeking lips of his—upward. She didn't think she hit him with enough force to hurt him, but in his astonishment he released her. She shoved him aside and pushed her way out of the stall. Once in the wide aisle, she stopped. "Do not ever presume to touch me again, Lord Chesterhaven, or you'll be terri-bly sorry. Not to mention *you'll* be the laughingstock of all the gentlemen's clubs, once it gets round what a pathetic blackguard you are."

The back of his hand pressed to the underside of his chin, he blinked. "You wouldn't dare. Society would say it was your fault."

"Oh, I doubt very many people in society have any illusions as to the sort of man you are."

She strode toward the open stable doors, only then realizing she had an audience. The head groom and two of his assistants were leading the horses in. All had stopped in their tracks, their dumbfounded expressions and gawking eyes trained in her direction.

Eva helped India into the latest outfit Mademoiselle wanted photographed. It was no easy feat, considering the poor girl had to balance on one leg. But she certainly was a trooper, as Claudette had implied. Always with a smile, a cheerful comment, and always looking as though she had enjoyed a full night's sleep and had nary a care in the world. Ah, the advantages of youth.

The temperature had dropped several degrees since the day before, and after donning her cardigan, Eva helped India out of the pavilion and along the garden path. For the shoot, Narcisse had chosen the footbridge that led over a man-made brook, its banks lined in bright purple Michaelmas daisies, with the Grecian folly as a backdrop. India wore an ankle-length evening gown in simple black with gracefully draping lines in a Grecian-like design, and having the folly in the background would lend a touch of historical drama to the photos.

Lady Phoebe hadn't yet returned from her ride, so with nothing pressing she needed to do, Eva stayed to watch the shoot. She also hoped to steal a word or two with Narcisse afterward. She looked on as he helped India pose as he wanted her and then returned to his camera to begin, snapping several pictures before suggesting something that

made India turn in profile. Eva only hoped Narcisse managed to capture the images he wanted quickly, as the dress
not only left India's arms bare, but dipped low in front and
even deeper down the back. Eva once more gave the girl
credit, as she showed no sign of being cold.

After several minutes, Mademoiselle came hurrying down
from the house, accompanied by her assistant, Françoise
Deschamps. Both women wore wide-brimmed sun hats,
Mademoiselle Chanel in a jersey skirt and shirtwaist,
Madame Deschamps in the loose-fitting trousers she fa-
vored. How relaxed yet flattering they were on the older
woman, whose figure remained like that of someone much
younger.

Before Mademoiselle reached Narcisse, she began a ver-
bal assault in French. Eva didn't quite understand the
words, but the sharpness of Mademoiselle's tone made her
cringe. Soon she gathered that Mademoiselle was upset
that Narcisse had started without her. Would he be made
to suffer the consequences of her wrath? He simply remained behind his tripod during the tirade and continued
snapping the shutter before finally allowing his arms to
fall to his sides. More French words passed between them.
She shook her forefinger at him. He nodded reluctantly.
Finally, Mademoiselle backed away, and Narcisse said
something to India that made her giggle, then press her
fingertips to her mouth.

Madame Deschamps drifted over to where Eva stood
beside the brook. "How goes today's session?"

"Quite well, by the looks of it. Although it appears
Mademoiselle doesn't agree," she couldn't help adding,
perhaps unwisely. She braced for Mademoiselle's friend
and assistant to reprimand her, but a retort never came.

"Coco *can* be exacting at times." Of all the French
guests, Madame Deschamps spoke the most polished Eng-

lish. "Narcisse is an excellent photographer, but Coco wants to maintain control over all creative aspects of her business."

"That's understandable," Eva readily agreed. It wasn't for her to judge, after all. Mademoiselle employed countless individuals, from those who wove her fabrics to those who sold the finished garments in shops. She had much to lose if business didn't go well.

"Ah, Mademoiselle Huntford." Mademoiselle had apparently finished admonishing Narcisse and adding her instructions for the shoot. "I am glad you are here. I wish you to speak to Lady Allerton and convince her to model for me."

The request, which had sounded more like a command, bewildered Eva. "I don't know that I could convince Lady Allerton to do anything she doesn't already wish to do."

"*Non, non,* that is nonsense. I see how both Renshaw sisters listen to you. Besides, I tried appealing to that German creature of hers—"

"Hetta?" Eva supplied, not liking to hear her fellow lady's maid referred to as a *creature.*

"*Oui,* that one."

"She's Swiss, not German."

"*Quelle différence?*" Mademoiselle swatted dismissively at the air, a gesture that had become familiar over the past few days. "I asked her to speak with her lady, and she had the gall to cross her arms and stare down her nose at me. I wished to smack that nose of hers."

Over her employer's shoulder, Madame Deschamps sent Eva an apologetic look. "Coco," the woman said, "perhaps you overestimate the influence a maid has on her employer. It is not their place to cajole or persuade."

"Fine." Another swat at the air. "I shall do it myself. Eventually, Julia will relent." Under her breath she murmured, "Useless creatures."

Eva turned about and made her way back to the pavilion. She had rather continue helping Claudette than stay and hear herself be spoken of in such a fashion.

She found Claudette, not in the tent, but on the terrace with a cup of tea. Eva waved as she approached, but Claudette continued staring off into the distance, perhaps to where the others had moved from the footbridge to the folly itself.

Eva climbed the steps. "Taking a well-needed break, I see."

Claudette blinked and gave herself a little shake, as if to rouse herself from a particularly absorbing daydream. "Eva. Grown weary of the photos?"

"Not exactly," she replied with a wry grin, but didn't elaborate. "I'm glad to see you off your feet."

"It will not last." Claudette raised her cup for a sip of tea and replaced it on the saucer with the lightest of clinks. She gestured with her chin across the garden. "Did you ask Narcisse your questions?"

Eva hesitated, then admitted, "No. Not yet."

"You should be careful, Eva. You are stirring up trouble. You and your lady."

"I only wish to speak with Narcisse because you told me I should. Don't you wish to know the truth of how Suzette died?"

"The truth should be known, *oui*, if it is not already." She combed her fingers through her short-cropped hair. "But why you? You are not a police officer."

"No, that's true." Not for the first time since arriving at Allerton Place, Eva wished she could speak with Miles Brannock, the local constable at home in Little Barlow. Miles would never have been so quick to dismiss Suzette's death as an accident. Though the chief inspector of Little Barlow might have agreed with the police here, Miles would have continued probing, asking questions, and following any lead to find the truth. And he would have welcomed Eva's and Lady Phoebe's help, so long as they didn't endanger themselves. Miles certainly didn't like it when Eva overstepped what he considered proper boundaries. But then, she didn't relish the idea of Miles facing danger either. A good thing, then, that peace prevailed in Little Barlow—most of the time.

While these thoughts passed through her mind, Claudette watched Eva closely. It was Eva's turn to blink and rouse herself, and Claudette's turn to grin. "I think you are someone who seeks trouble, *non*?"

Eva put up a hand. "I wouldn't put it that way."

"Trouble, excitement. Say it as you will, but you like it, Eva, do you not?" Before Eva could reply, Claudette leaned closer. "Remember this. Suzette enjoyed excitement, too. And she loved to stir up trouble."

She swallowed the last of her tea, came to her feet, picked up the empty cup and saucer, and retreated into the house.

CHAPTER 10

Claudette's parting words left Eva uneasy. Had she meant them as a warning? A threat? Impossible to know for sure, as Claudette's demeanor hadn't changed during their exchange. She had seemed preoccupied, perhaps even troubled, but she had been composed enough.

Eva would allow neither warnings nor threats to deter her. She waited on the terrace until India returned to the pavilion for a change in attire, accompanied by Mademoiselle Chanel and Madame Deschamps. By then, Claudette had come back outside as well. Reminding herself she didn't work for any of these people, Eva stole the opportunity to hurry down the steps and across the garden.

She found Narcisse disassembling his equipment. "All finished for the day?" she asked, using her friendliest tone. The question was disingenuous, for she already knew the answer.

"Hardly," the man grumbled. "Packing up only to move and unpack over that way." He pointed to yet another section of garden. "Mademoiselle is relentless."

"Sorry to hear that. I think what you took here, with the folly in the background, will be brilliant."

He had folded his tripod; now he laid it on the ground and straightened to regard Eva. "*Merci.* I wish Mademoiselle could be as certain as you."

"She will be, won't she, once the photos are developed."

He smiled and nodded. "She is usually pleased with the results. But she insists on giving me . . . how do you English say it? . . . grief . . . until she sees the proof."

Eva glanced at the various pieces of equipment. "Can I help you?"

"That is most generous of you. Yes, if you like."

"Where are we taking it?"

"The reflecting pool. That way." He pointed. "Inside the sculped hedges."

They worked in companiable silence for a few minutes, with Narcisse doing most of the packing—Eva didn't wish to handle the delicate equipment until Narcisse had secured it in its cases or bound it with straps. Once he had done that, she hefted all she could carry while he did the same, and together they traipsed across the garden.

The hedges formed a horseshoe around the pool, while four curved, white wrought-iron benches lined the space inside. Japanese maples, planted between the benches, cast their leafy reflections on the pool.

"How lovely," Eva exclaimed. "There really are more to these gardens than one realizes at first glance. Where do you want everything?"

He glanced about him for several moments, then walked the inner perimeter, stopping here and there to study the branches overhead, the light, and how the pool caught the reflections. Finally, he chose his spot, and he and Eva began unpacking and setting up. She wondered how much time before India and Mademoiselle joined them. Probably not long.

"You've done an admirable job adjusting to the changes," Eva said. "It can't have been easy."

"Changes?" He placed his camera on the tripod and set about securing it to the bracket.

"With Suzette gone, I meant. And India being inexperienced."

"India is quite natural at this."

"Luckily. But to lose a talent like Suzette . . . Such a tragedy."

"She had talent, yes."

Eva allowed herself to study him in silence a moment. "You were distraught that night, on the lawn, yet now you seem almost indifferent. Surely that isn't the case."

"It is complicated." He continued adjusting his camera and tripod, peering through the viewer repeatedly and making further modifications. He seemed able to do this almost without thought, as he continued speaking to Eva while he worked. "We had a history, she and I."

"You were close," Eva ventured.

"Once. But not of late."

No, you and she had a row. Had that ended things between you? Were you still angry?

"It seems nearly everyone had some difficulty with her." Eva strolled to one of the benches but didn't sit.

"At times, yes."

"Enough for someone to wish her ill?"

He stopped fidgeting with his equipment. "What are you asking me, mademoiselle? If someone killed her?"

"Did someone, in your opinion?"

He shrugged. "Perhaps. Enough of us wished to at one time or another."

Eva couldn't school the astonishment from her features, especially since he had included himself in the admission. Yet, Marcelle had been equally forthcoming.

He recognized her reaction and laughed. "Do not worry, mademoiselle, none of us is enterprising enough to commit murder. It is not in our natures."

"I'm glad to hear that. Because I heard something about you and she . . . that you argued before you left France. Loud enough for others to hear."

His gaze narrowed on her. "Who told you that?"

"I'm not about to say." She walked closer to him, picking her way over the grass. "Is it true?"

"We had a professional disagreement, nothing more." An angry blush mottled his fair complexion.

"You weren't very nice to her once Mademoiselle decided India would be the focus here. Was that a result of your falling-out, or were you simply trying to please Mademoiselle by switching your loyalty from one mannequin to another?"

"I resent these questions. You know nothing about me or Suzette or any of us. Who are you to accuse?" Turning his back on her, he sank onto his haunches and rummaged through one of his equipment bags. When he stood, he held a small folding camera in his hands and gave it a crank to advance the film. Before Eva realized his intention, he'd snapped a picture of her. He cranked the film again and snapped another.

Eva raised a hand to shield her face. "What are you doing?"

"What am I doing, mademoiselle?" He laughed. His skin tone cooled to its natural hue. "I am taking your picture. A keepsake. I wish to remember the woman who accused me of murder."

"Stop it. I didn't accuse you." A hot wash of chagrin crept up from her neck.

"You might as well have." He came closer, advancing the film and clicking the shutter several more times. "I thought perhaps you were sincere in your offer to assist me, that you did so out of friendliness. I see I was wrong." *Snap!*

She put up both hands to fend him off. "That's quite

enough. I'm sorry if my questions offended you, but a woman is dead, monsieur. Dead. There is nothing polite or friendly about that. We might all have to endure a bit of discomfort to discover the truth of what happened."

She might have said more, but voices alerted her to the imminent arrival of India and Mademoiselle Chanel. Madame Deschamps must have returned to the house. It was time Eva did so as well.

Phoebe paused to catch her breath upon reaching the terrace. She had walked all the way back from the stables, a farther distance than she had realized, having only motored there previously.

Her knuckles ached, a result of striking Lord Chesterhaven. Oh, she couldn't bring herself to think of him as *Chessy* anymore, not after his vulgar stunt in the filly's stall. How dare the man be so presumptuous? As if his tasteless attempt to woo her could have swayed *any* woman with a modicum of intelligence. Perhaps he believed his fortune would tempt her. Little did he guess she would rather live in a hut and eat radishes three times a day than shackle herself to a man who thought so much of himself and so little of everyone else. Not that he sought anything permanent with her. No, she was quite certain his intention had been a dalliance and nothing more.

Oh, he made her so angry she could kick something.

Her gaze drifted to the terrace doors and the drawing room beyond. She couldn't see very far inside due to the clothing racks in the way, but she wondered who might be in the room, and did she really wish to have to speak with anyone yet?

The answer was a flat no. To answer well-meaning questions about the ride, or about the filly, would fill her with enough ire to make her replies stick in her throat. Or to face Owen while her anger simmered so hotly would render her unable to hide what happened from him. He would ask what was wrong, and she, unable to lie to him or anyone she cared about, would spill the truth, and then . . .

What would he do? He would be furious. Blindly so. Would he decide he must teach Chesterhaven a lesson? Phoebe had already done that, not with the force of her fist but with the vehemence of her rejection. She had hurt him where it mattered most to a man like him—his pride.

She turned, about to descend the steps, having no idea where she would spend the next hour or so until she felt steady enough to face the others. Then a safe haven came into view in the person of Eva, striding across the gardens toward the servants' yard. Phoebe hurried down.

"Eva," she called. "Wait for me." Just as she caught up, her booted foot slid on the gravel. If not for Eva's speedy action in catching her arms, she might have landed face-down on the path.

"Goodness!" Eva exclaimed. "Are you all right?"

"I'm fine." Phoebe grasped Eva's shoulders for leverage and straightened until she stood on her own. "Let's keep going. I need to disappear for a while."

Eva didn't question her, not then. They made their way into the house through the delivery entrance and went swiftly down the corridor, dodging the green grocer's and butcher's assistants handing off supplies to the footmen. A couple of them looked startled when they recognized their mistress's sister in a part of the house where she oughtn't to be, but she waved them on while she and Eva hurried out of their way.

"Let's take the backstairs," Eva suggested, and led Phoebe all the way up to the second floor, to the tiny room Eva had been assigned beneath the eaves. She opened the door and stood aside for Phoebe to enter first. "Here we are, and no one will be disturbing us. I should be sharing with Mademoiselle's maid, Remie, but apparently Mademoiselle requires the poor woman to be on hand at all times. She sleeps in Mademoiselle's dressing room."

"How stifling for poor Remie." Phoebe stole a moment to catch her breath. "But truly, nothing about any of these people surprises me anymore."

"Nor me. I've had quite an interesting morning and have much to tell you, so it was fortunate us running into each other when we did."

"Literally. I almost ran you down out there, didn't I?"

"What did light the fire under your feet, if I may ask?"

"You most certainly may." Phoebe told her, and watched indignant fury darken Eva's eyes and scorch her cheeks.

"That scoundrel. You must go to Lord Allerton at once."

"I know I should, and I probably will eventually, but at the moment he's got enough on his mind."

"Lord Owen, then."

"No!" Phoebe's blurted refusal startled Eva, who flinched. Phoebe softened her tone. "If I do that, I'm afraid they'll come to blows."

Eva plunked her hands on her hips. "As well they should."

"Perhaps Chesterhaven deserves it, but what would it help? If he comes near me again, he'll experience a repeat of what happened at the stables, and I doubt very much he wants that. He'll especially not want to risk the others knowing how easily a woman can snub him. If it weren't for his title and fortune, I'd be hard-pressed to understand what Mademoiselle Chanel sees in him."

Phoebe sat in the room's only chair, a hard wooden ladderback. Eva sat opposite her on the edge of the bed. For a moment she avoided Eva's gaze. Phoebe hadn't mentioned the other reason she didn't wish Owen to know what happened. He had grown overly protective as it was; she didn't wish to give him any more reasons to intervene in her life—or her liberty. "Tell me about your morning," she said to change the subject.

Eva let out a heavy sigh. "Suffice it to say, none of Mademoiselle's employees has anything good to say about Suzette. Can you believe they all admitted to disliking her, at times even entertaining notions of killing her?" Phoebe's eyes popped wide, but Eva held up a hand. "None of them admitted to doing any such thing. It's the kind of thing people toss about casually in the heat of anger. As in, 'He makes me so angry I could simply kill him.' We've all said it, but it's a rare person who actually means it."

"Yes, but someone here is that rare person. Did you learn anything that brings us closer to discovering who?"

Eva shook her head. "Not specifically, no. I did learn some interesting things, though. Marcelle most certainly is in love with Narcisse, but his affections had been reserved for Suzette only."

"Then they *were* a couple, as we thought?"

"He fairly admitted as much. When I attempted to question him further about the argument they had in France, he insisted it was purely a professional disagreement. But he turned several shades of crimson as he made his claim."

"As did Chesterhaven when I asked him about Suzette. Couldn't deny his involvement with her more vehemently. Which of course made me more suspicious." Phoebe shook her head. "That was right before he turned into a mongrel and started pawing me."

"Beastly man."

"I did learn something else from him. Apparently, Mademoiselle would like nothing more than to become the Countess of Chesterhaven."

"She seriously thinks he'll marry her?" Eva's incredulity

spoke of her familiarity with the rules that governed the English nobility.

"Apparently. I don't have to tell you he has no such intention."

"No." Eva frowned. "Is it possible Mademoiselle discovered his dalliance with Suzette and . . ." She went silent.

"And murdered her?" Phoebe took a moment to give it serious consideration, then shook her head. "I don't think so, truly. Coco is a bully in her own refined way, but I can't see her committing murder over a disappointment. Chesterhaven told me she clawed her way out of the poverty of her childhood. A survivor like that tends to be logical, methodical, and yes, ruthless, but not unbalanced. If she discovered Chesterhaven had been untrue, I believe she'd simply move on to someone more amenable to her plans. As she will no doubt do once she realizes he'll never marry her."

"Yes, perhaps you're right." Eva compressed her lips, then craned forward. "I read something about her only this summer in one of my mum's magazines at home. For the past year she had been carrying on a very open affair with Grand Duke Dmitri Pavlovitch."

"Czar Nicholas's cousin?" Phoebe shuddered, remembering the tragic fate of the czar and his entire family. At the time, rumors of the massacre had crept into Europe, but no one had known for certain. Now they did. While the royal family had languished in a comfortable prison in Siberia, awaiting their fate, many of their relatives had fled Russia. Grand Duke Dmitri had been one of those lucky ones.

"The very same." Eva scooted slightly more forward until she perched at the very edge of the mattress. "Which makes him one of the closest heirs to the Russian throne.

According to the article, Mademoiselle entertained hopes that if the civil war in Russia caused the revolution to collapse, the czars might be restored and Dmitri would wear the crown. That would make her czarina if they married."

"My goodness, she aims high. I'm surprised she'd settle for an earl, although Chesterhaven *will* be a duke someday." She chuckled. "But never king of England."

"But to prove your point, once Mademoiselle realized for certain the grand duke had no intention of marrying her, she moved on." Eva's eyebrows went up as if she'd remembered something important. "Speaking of bullying, you might want to warn your sister that Mademoiselle hasn't given up on the idea of her modeling. She expected me to help persuade her. Which I have no intention of doing."

Phoebe smiled wryly. "Part of me feels it would serve Julia right to have her face plastered all over the fashion magazines and then have those same magazines delivered to Grams at Foxwood Hall."

"You won't think so when your grandmother demands to know why you didn't stop her."

Phoebe felt her grin turn flat. "You are quite right about that."

CHAPTER 11

Phoebe should have heeded Eva's warning before it was too late. During afternoon tea, Coco resumed bombarding Julia with reasons she should model clothing before the camera.

"I have something new, never before seen in the fashion world. I have been saving it, keeping it a secret." Coco slathered clotted cream across a halved scone and reached for the jam. "India, you have been doing a splendid job, but this new collection needs someone more mature, more sophisticated. You cannot have all the glory," she added with a grin before turning back to Julia. "This new collection needs you. And only you."

"Heavens." Julia's gaze darted around the table. They were once more seated on the terrace, wearing cardigans, shawls, and jumpers to ward off the afternoon chill. Compared to yesterday or even this morning, autumn seemed to have arrived in earnest. "If your collection needs only *me*, what would you have done if you hadn't met me?"

Phoebe snatched at the logic of that. "Yes, a good question. You designed your collection before you knew my sister existed."

"Perhaps." Coco set her half-eaten scone back on her plate. "Even so, the woman I imagined wearing these designs looked remarkably like Julia. And now that I *have* met her, I cannot imagine anyone else presenting this collection to the world. Other women will admire her so much, they will wish to be like her. That is what I need. Someone to inspire. Someone bold enough to forge a new path in women's clothing."

"You make it sound as if I'd be some kind of adventurer or explorer." Julia laughed and dropped another lump of sugar into her tea.

"That is exactly what you would be," Coco insisted.

"Oh, you should do it, my lady," India exclaimed. "Mademoiselle is right. You'll be perfect. And what is there to stop you?"

Phoebe's gaze connected with Theo's, and she read, not apprehension, as she expected, but interest. As if Coco's reasoning made sense to him and the prospect intrigued him. But only for a moment. Then the misgivings crept in. They hadn't only Grams to think about. What about Theo's mother? How would she react to her daughter-in-law, the current marchioness, hawking commercial products?

Suffice it to say Lucille Leighton, Dowager Marchioness of Allerton, would be both horrified and furious. And completely humiliated in the eyes of her friends.

"Julia, you can't," Phoebe said firmly.

"That's just silly," India insisted, unable to keep the disappointment from her voice. Phoebe had to admire the girl's willingness to share the photographer's spotlight.

"You must understand," Phoebe said to her, "that my sister's position is different from yours. While you can be seen in the fashion magazines without reprisals in the society columns, my sister cannot."

"Fashion *is* an adventure." Coco referred back to Julia's

comment with a hint of drama in her voice. "And when it is new, it is a risk. Women need incentive to gather their courage and explore, to take that risk to become their better selves."

"And fashion does that?" Owen's question, taken on face value, conveyed natural curiosity. But his tone implied the opposite—cynical disbelief no amount of persuasion could quell. Phoebe felt the same. Oh, she would agree that the right outfit for the right occasion could instill confidence, poise, and even a sense of authority. But those traits must already exist in a person for one's clothing style to bring them out.

Her mother had taught her that a woman must find her identity and purpose from within, and from no other source. It was one of the few memories that had remained vivid in her mind these many years since Mama died.

"I understand what you're saying, Coco, and I agree with all of it," Julia said slowly. The tip of her finger absently traced the rim of her teacup. When she spoke again, it was with the decisiveness of a marchioness. "But I simply cannot. You must understand that England is not France. Our society is vastly different, and there are things a woman in my position cannot do. The dignity of the Allerton title must be maintained, for the good of the many organizations and charities of which we are patrons."

Although no one made a sound, it was as if Phoebe, Owen, and especially Theo, gasped a sigh of relief. Even Coco's friend Françoise seemed to relax her shoulders and smile a bit, not with relief, but with inevitability. As if she had known all along what Julia's answer would be.

Only Chesterhaven continued in his rigid posture and the wary, speculative gazes he kept shooting across the table, first at Phoebe, then Owen, then Theo, and back again. Round and round. Phoebe found she rather enjoyed his discomfiture. He deserved to have it drawn out as long as possible. Another fist to the jaw, as Owen might have administered, would have been over and done with far too soon. Let the man stew and wonder.

Coco raised her hands in surrender. "All right. I see I cannot persuade you. I give up, then. It is a shame, but I must respect your decision."

"Thank you." Julia looked as relieved as Phoebe felt. "But don't for one moment think it's because I don't admire your work immensely. Because I do."

"I can see that." Coco beamed as she gestured at Julia, wearing yet another creation from Maison Chanel. "I will continue my search for the perfect woman to model for me. But perhaps I might persuade you to try on some of my new designs. Simply try on, nothing more."

"Nothing?" Julia's countenance once more sparked with interest.

"Nothing," Coco assured her. "I simply wish to see them on you, so I may envision other women like you, of your class, wearing them someday soon."

"Yes, well, in that case . . ." Julia hesitated, then broke into a smile she could not seem to suppress. "I don't see the harm. Theo?"

He looked surprised at her appeal. "My dear, you are free to do as you like. Always. You know that."

To Phoebe's surprise as well, Julia tossed a questioning glance at her. "I suppose it's fine," she replied. "It can't hurt to try them on."

"I'm sorry, Eva, but Hetta flatly refused."

Eva had been called down to the clothing pavilion at midmorning the next day, but this time, it wasn't Claudette or Mademoiselle issuing the summons, but Lady Allerton herself. "I truly don't mind, my lady, but what are we doing?"

Lady Allerton stood just inside the alcove formed by the privacy screen. "We are trying on some of Mademoiselle Chanel's fashions."

Eva started. "Surely not, my lady."

"Don't worry, you goose." Lady Allerton laughed. "I'm only modeling them. There will be no pictures taken. You'll never see my face on the cover of *Vogue* or *L'Officiel*."

Eva glanced past her into the alcove. She saw no waiting dresses. "What will you be wearing?"

"Mademoiselle is bringing them down from the house." Lady Allerton's cheeks turned pink with excitement. "Apparently no one outside of the company has seen them yet. I shall be the first. Along with you, of course."

"And Hetta refused to help?" Eva wondered how Lady Allerton's personal maid got away with her frequent displays of stubbornness. Even Eva wouldn't be so headstrong with Lady Phoebe, the most tolerant mistress in the history of mistresses, but Lady Allerton never seemed to mind when Hetta overstepped her bounds by insisting on this or that. She always meant well, and Eva supposed Lady Allerton simply accepted that.

"She would not be swayed, as she believes no good will come if it. She's up in the nursery with Charles while his nurse takes a couple of hours off to shop in the village." Lady Allerton shrugged. "Actually, this type of thing would be lost on Hetta anyway. She cares nothing for fashion other than what I'm wearing on any given day, and she can keep any fabric looking brand-new despite many washings. But I know you'll appreciate what we're about to see."

She ended on a little trill of excitement that Eva found contagious. Yes, she loved poring through fashion magazines at home once the ladies of the house had finished with them. She kept herself well-informed of the latest trends, whether they be in clothing, shoes, accessories, or hairstyles. Lady Phoebe might not be obsessed with her looks or her style, yet she always managed to present a tasteful and well-groomed appearance.

Thanks, in part, to Eva's skills, if she did say so herself.

"*Et voilà,*" Mademoiselle called out. Eva poked her head around the screen to see Mademoiselle, followed by Françoise Deschamps and Claudette striding through the tent single file, each carrying garments draped across their arms like sacred offerings. "Wait until you see."

Lady Allerton, too, peered around the screen. She pointed at Madame Deschamps's flowing trousers. "Will there be a pair or two of those? I do hope so."

"*Non,* not this time. But you will not be disappointed, I promise." Mademoiselle stopped in front of the screen and held up the frock she carried, allowing its full length to unfurl before her. Eva beheld a dress in midnight-blue charmeuse embroidered in such an intricate pattern, enhanced with beadwork, that her eyes were dazzled. Before she knew it, she had reached out with her fingertips.

"It's the most exquisite thing I've ever seen." She stopped herself just before her hand made contact with the fabric. "It's breathtaking."

"It most certainly is." Lady Allerton slowly came forward as if drawn by a dream. Eva stepped aside to allow her full view of the dress. "I've never seen anything like it. This pattern, it's so exotic."

Indeed, Eva glanced over at the other garments still draping across the other two women's arms. She glimpsed intricate geometric patterns with stylized flowers and birds.

"It is Russian," Mademoiselle explained with an unmistakable note of pride. "Russian inspired, I should say, for these were crafted at Maison Chanel in Paris."

How remarkable, Eva thought. She and Lady Phoebe

were just talking about Mademoiselle's affair with Grand Duke Dmitri. They had spent only a year together before going their separate ways, but apparently the grand duke had left a lasting impression on Mademoiselle.

The results were magnificent, fit for royalty. Claudette and Madame Deschamps took turns displaying the garments they had carried in. One outfit included a tunic and skirt in matching jersey, with embroidery and trim that added vibrant color. Madame Deschamps had also brought several blouses, each with a square neckline and billowing sleeves, that resembled peasant tops, but in fabrics and with adornments no peasant could ever afford.

Lady Allerton's eyes sparkled as brightly as the fashions displayed before her. "Which shall I try on first?"

"This one, of course." Mademoiselle offered her the midnight blue, a sleeveless evening gown done in three layers, each one cut at a slightly different angle, and embroidered and beaded meticulously. "Eva, you will help her."

"Yes, of course." Eva didn't mind that Mademoiselle had once again phrased her request as a command. She couldn't wait to see these enchanting designs on beautiful Lady Allerton.

"You will come outside." This time, the command was directed at Lady Allerton. "I must see you in the full light."

"Of course. Eva, shall we?"

They retreated behind the screen, and Eva carefully helped Lady Allerton out of her simple day frock and into the delicate evening gown. Then she stood back. "Oh, my lady. There aren't words to describe how extraordinary you look. That dress, its style—it was made for you. Mademoiselle was right, although it pains me to say it," she added in a whisper. They shared a laugh.

Outside, Mademoiselle and the others waited for them on the main garden path. Another had joined them, someone who made both Eva and Lady Allerton come to sudden, uncertain halts.

"What is he doing here?" Lady Allerton demanded, pointing to Narcisse and his camera equipment, set up beside the path.

Marcelle waited nearby as well, but instead of her table having been set up, she held several cosmetic brushes in her hands, and the pocket of the apron she wore bulged from whatever lay inside. As though she had run outside at a moment's notice with only the most basic tools of her trade.

With a woman of Lady Allerton's beauty, not much else would be needed.

"What is going on down here?" Eva pivoted to discover Lady Phoebe hurrying down the terrace steps. "Julia, you're not seriously considering allowing your picture to be taken?"

"I . . . I'm not sure." Lady Allerton looked about her, as if searching for an ally.

Eva stepped up beside her. "Don't do anything you don't wish to, my lady."

"Ah, you are being silly. Julia . . ." Mademoiselle glanced over one sister's shoulder to address the other as well. "Phoebe. As I said, this is only for me to see how my new designs will wear on an English gentlewoman. How they will enhance her, and she enhance them. A photo or two in each outfit. What could it hurt? They will be for my eyes only."

Lady Allerton crossed her arms in front of her. "You promise?"

"*Mais oui!* Of course."

Lady Allerton turned about to glance at her sister. "What do you think?"

Lady Phoebe shook her head and shrugged. "Do as you think best."

*   *   *

"She truly does remarkable work," Phoebe said to Françoise Deschamps. They had retreated to the garden table on the terrace, where they could observe Julia's fashion show but still chat without disturbing the others. Eva had remained below, to be on hand to help Julia change into each ensemble. There had been four so far, and it didn't appear that Mademoiselle would be satisfied anytime soon.

Phoebe had seen nothing of Owen since breakfast that morning. Or the other gentlemen for that matter. They had dressed in their country tweeds and had announced their intentions of engaging in target shooting out in one of the meadows. Ever since their ill-fated encounter in the downstairs hall, Owen seemed to be avoiding Phoebe. True, they had ridden together with Theo and Chesterhaven, but they had spent little time together since. He must still be angry, but she couldn't bring herself to regret either her actions or her words. If they were to have any future together, he must accept her as she was.

Then again, it wasn't only Owen doing the avoiding. Chesterhaven had good reason to put distance between himself and Phoebe, and since Owen hadn't hauled off and blackened one of his eyes, Chesterhaven must have judged it safe to go shooting with him. Then there was Theo— poor, beleaguered Theo—who seemed to have yielded a good deal of authority over his ancestral home to Julia, who showed little inclination to compromise these days.

"She is an artist in the truest sense," Françoise said in agreement with Phoebe's last comment. "I am very lucky to work with her."

Phoebe couldn't have hoped for a better invitation to ask a few questions. "How *did* you come to work for Coco? Were you in the fashion business before the war?"

"Me? *Non*." She spoke with a slight chuckle. She leaned her head back, allowing the sun to bathe her face. The light turned her graying blond hair to flashing silver. "It was after the war. We met in Paris."

"Had you always lived in Paris? Is that where you spent the war?" Phoebe found her curiosity to be genuine.

"No, I am from the north originally, but I spent most of the war in Provence, in the South of France, far from the fighting. My husband, you see, had been ailing, and one night a fire broke out—a kitchen fire—in our home. It was an accident, but caused by the carelessness of German soldiers who were occupying the property. The house went up so quickly . . . Phillippe did not make it out. I fled soon after, in the middle of the night, with only what I could hide beneath my clothing."

"Oh, I'm so sorry. About your husband *and* about losing your home." Phoebe shuddered to imagine what life would have been like if the enemy had broached England's borders, if they had occupied her beloved Foxwood Hall, if she and her family had been driven out. Yes, they had sacrificed during the war, they had suffered horrible losses, but on the whole they had been fortunate. So very fortunate.

"Yes. I evacuated south and arrived on the Mediterranean early in the war. It was only afterward that I went to Paris, as there was nothing to go home to." Françoise ran her fingers through her cropped hair, the smooth strands falling lightly back into place. "Life goes on, no? And I found Mademoiselle . . . through mutual acquaintances. She noticed I had a good head for business. For keeping track of things."

"That was lucky."

"It was, yes."

"And you're happy there, at Maison Chanel."

"Oh yes." Françoise's breathy reply might have been an

avowal of love, leaving Phoebe with no doubt as to the woman's loyalties. If she were to coax any information out of her, she would have to proceed carefully.

"And the others? Are they as content there as you?"

Françoise pulled her gaze from the clouds scudding over the gardens and studied Phoebe a moment. "That is a good question. Perhaps not as I am. I have become Coco's friend. Their positions are different. They are employees first and foremost, and as such, they are more prone to discontent. You see?"

"I believe I do. I can see that you and Coco are close. She relies on you. She trusts you, while she doesn't always extend that trust to the others, I understand."

"*Exactement.*" She leaned on her elbows, her chin resting in her hands. "You have insight, for someone so young and who has never worked."

Phoebe's hackles rose. "What makes you so sure I haven't?"

"You are the granddaughter of an earl, no?"

"That's true," she conceded, "but during the war, I worked hard and long organizing and collecting supplies for our troops on the Continent. I still do such work, only now it's for the returned soldiers and their families."

"Ah, but you do not get paid." Françoise held up a finger. "You are not dependent on the work for your food and clothes and the roof over your head. It is one thing to wish to work, it is quite another to *have* to."

"Well, yes, you're right" Phoebe conceded. Suddenly, she wondered how Françoise managed to turn the focus on her, rather than on Phoebe's questions. Had it been deliberate, or merely a trick of the conversation? She decided to remedy matters quickly. "Do you need to work as well?"

Françoise nodded. "I do, now. Not before the war, but ever since. You see, I lost not only my home and husband, but everything. I arrived in Paris nearly penniless, my money having run out months earlier. I had been living on the largesse of friends. I have no wish to do that anymore."

"Coco trusts you," Phoebe said, returning to the earlier topic, "but she doesn't trust the others. Do they trust her? Trust her not to cast them out without a moment's notice? Trust her not to turn on them on a whim?"

"You do not think highly of Coco, do you?" Françoise sat back, looking pensive.

"To be honest, I'm not sure. I saw how she treated Suzette that first day when you all arrived. She flatly rejected her in favor of India. That didn't seem fair."

"There was more to it. Things you did not see, that happened in France before we came."

"Such as the terrible argument between Suzette and Narcisse?"

"*Mon Dieu.*" She shook her head. "How did you hear about that?"

"People talk," was all Phoebe would say. She had no intention of getting Marcelle or Claudette—or Eva for that matter—in trouble.

"People should close their mouths. But yes, they argued. Lovers do. Then again, Suzette had many arguments, some of them with Coco. She had . . . how do you English say? Gotten too big for her britches."

"Then Suzette and Narcisse were lovers?"

"Of course. That was no secret."

"How angry was he?"

Françoise met her gaze sharply. "As angry as I have ever seen him. And that is saying something for a man who occasionally throws tantrums. Artist types, you know."

Phoebe weighed the wisdom of her next question and asked it anyway. "Was their argument over the Earl of Chesterhaven?"

A smile played over her lips. "However did you come to that conclusion?"

Phoebe noticed Françoise hadn't denied the allegation. "I've observed a few things. For one, he very determinedly ignored her at dinner the night she died, as if he very much wished to give the impression of indifference toward her. And for another, his reaction to her death seemed extreme for someone who barely knew her. Which led me to the conclusion he *did* know her, rather well."

"How astute you are, Phoebe. You would make a good businesswoman." Her gray eyes narrowed. "I think there is something else you observed about the earl, no?"

"He's a mongrel," she freely admitted.

Françoise threw back her head and laughed. "Yes, I have a similar impression. He takes no woman seriously. Certainly not Coco. But she will be all right. That is always her revenge against unprincipled men, that she emerges intact and relatively unharmed." She fell into thought, staring down at the gardens as Narcisse posed Julia in yet another outfit whose beadwork glittered in the sunlight. Then she said, "Yes, I believe the argument was over Chessy, that he and Suzette had been . . . well . . . you know. Coco obviously knew about it, too, though she didn't speak of it. She didn't speak to Chessy either, not for several days afterward. Not until we left for England, when she relented. I suppose he managed to appease her in some way, or she simply decided to ignore his little indiscretion. And Suzette . . . She spoke to no one about it at the time and no one spoke to her. You know how these things are. The woman is always blamed."

"There was no one she could confide in?" How sad for her, Phoebe thought. Despite her arrogance and lack of compassion for others, no one deserved to be completely alone.

"I see pity in your eyes, Phoebe." Françoise's own eyes

turned as cold as steel. "You are wasting your time with such sentiments. She did not deserve it."

Phoebe hesitated, realizing she had inadvertently struck a nerve. "What do you mean? What did she do to you?"

"She . . ." Françoise trailed off. Inhaled deeply. "She made trouble between people. She used them to her advantage. She never cared about consequences."

"Your animosity toward her seems more personal than that. There must have been something."

Phoebe held her breath hoping Françoise would reply. But in the next moment, Coco called to her from across the garden and beckoned with outstretched hands.

"Excuse me. I am needed." Françoise came to her feet and hurried down the steps.

CHAPTER 12

Eva stepped out of Lady Phoebe's room as Claudette pushed her way through the door from the service staircase. She wondered what the clothing mistress was doing in that part of the house, but she soon learned the reason as, once again, her assistance was requested.

"Mademoiselle wishes me to pack Suzette's things, and Remie is busy washing Mademoiselle's and Françoise's delicates," Claudette explained. "Would you mind?"

"Not at all." Eva had never been so much in demand, neither at home nor when traveling with Lady Phoebe. True, her duties kept her busy throughout the day, but she usually found time for a cup of tea or to join the other servants belowstairs for a quick chat. Not that she minded the extra work here. It helped pass the time before she and Lady Phoebe could go home again.

When she entered Suzette's bedroom, however, a chill slithered up her spine. The faint scent of smoke lingered in the air, clinging to the bedclothes and draperies. Eva tried to avoid looking at the bed where the poor woman suffocated, and went directly to the tall bureau to begin emptying the drawers. Still, she and Claudette found it necessary to use the bed to lay out the clothing before folding it and packing it away. For that purpose, Suzette's trunks had been brought in and stood gaping like giant mouths waiting to be fed. It saddened Eva to think they would be devouring the remnants of someone's life.

"*Bien*, you are both here." Coco strode into the room, her presence filling it despite her petite form. "*Merci*, Eva, for helping once again."

"You're quite welcome, Mademoiselle. Between the two of us, we should make short work of the job."

"I want it done properly now," Mademoiselle said in her commanding way. "This is a job for women who understand clothing, which is why I did not ask Marcelle to help. Some of these things I lent to Suzette. They are costly and I do not wish them ruined in the packing."

"Be assured they will not be, Mademoiselle." Claudette spoke with a dismissive hint in her voice. She no doubt wished Mademoiselle to leave them to the task, but Mademoiselle showed no sign of going.

"Eva, I see you have begun with the bureau. Good. Finish with that. Claudette, continue with the armoire. I will look over what you have already placed on the bed. Once everything has been emptied, you can begin folding."

Eva didn't relish having an audience any more than Claudette did, judging by her tight-lipped expression. She finished emptying the drawer she had been working on and then opened the one below it. Slowly the piles on the bed grew higher. They worked mostly in silence with occasional comments from Mademoiselle. She suddenly let out a shriek.

"What is this?" She held up a silk scarf from the top of the stack Eva had just placed on the bed. The semi-sheer square bore a bold floral pattern. "Where was this?"

"In there." Eva pointed to the dressing table, where she

had moved on after the bureau. "In the top drawer, Mademoiselle."

"This is mine," the designer declared. "And I never gave it to her, nor lent it. She stole it."

"Surely not, Mademoiselle," Eva found herself saying, though she knew no such thing.

The Frenchwoman pinned Eva with a scathing glare. "Do you think I do not know my own collection? This is from last spring. Part of the fashions she modeled, but I most certainly did not give it to her to keep." Her gaze darted over the bed. "What else did she steal, I wonder? We must go through everything again. All of it."

With that, Mademoiselle began flinging garments this way and that, some of them landing back on the bed, others crumpling to the floor. Eva and Claudette scampered to retrieve them from underfoot before Mademoiselle trampled them. So much for not wanting anything to be ruined.

"This! This is another." Mademoiselle held up a blouse that looked very much like it belonged with the Russian-inspired collection Lady Julia had modeled earlier, with its square neckline trimmed in embroidery. "I never gave this to her. No one was to have worn any of this yet." She reached out again, this time sliding a belted jacket lined in fur from one of the piles. Her gaze narrowed on Claudette. "How could you not have known these things were missing?"

"I am sorry, Mademoiselle." Claudette shuffled her feet and raised a hand to dab at the perspiration beading her forehead. "There are so many things to keep track of . . ."

"That is no excuse. You are my clothing mistress. It is your job to know where each and every article of clothing is at all times. *At. All. Times.*" Mademoiselle's voice rose with each word, hitting a crescendo that made both Eva and Claudette flinch. She went to the armoire and shoved the remaining clothing aside, only to begin flipping through them one at a time, the hangers scraping across the bar.

She found several more garments and accessories—a beret, several belts, a pair of satin boots—and gathered them with the other stolen items. Eva watched, feeling as though she should be helping, although Mademoiselle's expression didn't invite her to step forward. Claudette looked on from the corner she had retreated to, her face gone pale. Would she really be held to blame for another woman's actions?

Mademoiselle's head reared suddenly, her eyes sparking. She scurried to the dressing table. "Where is her jewelry—where?"

"Right there, Mademoiselle." Eva pointed at the jewelry box sitting on top. "I was leaving it for last."

Mademoiselle wasted not a moment in flipping the box open and digging inside. The contents rattled beneath her fingertips. She drew something out that streamed from the box like drops of water.

"These black pearls, they were most certainly not hers." Mademoiselle held up a length at least two feet long, the rope swinging from her grasp like a hangman's noose.

"They are not real, Mademoiselle," Claudette offered weakly. "You know that."

"Do you think it matters if these are faux pearls? No, they are not as precious as the real thing, but I have them manufactured to be as lifelike as humanly possible, to make them accessible to ordinary women. Do you think I mean to throw them away when I am done with them? *Non!* All of these things, they are mine."

She went still for a long moment, her gaze once more riveted on Claudette. Then she crossed the room to the other woman and stopped only a foot or two away. "It is impossible you did not know about this. That leads me to conclude she stole with your blessing."

"*Non*, Mademoiselle! *Certainement pas.*"

Certainly not, Eva translated silently. But was the clothing mistress being truthful, or desperately trying to save her job? Apparently, Mademoiselle wondered the same thing.

"Ah, *oui*." Mademoiselle shook her head at a cowering Claudette. "Tell me the truth. Were you and she stealing, and perhaps selling my things secretly? Did you think to make yourself a little more money? Do you believe I do not pay you enough?"

"*Mademoiselle, s'il vous plaît...*" Claudette fell to whimpering, until Eva pitied her. But she also noticed Claudette didn't deny the charge.

"Perhaps I pay you too much," Mademoiselle mocked. She pulled her slender form to its full height, hefting her delicately pointed chin. "I think I should not pay you at all, not anymore. I think I will let you make your own way on the streets of Paris from now on."

"*Mademoiselle, non, s'il vous plaît*," Claudette repeated, her voice fading to a sob.

"Come." Mademoiselle pivoted on the low heel of her pump. "Both of you. We are going to search through Claudette's room. If I find more stolen things, you will sleep in a cell tonight."

Eva's stomach fell. She had no wish to participate in the downfall of Mademoiselle's clothing mistress, even if she was guilty. What was it about these people that they were capable of disrupting the lives of everyone around them?

Yet, to her satisfaction, they found nothing questionable in Claudette's room, down the corridor from Eva's on the second floor. It was a quick search, as it appeared Claudette traveled lightly. Mademoiselle even peeled back the mattress, checked for loose floorboards, and burrowed through the dresser. Mademoiselle made no apologies for the intrusion, nor did she reassure Claudette that she could remain with Maison Chanel. Instead, she issued a terse order.

"Go back to Suzette's room and finish up." She clapped her hands twice. "If you find any more stolen items, put them aside. Then come down to the pavilion. I have a new project for you. Be sure to bring your very best shears."

"*Oui*, Mademoiselle," Claudette replied weakly. She waited until her employer's footsteps faded down the corridor before pivoting to face Eva. "I am sorry you had to witness this. But as you can see, I am no thief."

"No, and I'm glad you're still employed by Maison Chanel." That certainly seemed to be the case, anyway. A new project? Mademoiselle would hardly show her new ideas to someone she intended to fire. "If she had wished to give you the sack, she would have done it already."

Claudette nodded and led the way out of the room. On the way back down to Suzette's room, relief coursed through Eva that the distressing interlude had reached a happy conclusion. And yet . . . Mademoiselle had made a valid point when she said nothing should go missing from the collections without Claudette knowing about it. It *was* her job to keep track of every item, from frocks to shoes to accessories, and everything in between.

So how to explain it? Had the pair been stealing and selling on the side as Mademoiselle accused? If so, whose idea had it been? Had they been in on it together? Had Suzette forced Claudette to go along with it? Or had Claudette forced Suzette to do the stealing?

Had an illicit partnership somehow turned to murder? If so, perhaps the evidence might still be among Suzette's things.

* * *

Voices in the dining room let Phoebe know Theo and the other men had returned from their morning adventures. Had Owen been purposely avoiding her since their spat? Or had she been avoiding him? She couldn't honestly say, but perhaps the time had come for a truce.

She went into the dining room to find the three men sitting casually at one end of the long table, a platter heaped with sandwiches and a pitcher of dark frothy stout on the table between them. They didn't notice her at first and went on with whatever they were discussing, their words punctuated with quiet laughter.

"Are women welcome?" she asked as she approached the table.

As one, they came to their feet. Theo pulled out the chair beside his own. "You're always welcome, Phoebe, you know that."

"I hope so," she said earnestly, and met Owen's gaze. Was he still angry? Was she? She wasn't quite sure, but she didn't wish to be. So perhaps there lay her answer. She avoided looking at Chesterhaven. If her sudden presence made him uncomfortable, so much the better. "Where did you all go on your travels after target shooting this morning?"

"Where didn't we go, is more the question," Owen replied with a rueful chuckle. "I think I'm as well acquainted with Allerton Place now as Theo here."

"Don't exaggerate." Theo reached for another sandwich. "Phoebe, care for some? There's plenty, and you'll find extra plates on the buffet. Glasses, too. Help yourself. We're on our own, as I told Tewes we'd fend for ourselves. If you don't care for ale, I could ring for lemonade."

"Don't mind if I do, and ale is fine." She grabbed a plate and mug from the buffet and returned to the table. Owen lifted the platter and held it before her. She chose rare roast beef between pieces of thick, freshly baked bread. Then she half filled her mug with stout.

"Didn't know you were a beer drinker," Theo commented with a smile.

"I'm not, generally, but there's no harm in it occasionally." To prove her point, she raised the mug to her lips and drank deeply. The rich, robust flavor enveloped her tongue, leaving a tangy bitterness after she swallowed.

"Tell us," Theo said after a swig of his own stout, "what went on around here while we were gone?"

"I think I should let Julia fill you in on most of it."

"Most of what?" Julia appeared in the doorway, back in her usual attire of day frock and comfortable, low-heeled pumps. The men stood briefly, then resumed their seats as Julia joined them at the table. This time, it was Owen who pulled out a chair for her. Chesterhaven kept himself busy by avoiding direct eye contact with Phoebe.

"Apparently, Phoebe doesn't think it's her place to tell us what went on here in our absence." Suddenly, Theo returned to his feet, his complexion turning pale. "There hasn't been more trouble?"

"No, not at all." Julia waved him back into his seat. She looked over the contents of the platter. "We've all eaten lunch, but those do look scrumptious."

Phoebe passed her the platter, wondering if she should have invited further discussion of their morning, or if she should simply have told the men nothing noteworthy had occurred.

Before biting into her sandwich, Julia said, "As to your question, Theo, I had a splendid time this morning modeling outfits for Coco."

Theo's eyebrows gathered for an instant before he schooled his features. "She got you to do it, eh?"

Julia looked concerned. "You don't mind, do you?"

"My dear, I told you it was your decision."

"Good, because it turned out to be splendid fun. That man, Narcisse, even took some pictures, but Coco promised me they were for her use only." She turned toward Chesterhaven and said with a teasing smile. "Coco *does* keep her promises, doesn't she?"

The man nearly choked on a bite of his salmon and watercress sandwich. After a draft of stout, he coughed away the remaining tightness in his throat and managed to stammer a reply. "Of c-course she does. Usually. Ah . . . em . . . You know Coco."

Julia frowned. "Whatever does that mean?"

"Yes, Chessy," Theo joined in, "what do you mean? Is Coco not a woman of her word?"

"Of course she is." Chesterhaven took another sip of his stout. "Er . . . where is she now?"

"She and Françoise were out in the tent earlier with the clothing mistress and wouldn't let anyone else in," Julia said, "and now the two of them are holed up in Coco's room, working on something she said is entirely new. An idea that came to her since she's been here. It's a great secret but she says we'll know more in the morning." Julia raised her shoulders and pressed her hands together. "It's so exciting, especially to think that her visit to our home is what inspired her."

The conversation soon turned to the tenant farms and the improvements Theo had introduced in the past three years since the war ended. There were concerns that the recent repeal of the Agricultural Act, put in place during the war to ensure minimum wages for farm laborers and stable prices for produce, might lead to a serious decline of the farming industry. That would mean food shortages, higher prices, and increased poverty in rural areas.

Phoebe sighed over the prospect. "I'll prepare everyone at the RCVF for increased need in the coming year." During the first year of peace, she had formed an organization called the Relief and Comfort of Veterans and Their Families, which continued the work she had performed during the war, gathering and distributing supplies for the soldiers.

Owen leaned toward her and quietly said, "I'll help in every way I can."

She beamed at him. He had, on several occasions, already donated untold bolts of wool, along with finished clothing and blankets, from his woolen mills in Yorkshire. How could she be angry with such a man? How could she not show him the patience he deserved?

After they'd eaten, Julia went for a lie-down and Theo and Chesterhaven went out to the stables. Phoebe waited for Owen to come up with an excuse to be off on his own, but to her relief it didn't come. Instead, he offered her his hand and together they went out to the gardens. For once, this part of the grounds was deserted, except for the gardener and his assistant, giving the rose bushes their autumn pruning. She and Owen meandered in the opposite direction.

"Quiet out here this afternoon," she commented.

"A nice change."

"Just what I was thinking. I've also been wondering how much longer Coco and her cohorts will be here." When he angled a glance down at her she held up her free hand, the other still warm in his grasp. "Not that it's any of my business."

"Actually, I've wondered the same. There's nothing to keep them here, not with the police having dismissed Suzette's death as an accident."

His mention of Suzette surprised Phoebe. She had expected him to avoid the subject entirely. "Oh, as far as Coco is concerned, it's as though Suzette never existed.

She's determined to finish photographing her collection. I wonder what this new idea of hers involves."

"Does it matter? You're right. She's an awfully cold fish to have dismissed the matter and gotten on with her so-called work."

Although she basically agreed with him, something in his dismissal of Coco's endeavors didn't sit well with Phoebe. "It *is* work—hard work. And I think she's brilliant at it. Just as you are with your business." She raised an eyebrow at him to help make her point. "And in a significant way, you are both in the same business—clothing people. For all you know, Maison Chanel will become a customer of your mills."

"Then I'd better be nice to her, eh?" He spoke with a chuckle that irked Phoebe. Would he be so flippant about Coco's fashion house if it were run by a man?

The wind kicked up, blowing clouds across the sun and thrusting the gardens into shadow. Phoebe shivered, and Owen slipped an arm around her shoulders. "Perhaps we should go in."

"No," she insisted, "I'm fine. I like it out here. Inside, I keep imagining I smell smoke, even when I'm nowhere near Suzette's room. It's unnerving."

"Then let's sit in here." He turned them toward the horseshoe formation of hedges with the reflecting pool inside, where Eva had confronted Narcisse and angered him with her questions. They sat on a bench beneath a Japanese maple. The water seemed to shiver, as Phoebe had done, as the wind skimmed its surface. "Why are you sticking up for her, anyway?" Owen asked. "I didn't think you liked her any better than I do."

"I don't. But there are things I admire about her." She quirked her lips at his begrudging shrug. "All right, there *are* many things I *don't* like about her."

"Good. At least your good sense hasn't completely deserted you."

Phoebe went rigid, until he turned and grinned at her. "Only joking, my dear. One could never accuse you of not having good sense. A tendency toward recklessness, perhaps, an insatiable curiosity, indeed, and more courage than any one person has a right to, most assuredly." He took on a mock-pained look and sighed. "One can't but assume it's your good sense that's seen you through the many scrapes you've gotten yourself into. And I'm grateful for it."

She returned his grin, his words having sent shoots of happiness down to her very toes. "Then no more telling me what I should or shouldn't do?"

He hesitated in replying, and in that pause, voices from beyond the hedges reached their ears.

"Have her then, though what you see in that little girl I cannot fathom."

Phoebe's eyes went wide. "That sounds like Coco."

"I don't see anything in her, my love" came the reply. "I was only talking to her."

Owen pursed his lips. "Chessy."

"Uh-oh." Phoebe craned forward on the bench, trying to see beyond the opening in the hedges to the garden beyond. Whom could they be talking about? Surely Coco hadn't heard about what happened between Phoebe and Chesterhaven in the stables? She remembered the looks she had gotten from the groom and his assistants. But she couldn't imagine them telling tales, especially not ones that could reach the ears of a guest. "I can't see them. Can you?"

Owen shook his head, a finger to his lips.

"Talking to her on the threshold of her open bedroom door? Were you on your way in or on your way out when I caught you?"

"Coco, you didn't *catch* me at anything. Don't be daft. I was only seeing if she needed anything."

"Now I am daft? What does she need? For you to massage her sore ankle, hold her swollen wrist? Or more than that?"

"You're being ridiculous." Chessy's voice had gone from pleading to angry. "I'm here with you. Isn't that enough for you?"

"You are an intolerable flirt. You think I do not know what went on between you and Suzette? I know. Everyone knows, you fool."

"That's . . . not true . . ."

"Yes, it is," Owen whispered. When Phoebe questioned him with a look, he shook his head. "No, he didn't tell me anything. But his reputation precedes him—everywhere. It's what he does."

Phoebe hissed a breath between her teeth and scowled, then caught herself. She tried to smooth her disgust away, but too late. Owen grasped her chin and held her steady when she attempted to look away from him.

"Has he . . . ?" His whisper broke off as his gaze traveled over her features, searching deeply. His eyes blazed. "He did, that fiend. When was it? Why didn't you tell me?"

She felt a rush of panic. What would he do? "Owen, it doesn't matter. Let it go."

"Let it go? Are you serious?" He broke off, then went still. "The stables yesterday. After our ride. It was then, wasn't it? It was the only time he's been alone with you."

How had she ever thought she could keep it from him? A weight of dread sank in her stomach. She tightened her fingers around his hand, as much to plead with him as to hold him in place and prevent him from running after Chesterhaven right then. "Please, leave it alone. He didn't get away with anything, I assure you. And he won't try it again. Not with me."

That drained some of the anger from Owen's features. A ghost of a smile hovered about his lips. "What did you do?"

She curled her free hand into a fist. "This. Square in the jaw."

His smile burst forth, irrepressible. He slapped his thigh. "Good! Good for you. You should have kicked him, too, for good measure."

"I think striking him lent just the right amount of humiliation to the occasion."

"I've no doubt you're right. No wonder he's been acting so oddly, especially around you. I couldn't figure it out, because he certainly hasn't been flirting with you that I've seen." He sat back, still smiling. "He's afraid of you."

"Then you'll leave it alone?"

He hesitated, the breath leaving him. Then he gave a nod. "For now."

"Coco, wait," they heard Chesterhaven cry out, followed by the thudding of his footsteps across the lawn. Coco answered with something shrill, the words of which Phoebe couldn't make out, or Owen either, judging by the quirk of his mouth.

"It sounds like fate has conspired to serve up what he deserves, anyway," he commented.

"Fate in the person of one Coco Chanel?"

Owen chuckled and pulled Phoebe closer.

CHAPTER 13

That evening after supper in the servants' hall, Eva was on her way to the back stairs when she heard something that made her pause. Someone was using the telephone in the housekeeper's parlor, but the voice was far too youthful to be Mrs. Bristol. Nor did the speaker's West London accent sound like it could be one of the servants.

"For the last time, Mother, I am not coming home."

India Vale. And by the sounds of it, this was no cordial conversation.

"Because I'm not marrying him," the girl hissed over the line. "I don't care what you and Father want. *No.* Good God, Mother, he's as old as Methuselah, that's why."

Eva stood riveted just beyond the threshold, the door to the parlor open barely an inch. It was enough for India's voice to carry into the corridor, although she spoke so quietly that, had Eva been a few feet farther away, she probably wouldn't have heard a thing.

A quick glance down the hallway confirmed that the rest of the staff had either lingered in the servants' hall or were carrying the dishes and remnants of supper into the kitchen. Eva saw no sign of Mrs. Bristol, but then, if she had given India permission to use her telephone, she would make herself scarce long enough for the girl to complete her call.

So, the Vales were attempting to marry their daughter off to some old codger—why? For his money? Perhaps, although the Vales were well-off enough. Still, some families could never have too much and weren't above using their daughters as conduits for more. Then again, it could be a title they were after. Yes, having achieved all they could monetarily, the next step for many a nouveau riche family was to ingratiate themselves to the aristocracy.

"Do you think I care how much effort you've put into planning a wedding?" India laughed, but the sound held no humor. "You shouldn't have bothered. I told you right from the first I would never say *I will* to that man. I don't even like him. If he were my grandfather I'd *never* visit him."

My goodness, who could this man be? And how on earth could the Vales think to chain their daughter to a man old enough to be her grandfather? Or was India exaggerating, as young people tended to do? That was probably it, but even so, if she didn't wish to marry the fellow, it should have put an end to the matter. This was 1921, after all, not 1821.

"It was only a handbag, Mother, and a tiny one at that. And yes, the bracelet. What of it? Everyone does it nowadays. It's not like they're going to hang me."

What? What could India be talking about now? Eva craned forward, bringing her ear closer. She glanced over her shoulder. The kitchen assistants were still making a steady stream back and forth from the dining hall to the kitchen, none of them paying her any attention. From the hall itself came laughter and conversation, and a moment later some of the men broke out in a lively ballad.

Eva turned her attention back to Mrs. Bristol's parlor.

"I'm sorry you were stuck with the bill." India didn't

sound at all sorry. She sounded bored. "You would have been anyway, wouldn't you, if I'd gone in and added those things to your account."

Had India stolen from a store? Eva frowned, suddenly seeing the girl in an entirely new light. That open, friendly, agreeable young lady—a thief?

"No, Mother, I'm not about to tell you where I am. I'm perfectly fine, and I don't need anything. Mother, no— wait!" There was a pause, and then, "Father, I don't know what Mother's told you. I'm only—no, I didn't just raise my voice to her. Truly. I merely told her I'm fine and will be home soon. But you know how she is, she worries about me all the time. Yes, put her back on and I'll apologize."

Eva winced at how easily India lied to her father, how her voice smoothed to a pleasing lilt, and how she played on her father's apparent tendency to spoil her. India's next words proved how disingenuous she was. "Mother, you can blasted well tell everyone the wedding is off. And no, I'm not coming home. Don't worry, I'll get by. You just might be surprised when you see how well."

The receiver slammed onto its cradle, and Eva took that as her cue to scramble back down the corridor, not toward the staircase but toward the servants' hall. She stopped just short of the doorway and then doubled back again, this time much more slowly, as if she had only just finished her supper. A tap-tapping of crutches and the thud of India's good leg heralded the girl's appearance. Eva smiled and nodded to her.

"Miss Vale—India. What in the world are you doing down here?" Her own duplicity prompted her to cross her fingers behind her back.

India wiped a scowl from her face, but not before Eva took note of it. "Using the telephone."

"I'm sure there is one or two abovestairs you might

have used." Eva approached her as if she hadn't heard the scandalous conversation—albeit only one side of it.

"I didn't wish to disturb Lord or Lady Allerton."

"Ah. Can I help you upstairs?"

"No, I'm fine. I'll use the service lift. Mrs. Bristol already said I might."

Eva had known about the lift but had no wish to ride in it herself. Like motorcars, lifts sent people in directions and at speeds no human should go. She'd had little choice but to use a hotel lift while accompanying the family to the Isle of Wight two years ago, and each time she had felt as if her body arrived at her destination several seconds before her stomach. "All right then. Good night."

Eva hurried upstairs to the first floor and let herself into Lady Phoebe's bedroom. She passed the time tidying an already tidy room and setting out Lady Phoebe's bedclothes. Finally, the door opened and Lady Phoebe came in, yawning.

"Eva, you didn't need to wait up for me. I was upstairs in the nursery playing with Charles. I do believe he was trying to say *auntie*. Isn't that lovely?"

"Very lovely, my lady. But I had good reason to wait. I've something to tell you."

Lady Phoebe wasted no time in settling onto the room's small settee and drawing Eva down beside her. "You've learned something new."

"I have. But I must preface it by admitting I resorted to eavesdropping. As always, I'm not at all proud of it but—"

"Yes, of course not. But needs must, mustn't they? Tell me all." Lady Phoebe's eyes widened in anticipation.

"Were you aware that India came belowstairs to use Mrs. Bristol's telephone?"

Lady Phoebe gave a quick shake of the head. "Why

would she do that? There is one in Theo's study and one in Julia's sitting room."

"She didn't wish to be overheard. In fact, she obviously tried to time it so that even belowstairs, we'd all be busy eating supper and then cleaning up afterward. Unfortunately for her, I'm not required to help with the cleaning."

"I should hope not." Lady Phoebe drew herself up with an indignant sniff. "You've been doing enough around here as it is."

"Yes, well." Eva waved off Lady Phoebe's concerns. "India was talking with her mother, and the things she said! If I'd ever spoken to my mum that way—even now—she'd take a switch to me."

"Goodness, what did she say?"

"Apparently, her parents were planning a wedding for India and some older man she has no intention of marrying."

"Oh." A cloud passed over Lady Phoebe's face. "The way Julia married Gil Townsend?"

"No, not like that. Because your sister went into the marriage voluntarily. Your grandparents certainly didn't force her."

"No, but they encouraged it. Especially Grams." Lady Phoebe shook her head and sighed. "It was all so wrong, so ill-fated, and look how it ended. India is right to refuse."

"I agree with you there. However, there is more. It seems India has run off from home, and her parents have no idea where she is. And she's been in a spot of trouble."

"Trouble? Of what sort?"

"Stealing. As in she acknowledged to her mother that she had stolen a handbag and a bracelet from a shop, but I heard not the tiniest bit of remorse in her voice. It was all the same to her whether she stole or let her parents pay for the items. She was quite flippant about the whole affair.

And then she ended the conversation by telling her mother she had no intention of going home, and she slammed the receiver."

"You mean to say they don't know she's here at Allerton Place?" Eva shook her head, prompting a look of disbelief. "But why not? There's nothing wrong with her being here. Julia and Theo are respected members of the community. And she's well chaperoned, for goodness sake."

"Yes, but I think if they knew where she was, her parents would come immediately to bring her home."

"This is awfully brazen of her, to stand against their wishes like that. She isn't even twenty-one yet."

"I think it's more than that." Eva lowered her voice, even though there was no one to overhear. "Don't you see? India has a lot to lose. Namely, her independence. I think modeling isn't something she's doing for her own entertainment. I think the opportunity came along at just the right moment in the person of Mademoiselle, and India seized her chance. Think about it. Permanent employment with Maison Chanel means she'd never have to rely on her parents again. And she would certainly never have to go home if she didn't wish to."

Eva let the rest of her meaning hang in the air. She watched Lady Phoebe work it out, which didn't take long. "Suzette stood in her way. What's more, Suzette nearly ended India's potential career before it had even started when she caused India's fall from her horse."

"That's right." Eva nodded at each revelation. "She was so angry at Suzette—perhaps not merely because of the incident on face value, but what it could have meant for her plans to free herself of her parents."

"Why would her parents try to force her to marry such an older man?" Lady Phoebe mused aloud. "They're wealthy enough, I should think."

"I wondered the same thing. But then I realized we're not talking about any well-brought-up young lady from a good home. We're talking about a girl who steals, who runs off without telling her parents where she is going. And who talks to her mother as most people wouldn't talk to their hall boy."

"Yes." Lady Phoebe compressed her lips in thought. "They're hoping marriage to an older man will curtail her wilder tendencies. Perhaps unfairly—I mean, how awful to be saddled with a man one doesn't have the slightest regard for. But at this point they might be desperate to control her."

"I think that's it exactly. You haven't heard back from your sister yet, have you?"

"Amelia? No. But I think it's time to telephone her again and see if she's learned anything. I've a feeling that if India is as unruly as what you overheard indicates, at least some of her peers know about it. I'll call up to London again first thing tomorrow."

Phoebe telephoned the Olivers' home early the following morning, but she still missed Amelia by a quarter of an hour. She had gone riding in Hyde Park, and the housekeeper promised to relay the message.

In the meantime, India resumed modeling in the gardens shortly after breakfast. Mademoiselle wanted to take advantage of the morning light on such a crisp autumn day. On her way out, India mentioned how chilly it was compared with the day they'd arrived.

"It will bring out the color in your cheeks," was all Coco had to say about it. She didn't even suggest moving the day's outfits into the house to allow India to change in warm surroundings.

But perhaps someone should. Whatever assumptions she and Eva had made about the girl last night, she shouldn't be made to catch a chill. Phoebe followed them through the drawing room and outside. She approached Coco with her concerns, but the woman waved off her warning.

"Never mind about that. I have other ideas for you."

Phoebe took a step back. "Ideas?"

"Ah, *oui*." Coco suddenly lurched closer, and without further warning began mussing Phoebe's hair, carefully pinned back earlier by Eva. Strands fell about her face, and then Coco turned her this way and that, inspecting her as if she were an item for sale at a church bazaar. Had she and Julia finally decided to make good on their intentions to fix her?

"Whatever are you doing?" Phoebe demanded, in no mood to be treated as one of Coco's projects.

"You are perfect. Perfect! India, she is too young for what I have in mind. But you, you are just right."

"What are you going on about?"

"Where is your Eva? You will need her."

"For what? Coco, I only came out to remind you it's colder today than it's been and you don't want India catching cold. She has enough to contend with, with her sprained ankle."

"India will be fine. As will you." She turned and called over her shoulder, "Claudette! Do you have the pieces ready?"

Claudette came around to the side of the clothing pavilion. "I do, Mademoiselle. I will just finish readying India, and then . . ."

"Good," Coco replied, interrupting her clothing mistress. "Hurry it along. I want Narcisse to finish with India's photos quickly so he can move on to . . ." She trailed off and turned back to Phoebe, who was suddenly gripped by a wary sensation. Coco brushed Phoebe's cheek with the backs of her fingers. "Now then . . . where is Marcelle?"

Only a few minutes later, Phoebe stood behind the screen in the pavilion while Eva and Claudette adjusted the outfit Coco had persuaded her to model.

Had she been persuaded? Phoebe could barely remember the conversation, much less agreeing to anything. It had happened so fast, and then suddenly she was being bundled through the tent and Eva and Claudette had appeared, each holding garments.

And such garments they were! At first Phoebe thought Coco meant for her to dress like a man, and not as Françoise dressed, in flowing trousers and soft silk blouses and scarves. No, *truly* as a man, in sturdy tweeds. The very notion.

But here she was, in a tweed skirt with wide pleats that had been completed only ten minutes ago, according to Claudette. She hadn't even had time to add closures, and at present the skirt was being held in place by Claudette while Eva knelt behind her and sewed her in with needle and thread. That accomplished, Claudette straightened the very masculine V-neck jumper Phoebe wore, making sure its stripes lay perfectly horizontal, before Eva, done sewing, helped her on with a jacket that matched the skirt; the jacket had obviously been cut down—taken in and made shorter—from a man's Norfolk jacket. The belt had been removed, and Claudette arranged the open sides so that they hung just right to reveal the jumper beneath.

She gestured for Phoebe to sit, and Claudette knelt at her feet to slip on the brown-and-white oxfords and lace them up. Eva stood ready with several long strings of pearls. Claudette topped off the outfit with a shallow-crowned picture hat in deep brown velvet.

Coco's voice cried out from beyond the screen. "Is she ready?"

"She is, Mademoiselle," Claudette called back.

Phoebe gazed at herself in the swivel mirror behind the

screen, hardly recognizing herself. Grams would no doubt say she looked like a boy, but she had to admit, she rather liked the style. It was entirely new, nothing she had ever seen before—not even in London. Perhaps with a change of footwear, she felt as though she could comfortably traipse across the countryside all day.

"Stand aside," Coco ordered Eva and Claudette as she came around the screen. "Let me see her."

She came to stand before Phoebe, blocking her view of herself in the mirror, and grasped her shoulders. A smile spread across her lips. "It is as I thought. You are perfect for this." She glanced down at the skirt. "Claudette, you have done well."

The clothing mistress breathed an unmistakable sigh of relief, and who could blame her with such an exacting employer? The poor woman must have been up all night making the skirt and altering the jacket. And how had she known Phoebe's measurements, or were her skills so great she could judge merely by looking? Phoebe didn't doubt Coco would require such expertise of her staff.

"So now what?" she asked, holding out her tweed-clad arms.

"Now we take photos." Coco made a small adjustment to the angle of her hat, and then dragged a few more curling strands of hair to frame Phoebe's face.

Phoebe shook her head. "Not without a promise that you won't use them except privately, for your own reference. Just as you promised with Julia."

"But, of course. Do not worry so. Come, Narcisse is waiting."

Coco drew her to where Narcisse had set up his equipment. He apparently had finished with India, who stood near him while he changed the angle of his camera. Their voices and laughter drifted along the pathway. At least

India's good spirits seemed to be restored after her contentious telephone call with her mother.

Marcelle had set up her dressing table beneath a tree today, and Coco led Phoebe to it. "Sit and let our makeup artist perform her magic on you."

Phoebe sat, but Marcelle didn't look as though she were up to performing any miracles. She held her features taut, her lips pinched, as she draped a cloth around Phoebe's shoulders and then opened one of her cases. Phoebe felt as if no part of her countenance went untouched. Eyebrows, lips, cheekbones . . . Was her natural appearance as unacceptable as all that? Finally, taking up a medium-sized brush, Marcelle dipped it in a container of sheer powder and swiped at Phoebe's face as if sweeping an untidy floor. Phoebe was about to grab her wrist to stop her when her ministrations came to an end. Marcelle passed her a hand mirror.

Phoebe peered at her reflection, barely recognizing the stranger peeking back at her. Her eyes were larger, her lips plumper, the contours of her face more pronounced. She appeared older somehow, more confident, more poised. More . . . dare she think it? . . . like Julia. The resemblance was unnerving.

She drew a deep breath. "Thank you, Marcelle."

"Mmm."

With a frown, Phoebe rose and left the table, wondering what had put the makeup artist in such ill humor. Did she take issue with having to ply her trade with nonprofessionals such as Phoebe and her sister?

"You are welcome, madame," the makeup artist said belatedly to her back. Phoebe turned, and Marcelle offered her a weak smile. Phoebe took this as reassurance her displeasure hadn't been directed at her.

Then at whom?

Eva came up to her and patted the lapels of her jacket. "You look extraordinarily pretty."

"I feel like I'm going to a fancy dress party," Phoebe admitted. "It's garish, isn't it?"

"Not at all." Eva touched her fingertips to Phoebe's cheek in a gesture that was both familiar and reassuring. "You don't need any of this, but you do wear it well."

"You'll stay to watch the photos?" When Eva nodded, Phoebe added, "In case I need reinforcements. These people, especially Coco, are relentless, and I might wish to make a getaway."

"Just give me a signal. How about if you touch your nose, I'll come running to your rescue?"

Phoebe laughed, then asked in a near whisper, "Now that Coco can't hear us, what *do* you think of this outfit? Imagine, women wearing men's tweeds? I'll admit it's frightfully comfortable. And warm, too. Do you think it will ever catch on?"

Eva surveyed her with a critical look. "I believe it could. Somehow, she's transformed masculine clothing into something entirely feminine."

"I completely agree," a man's voice said behind them.

Phoebe turned to find Owen a few feet away, smiling appreciatively. "Owen, what are you doing here? Why aren't you out riding or target shooting or whatever you men have been doing to occupying yourselves?" She couldn't help noticing how alike they were dressed, right down to the Norfolk jacket, although he had secured the belt on his. "Or are you here to have your picture taken as well?"

He held up his hands in mock horror. "I'll leave that to you ladies, thank you very much. But I did want to tell you that this"—he gestured to her attire as he stepped closer— "suits you, very well. It makes you look like the woman you are—one who isn't afraid to take charge, and who stands on her own principles."

Phoebe held out her arms and looked down at herself. As she did, she noticed Eva quietly backing away from them, a smile on her lips. "All that from a few yards of tweed?"

"No." He took her hand. "All that from you. But your photographer awaits. Shall we?" He held out his arm, and Phoebe happily linked hers through it.

CHAPTER 14

Eva made her way down to the laundry cellar after receiving a cryptic summons from the head laundress. Had she overburdened them with too many of Lady Phoebe's things? She couldn't imagine that could be it. Had she somehow taken an item belonging to another guest and mixed it in with Lady Phoebe's? Again, unlikely. Eva knew every piece of clothing belonging to her mistress and an unfamiliar item would certainly have caught her attention.

When she went down the steps into the washing room, the woman who had sent for her whispered something to her assistant, who immediately left with a curious glance at Eva. Then the laundress beckoned Eva over.

"Miss Huntford, I could get into trouble for this, but I wanted you to know about something I found." She went to a corner of the workbench and picked up a wadded ball of fabric. When she held it up, it revealed itself to be a man's shirt. A few faint stains indicated the shirt hadn't yet been washed.

Eva didn't know what to think. "Yes?"

The woman brought the shirt closer and handed it to Eva. "Smell it."

She brought the shirt close to her face and inhaled. Comprehension flooded her even as the odor inundated her senses. "Smoke."

The laundress lifted an eyebrow and nodded.

Speculations ran through Eva's mind, until a realization brought them to a shuddering halt. "This could belong to any of the men who stayed behind the night of the fire to help everyone out of the house."

"All of that clothing came down to me that very morning. Why not this one, too?"

"You're certain? Could this belong to a footman, or what about the hall boy who cleans the hearths belowstairs?"

"This shirt is far too big for the lad, though not big enough to fit our marquess, nor his guests." She took on a knowing look.

"What are you trying to tell me?" Eva demanded. "Please, just come out and say it."

"This shirt came down in a bundle of clothing and linens from the photographer's room."

With a start, Eva's gaze skittered over the garment again, taking in the cut of the tailoring, the quality of the fabric—a fine linen weave—and the light stains, one on each cuff and another beside the placket that might have been a drop of tea.

"If you ask me, he saved it until he had enough laundry that no one would notice. It was half wrapped in his bedclothes, along with the rest."

Eva leaned a hip against the workbench as she continued to regard the shirt. If this belonged to Narcisse, if he had been in Suzette's bedroom and closed the flue, why would he keep such incriminating evidence? Why not dispose of it?

But how? Yes, he had access to the rubbish bins belowstairs, but someone might have seen him. As a guest, even an employee of a guest, he should have no business in that part of the servants' areas. Far less noticeable to put the shirt in his laundry and hope for the best.

Then another point struck her. "Why are you showing this to me?"

The laundress lifted her chin with a laugh. "Your reputation precedes you, Miss Huntford. Yours and your Lady Phoebe's. I know the pair of you have been asking questions—ones the police won't ask. We all know it."

Eva grinned in spite of herself. Of course the servants knew. They always knew everything that went on in the house they served, and word quickly spread.

The woman hadn't finished. "We don't like one of our own wrongly accused. Bobby wouldn't have left a flue closed, and it's unfair of anyone to say he did." She moved closer, nearly shoving her own face in Eva's. "Lady Allerton is wrong to say it, and she's wrong to bust him back to third footman."

For all she agreed generally, Eva stiffened in indignation at the mention of Lady Allerton. "It's not your place to judge your employers, is it," she said rather than asked, in a severe tone. "Lady Allerton doesn't need to explain herself to you or anyone, but suffice it to say you cannot imagine her life in recent years."

"*Her* life?" The laundress backed away, her eyes becoming pinpoints of anger. "You want me to believe our high-and-mighty lady has ever had to worry about a thing? That she knows what it's like to fear for the very roof over her head? *Pshaw.* Here, give that back to me and forget I ever said anything." She reached for the shirt.

Eva swept it out of the woman's reach even as a sharp retort leapt to her tongue. She bit it back. Engaging in such an argument would serve no purpose. Well enough did she know that complaints and resentments festered belowstairs in every great house. Not every servant held their employers in high esteem. That didn't mean they didn't give their best effort every day in performing their jobs.

"I'll keep it for now, and thank you," Eva said. The laundress relaxed at those words.

"Yes, well, I might have spoken out of turn. But someone needs to do right by Bobby. Even if he isn't charged with a crime, something like this will follow him the rest of his life."

"I understand." Eva offered a small smile. "And I'll do my best to find out what really happened."

To that end, Eva climbed the backstairs to the second floor. While the footmen's and maids' quarters were strictly separated, Narcisse had been lodged not far from Eva's own room. On her way up, she had paused on the landing and peered out the window into the rear gardens. Although Lady Phoebe had apparently finished with her photographs, Narcisse was still outside with his equipment. Eva hurried the rest of the way up.

Before she reached his door, she plucked a hairpin from her simple chignon. Once again, she paused, this time to listen for signs that anyone else was nearby. At this time of day, no one should have been. Silence permeated the corridor.

Eva knelt in front of Narcisse's door and inserted the hairpin into the lock, a skill her brother had taught her before he'd gone off to war. Not that Danny had been a thief. But he'd been exceptionally skilled with his hands, able to take apart motors and put them back together again. As far as picking locks, that had come in handy in stealing cakes and biscuits from the larder at home. He never pilfered enough to make it obvious, but Mum would always scratch her head and swear there must be mice in the house.

She worked the hairpin into the locking mechanism, trying several times before she heard the satisfying click. The door opened at her touch, and she slipped inside.

Back in her normal clothes, Phoebe wandered alone into the drawing room. Julia and Coco were already upstairs resting before they changed for dinner. The men were enjoying a quiet game of billiards. Phoebe no longer worried that Owen wished to avoid her. Chesterhaven, on the other hand, very much *did* continue to dodge her, and Coco as well. With Allerton Place no longer a welcoming prospect for him, she wondered why he hadn't yet fled.

Claudette, with Marcelle's and Remie's help, had brought the clothing back in from the pavilion, and now it filled the far end of the drawing room, with an aisle down the center leading to the terrace doors. Dusk was falling; she switched on several of the room's lamps.

With an inner sigh, she admitted that modeling Coco's newest design idea had been exhilarating. She wasn't often the center of attention and didn't typically crave being so, but for this one time she had very nearly reveled in it. Owen hadn't taken his eyes off her the entire time, a small but warm smile curling his lips. Julia had come out at one point, baby Charles on her hip, and even *she* had gazed at Phoebe with something approaching admiration, not to mention approval. Perhaps Coco's and Julia's initial assessment of her when she had arrived at Allerton Place had been correct. Perhaps she should make more of an effort to be fashionable, to stand out by emphasizing her better traits.

She sighed again, not sure if she could keep up such efforts for very long. Still, the racks of clothing drew her to that end of the room. She flipped through several frocks, admiring the handiwork. These were the evening gowns, and while Phoebe was no stranger to dressing up for dinner and evening entertainments, such dresses didn't feel like *her*. Another rack held matching separates, and here she found several outfits she thought complemented her own image of herself. Outdoorsy, casual, active. Much like the makeshift tweed attire she'd modeled.

"Find anything you like?" Françoise strolled down the center aisle, a folder grasped in one hand and a pencil in the other. She moved to the rack of evening gowns and began making notations. Today, she had exchanged her trousers and shirtwaist for a rose wool frock whose ruffled hem swirled about her calves as she walked. Despite more feminine trappings, she retained her usual air of calm authority and nonchalance.

"I liked what I wore today," Phoebe said as she approached the older woman. "It was so . . ." She groped for the right words and came up with only one. "Unexpected."

"Coco always does the unexpected. It is her secret power. She is very excited about this innovation. I believe we will get to work on it as soon as we return to Paris." She made some notations on a paper in her folder.

Phoebe fingered the silk embroidery on the neckline of a gown. "What's that you're doing? Weren't these photographed already? The other day?"

"That is the point. Narcisse has developed his photographs. Did you know he made a darkroom on the third floor?" When Phoebe nodded, she continued. "I am making notes of which of these must be reshot and which can be used in our advertising. You see, each has a number sewn inside."

Phoebe followed her as she continued her work, and Françoise explained why some photos hadn't passed Coco's standards. "Sometimes it is the lighting, or a shadow in the wrong place, or since the modeling is outside, there could be an insect in the frame."

"I hadn't thought of that." Phoebe chuckled. "You seem

very proficient at what you do. Tell me, did you have prior experience in fashion, or did Coco hire you on faith?"

Françoise smiled as she made another notation. "On faith, if the truth be told. My knowledge of fashion only went as far as my own wardrobe, but I had vast experience in managing an estate, along with its farms, vineyards, and wine-making business. And a little with fabric and stitchery."

"You mentioned your husband had been ailing," Phoebe said gently. She thought of what Françoise had told her about the house fire, and the tragedy of her husband not being able to evade the flames in time. Françoise's face became shadowed. "I'm sorry. I shouldn't have brought it up."

"No, do not be." Françoise turned to a new page in her folder. "It was a difficult time, true. But I learned the skills I would need to carry on with life. As we must, no?"

Phoebe nodded thoughtfully, wondering if she would have the fortitude to carry on alone, without her family, without Owen, and most especially, without Eva.

"I had help," Françoise went on. They moved to the next rack. "The women of our village, and the Society for Employment of Women."

Phoebe had been absently regarding a frock with nautical embellishments. She glanced up from her musings. "What is that?"

"During the war, especially in the north, there were few men available to support their families. They were off fighting, or they were maimed or dead."

"We knew something about that here, too, although not with the severity of the French families you're speaking of."

"*Oui.* The Germans devastated the regions they occupied, destroying what crops and livestock they did not take for their own use. The society organized women of the war-torn villages to make and embroider household items. Simple things—towels, napkins, and tablecloths, and other items such as drawstring bags. The products were shipped to Paris and then sold overseas, mainly in America. It is only in this way many were able to stave off starvation for their families."

Phoebe felt a sharp stab of guilt. Her efforts, and those of Little Barlow, had been mostly in the form of gathering supplies to be shipped to the soldiers at the front. Vegetable gardens had popped up everywhere, in every available plot of ground, to supplement what must also be shipped to the forces. They had taken pride in doing their bit for the cause. There had been sacrifices and privation, but they had never been in danger of starving; never at the mercy of an invading army. "They are to be commended. All of you are."

"*Merci.* It is the village women who deserve the praise. When the shelling became particularly hard, they would gather in the cellar of our home, at Château des Champs, and continue their work there until it was safe to go home."

"And this went on all during the war?"

"Until the house burned. But it was during that time I began to learn about textiles. It was not much—not nearly what I have learned in the years since meeting Coco, but it was enough of a beginning that, with my knowledge of running a house and business, it made me useful to her."

"And now she couldn't do without you," Phoebe said with an encouraging smile.

Françoise looked down at her folder. "I hope not."

Phoebe was about to comment again on the bravery of the French women when voices from beyond the open windows on either side of the terrace doors stopped the words from passing her lips.

"How could you?"

"It is none of your business."

Except, the words weren't in English. They were in French, the voices those of a man and a woman.

"It *is* my business. What you did, it is unconscionable. Depraved. Even after her death, you are still as immoral as ever."

Goodness, Phoebe thought, depraved? That was a serious charge.

"Leave me alone!" The man's voice belonged to the photographer, Narcisse. If Phoebe would have had difficulty identifying it previously, after working with him so closely this morning, she needed only a snippet to recognize him as the speaker. And the woman . . .

"That is Marcelle." Françoise moved to the terrace doors. Phoebe followed. It seemed this group from France were no strangers to frequent arguments. First Coco and Chesterhaven, now these two. Their voices were bitter and harsh against the evening breeze.

Françoise stopped at the doors and peered out through the panes.

It had grown dark outside. Phoebe came up beside her and cupped her hands against the glass to block out the glare of the room's electric lights. "What are they saying now?" For the most part, she could follow their French, but she had missed some of their words as she'd crossed the room.

Françoise shook her head, a frown gathering between her eyebrows. "There is something they are not saying outright, something implied. Although Narcisse is denying it with as much fervor as Marcelle is accusing him."

"Do they argue often?"

"No, not to my knowledge. Marcelle is usually so retiring. Coco calls her *notre souris*, our mouse."

Eva had seen evidence that Marcelle had strong feelings for Narcisse, and that those feelings translated into resentment toward Suzette. But tonight's encounter between them suggested that Narcisse knew how Marcelle felt about him. That she had made her sentiments crystal clear.

And that he cared not in the least.

"Poor Marcelle," she murmured.

Françoise turned to her. "Why poor Marcelle? Perhaps it is Narcisse that is to be pitied. Men are typically cads, yes, but women can also bare their claws and scratch deeply."

The voices became louder, and Marcelle's shriek echoed against the house. Acting entirely on instinct, Phoebe pushed her way through the doors and out onto the terrace. She had barely made it to the steps when Marcelle shouted something that prompted Narcisse to turn away in preparation of striding off. Marcelle reached for his hand, but he snatched it away, then raised his arm high in the air, ready to deliver a backhanded blow across Marcelle's face.

"Stop it this instant," Phoebe cried out. "Both of you." She ran down the steps. It didn't matter that she had issued her command in English. Her outburst had frozen Marcelle and Narcisse in place, his hand hovering in midair. Looking like a pair of startled rabbits, they both swiveled their heads to stare at her. Then Narcisse let his arm drop to his side. He shoved the hair back from his brow, murmured something, and strode farther into the gardens. Soon, the gloom swallowed his figure and the breeze muffled his footsteps.

Phoebe hurried over to Marcelle. "Are you all right?"

Her eyes red with tears, Marcelle evaded Phoebe's gaze and started walking, then running, toward the entrance to the service yard. Phoebe hurried after her. "Marcelle, please wait. I want to help."

It was no use. The girl not only didn't stop but ran faster. Phoebe followed her through the gate in the hedge, emerging on the other side to see Marcelle at the servants' entrance of the house. Phoebe didn't follow. The girl had made it quite clear she didn't want Phoebe's interference. And what could she have said, after all? It was time she went upstairs and began dressing for dinner. Eva was probably already there waiting for her.

When she walked into her room, however, it wasn't an evening dress Eva held up for her to see.

Eva had expected Lady Phoebe long before this, and had even begun to worry. No wonder, then, that when the door opened she sprang to her feet with Narcisse's shirt unfurling from her grasp.

Lady Phoebe came to a puzzled halt on the threshold, frowning faintly. "Eva, you startled me. What have you got there?" She came the rest of the way into the room and closed the door.

Eva held the shirt out. "You need to smell this."

Lady Phoebe made a face that almost made Eva laugh, had the circumstances not been so serious.

"It smells of smoke," she explained, adding emphasis to the last word. "The laundress showed it to me. It came to her with Narcisse's laundry this morning."

"This morning?" Lady Phoebe fingered a sleeve, then took the garment from Eva and held it close to her nose. She gave a little shudder and handed it back. "Why would he wait so long to have it washed?"

"I wondered the same, along with why he didn't simply dispose of it." Eva set the shirt on the low table by the settee and crossed to the armoire. She opened the doors and took out the cobalt-blue chiffon dress she and Lady Phoebe had decided on for tonight. "But it's not so easy to dispose of something like this without being seen, is it? The garbage bins are located belowstairs, where there are always people busy at work. Even at night, there are the night footmen and the risk that Mr. Tewes or Mrs. Bristol might be up working late. Or working extra early. Belowstairs is never truly a private place."

Lady Phoebe nodded. "I never thought of that, but you're right. So little goes unnoticed in a house like this. There's so little privacy for anyone."

"And as for the laundry, the woman told me this shirt was balled up with many other things, linens included. As if he hoped it might simply be tossed in with everything else."

"And once it had been washed, the odor would be gone."

"Exactly. But the true question is, how did the odor get there in the first place? Even with the weather growing colder, no one has asked for a fire since Suzette's death. And Narcisse's room doesn't have a fireplace." Eva compressed her lips, hesitating to state the obvious.

She didn't have to. "If he closed the flue in Suzette's room while she slept," Lady Phoebe said, "and then waited long enough to make sure the smoke would fill the room, this shirt might bear the evidence of it."

"Indeed." Eva moved behind Lady Phoebe to unfasten the buttons down the back of her day frock and help her off with it. Then she handed Lady Phoebe her wrapper. "I'll run a bath." How odd, she thought on the way into the adjoining bathroom, that such routines kept on even in the face of new evidence of murder. Such was English society. Yes, someone had died, but dinner must still be served, and one must dress before going down.

She didn't know sometimes if she envied her mistress or pitied her, having to adhere to such conventions. But then she remembered that while Lady Phoebe observed the traditions of her class—or most of them—she kept her eyes and ears open for any clues that would find justice for those who had been wronged.

"It'll be a quick one," Lady Phoebe called after her. "I'm running late as it is. I have things to tell you, too, and they also involve our dear photographer."

A quarter of an hour later, Lady Phoebe sat at the dressing table while Eva unpinned her hair and took up the hairbrush. She swept each section of lovely reddish-gold hair in smooth, even strokes before re-pinning them in a more elaborate style than she wore during the day. Eva's shock grew as Lady Phoebe recounted the argument she'd witnessed in the garden before coming upstairs.

"I guessed that Marcelle had become attached to Narcisse and that he most likely didn't return her feelings, but this!" Eva slid the last pin in place and gave a pat.

"She was in a frightful mood this morning when she did my makeup for the photos. Obviously, the cause must have been Narcisse." Lady Phoebe opened a drawer and lifted out her makeup case. She had washed off the remaining cosmetics Marcelle had applied and now opted for a light application of rouge and eyebrow pencil. A dusting of powder completed her ministrations. Then she stood and Eva helped her step into her sleeveless gown. The hem skimmed just above the ankles to show off the rhinestone buckles on her shoes.

"Are you sure the shirt belongs to Narcisse?" she asked when Eva stood back to view the overall effect of the outfit.

"Not completely, but I have more to tell you." Eva went to the dressing table and retrieved the locket Lady Phoebe planned to wear, silver and marcasite with a long, sleek chain. "I sneaked into his room and compared it with the others in his wardrobe."

Lady Phoebe gasped. "You didn't take such a risk!"

"I did." Eva couldn't help grinning. "While he was carrying on in the garden with Marcelle, I was picking the lock on his bedroom door. He hasn't many other shirts to compare this one with, and to tell the truth, none of them are exactly the same size or fit. As if he purchased whatever he could find secondhand."

Lady Phoebe went to the sofa table and picked up the shirt. "This fabric is rather good, though. It doesn't look as though he found it secondhand, although one can never be certain."

"It could be his best shirt and one he spent more money than usual on. In terms of size, they all varied as I said, but all looked as though they would fit him well enough. This one included." Eva moved behind Lady Phoebe and secured the locket around her neck. "Do you think he really would have struck Marcelle?"

"I don't know." Lady Phoebe turned around to face her. "It certainly looked as though he had every intention of doing so, but I stopped him before it happened. Perhaps he would have stopped himself at the last moment."

"But if not, it would have proven his tendency to become violent."

Lady Phoebe held her gaze. "Violent against *women*."

Eva nodded. "So what do we do about the shirt?"

"I think I have no choice but to show it to Lord Allerton."

CHAPTER 15

After Eva left her room, Phoebe considered when the best time to speak with Theo might be. The sounds of his and Julia's voices in the corridor sent her out to head them off before they went downstairs.

"Theo," she called to him, "may I have a moment?"

"Of course, Phoebe." He readily changed course. Looking less enthusiastic, Julia followed him.

Phoebe waved them both into her room and closed the door. She handed Theo the shirt. "Your laundress noticed this today and told Eva about it. It smells of smoke."

Julia let out an indignant huff. "Really, Phoebe, now you're interfering with the laundry?"

As Theo brought the shirt close to his nose, Phoebe said to Julia, "It's important. This might tell us who opened the flue in Suzette's room."

"Not that again." Julia waved a dismissive hand at her. "Will you please leave it alone?"

Phoebe ignored this and asked Theo, "Do you smell it?"

"I do," he replied with a nod. "Do we know whose it is?"

"It went down to the laundry room with a bundle of things from the photographer's room."

Theo's gaze met hers. "Is the laundress certain about that?"

Phoebe nodded.

"Did anyone ask Narcisse?" Julia demanded. "Our gardener is always burning leaves this time of year. Perhaps Narcisse wandered out there."

Theo shook his head. "Burning leaves smell different from this."

"Then maybe he had a fire in his room and stood too close to the hearth." Julia made a sound of impatience.

Theo turned to her. "My dear, there are no fireplaces on the second floor."

"Aren't there?" Julia scrunched her nose. "Then how do the servants stay warm in winter?"

"With extra clothing and blankets," Phoebe informed her bluntly, willing her own impatience not to assert itself. "And with the ambient warmth traveling up the chimneys. It's the same at Foxwood Hall, or didn't you know?"

"I didn't." Her brows gathered. "It doesn't seem right."

"My love, that is neither here nor there at the moment." Theo returned his attention to the shirt. "What matters is that Narcisse did not have a fire in his room. And the only fires lit in recent days were in Coco's room and Suzette's. I think we can say of a certainty Narcisse has not visited Coco in her room."

"What are you going to do?" Phoebe knew exactly what he should do. She held her breath as she waited for his answer.

After a pause, he gave a decisive nod. "I'm going to send for the police again. They need to see this. They need to question the photographer again."

"Theo, don't be ridiculous." Julia took the shirt and

tossed it over the back of the nearest chair. "Do you truly think Narcisse would murder the very woman who has formed the basis of his career these past several years? He'd have to be mad to do so."

"He might have done," Phoebe said. She went to retrieve the shirt. "Especially if she was no longer to be the basis of that career, and if she had recently enraged him with her behavior. Julia, I have reason to believe Suzette and Chesterhaven might have been—"

"Don't say it." Julia slashed her hand at the air in a cutting motion. "I've had quite enough of your speculations. Theo, telephone the police if you must. But let them handle it. I won't have my sister putting ideas into their heads and skewing matters in the direction she wants them skewed." Julia turned on her satin heel and strode from the room, the beading of her evening gown clattering like a shower of pebbles.

"Sorry about that." Weariness dragged at Theo's features, stretching the scars at his mouth ever tighter. "She simply won't hear about Suzette's death being anything but an accident."

"I suppose Julia's doing what she needs to do." Phoebe reached up to place a sympathetic hand on his shoulder. "Just as the rest of us must do what we need to do."

Theo nodded grimly. He went to use the telephone while Phoebe went down to join the others in the drawing room before the dinner gong sounded. It didn't escape her attention that Julia made an effort to avoid her. Apparently, Phoebe wasn't the only one who noticed.

Owen extricated himself from a conversation with Coco, Françoise, and India. Chesterhaven stood across the room, a tumbler of whiskey in his hand, a glum expression on his face.

"What's going on between you and your sister?" Owen asked when he reached her side.

Phoebe explained about the shirt.

"Could someone have planted that shirt among his things?"

"I suppose. But it was well hidden among the rest of his laundry, as if whoever put it there hoped no one would notice it. If someone wanted to frame him, wouldn't they have made it more obvious?"

"Not if they wanted their scheme to work. Make it too obvious, and it would look suspicious. Do the servants leave their laundry outside their bedroom doors before coming down to work?"

"Yes, I imagine they do."

"Then you see, it wouldn't have been difficult for someone to slip the shirt in among the other things." When Phoebe frowned at the logic of that, Owen put an arm around her shoulders. "Giving it to Theo, and letting the police handle it, was the right thing to do. I'm proud of you for not giving in to your rasher instincts this time."

Phoebe stepped away, allowing Owen's arm to slide from her shoulders and fall to his side. He frowned, looking perplexed, but before he could question her, India hobbled over with the help of her crutches.

"Hullo, you two. Phoebe, you're hogging one of our few available men. Not very sporting of you, is it?" Laughter accompanied her words. Phoebe couldn't but agree the girl was right. The gathering before dinner was not a time for private conversations, but for the party to catch up with one another after their various activities during the day, before proceeding to the dining room. She also silently thanked India for defusing another awkward situation with Owen.

"How is your ankle?" Phoebe asked the girl.

Balancing on her crutches, India lifted the hem of her gold silk and tulle evening gown to reveal her injured ankle, wrapped in a bandage, along with several inches of calf covered in a clocked silk stocking. "It's coming along, thanks. The swelling's way down. I don't think I'll be needing these daft crutches much longer, but I also don't want to risk hurting myself all over again." Her gaze darted to Coco.

"Are you still planning on modeling after this?" Phoebe asked. She watched India intently.

"I hope to," the girl replied eagerly. "It's been such fun, I'd hate to give it up."

"Thought about going professional, have you?" Owen asked her, and again, Phoebe offered silent thanks. It was exactly what she wished to ask India but had hesitated to question her so blatantly.

"I'll admit, I wouldn't say no if the offer came along." Again, India's gaze flicked to Coco.

Phoebe pretended not to notice. "I'll bet the pay is nothing to sneeze at."

"Oh, I've hardly given *that* a thought," India said quickly. "As I said, it's great fun."

Enough fun to murder a rival?

No, if India caused Suzette's death, she did it for the money—funds that would allow her to live independently of her parents. Did Phoebe believe India to be the culprit? Or Narcisse? Or . . . whom?

"What about your father's business?" Owen said, scattering Phoebe's speculations. "One would think you'd be keen on joining him in some capacity. You're such an accomplished horsewoman."

"Well, yes, that's true. Perhaps someday, but not yet. I want to travel first, go interesting places, meet interesting people. Have a little fun. You know."

Phoebe nodded, still studying the girl closely. "Yes, I understand. But all that takes a good deal of money, or at least friends with money who are willing to bring you along."

"Phoebe," Owen murmured. Did he find her comments crass? True, as a rule, their set didn't speak of money so openly, especially not in social situations. But this was no simple occasion, and it hadn't been since Coco's entourage showed up uninvited.

The dinner gong sounded and the drawing room doors opened. "Dinner is served, my lady," Tewes announced to Julia.

"Ah, good. Thank you, Tewes. Everyone, shall we proceed inside?"

As the highest-ranking male guest, Chesterhaven moved to Julia's side. With such a shortage of men, he also escorted Coco on his other arm. Owen escorted both India and Françoise. That left Theo, who hurried into the room at the last moment, to escort Phoebe.

"What did the police say?" she asked him under her breath.

"They're on their way. I'll probably be called away from dinner, but I'm not saying anything until I have to."

"Good thinking," Phoebe agreed. Why annoy Julia before one had to? "Will you tell me what happens afterward?"

"You know I will. You can count on me."

"I can *always* count on you to understand, Theo." Phoebe faced forward, not allowing Theo to see the frown that tightened her brow. Why couldn't matters be this easy with Owen? Why could he not simply understand her need to be involved when she saw something that needed doing? Her desire to be useful? He *used* to understand, at least she believed he had. Why this sudden change in him? Why the possessiveness? Why the condescension? For that was exactly what she had heard in his voice earlier when he declared himself proud that she had resisted her rasher instincts.

Rasher instincts, indeed. Perhaps he should resist his more arrogant instincts.

During dessert, Mr. Tewes delivered a message to Theo with a whisper in his ear. "Took them long enough," Theo murmured as he tossed his napkin on the table and came to his feet. "If you'll all excuse me. I'll try not to be long."

Julia shot him a perplexed glance from the opposite end of the table. "Where are you going?"

"There's a . . . er . . . matter I need to see to. Please, everyone, enjoy your dessert, and I'll see you back in the drawing room."

The others looked as puzzled as Julia did annoyed. It was all Phoebe could do not to jump up and follow Theo. The constable and his assistant must finally have arrived, and she longed to hear what questions they asked, and how Narcisse answered them. She had no choice but to be patient.

Theo appeared some half hour later in the drawing room, as promised. Again, impatience made Phoebe want to corner him and find out what happened. Julia beat her to it. "What was that all about?" she demanded. "The police were here again, weren't they?"

"They were, my dear." Theo shot his cuffs and sighed. "But nothing has changed. No one has been arrested, no charges made. The police have taken the item in question and have left."

Phoebe couldn't contain her curiosity another moment. She approached Julia and Theo, ignoring the curious gazes of the others, and the disapproving one from Owen. "What did they conclude?"

"That while the shirt could belong to the photographer, there is no firm evidence to prove it."

"I fairly well said as much." Phoebe jumped at the sound of Owen's voice close beside her; she hadn't realized he'd followed her. "That shirt could belong to anyone."

"What is this?" Coco and the others gathered around them. "What shirt, and why were the police questioning my photographer?"

When Theo hesitated, Phoebe explained, "A shirt turned up in the laundry today smelling of smoke, and it was found in a bundle of Narcisse's things."

"Phoebe," Owen murmured in yet another admonishment.

She whirled to face him. "They might as well know. It's no secret now, is it?"

Julia, one delineated eyebrow raised above the other, asked, "Did they have him try it on?"

"They did." Theo nodded. "It fit generally, but not well. Certainly not tailored to fit him."

"Of course not." Coco thrust her hands on her hips. "He is a photographer. Paid well enough, but not so well he has his clothing tailored to his exact measurements."

"So you're saying the shirt could be his," India said eagerly. "Holy cricket, does this mean what I think it does? Do the police believe Narcisse killed Suzette?" When no one answered, India shook her head and clucked her tongue. "Oh, but that's daft. He'd never hurt a fly. Why, he's . . ." She trailed off, perhaps only then realizing all eyes were upon her.

"And what would you know of it?" Coco demanded of the girl.

"Nothing." India's enthusiasm waned. "I just mean to say, you know, he's an artist, not a murderer."

"Even an artist will commit murder if he is pushed hard enough." Coco pinned her gaze on Chesterhaven, who coughed and looked away.

Eva sat up in bed and tossed the covers aside. A chill permeated the room, prompting her to grab her wrapper from the foot of the bed and swing it around her shoulders. So many possibilities kept playing over in her mind, chasing away sleep. She and Lady Phoebe had gone over them all earlier as Eva had helped ready her for bed.

Everything they'd learned pointed to Suzette having engaged in a dalliance with Lord Chesterhaven. Had this prompted Narcisse to murder her in a fit of jealous rage? Lady Phoebe had related India's theory that an artist couldn't commit murder. Well. The man obviously had a temper, revealed when he had nearly struck Marcelle that evening.

Speaking of Marcelle, she obviously entertained feelings for Narcisse, and by her own admittance she had loathed Suzette. Had she murdered Suzette in hopes of paving the way for a relationship with Narcisse?

Then there was India, intent on a modeling career. Though she had denied money as a motive, Eva knew she wished to squeeze out from under her parents' thumb. Suzette had nearly ended that career aspiration. Had India murdered her to prevent Suzette from trying again?

Finally, on their list of most likely suspects, Claudette appeared to have been involved with Suzette in stealing from Maison Chanel. Even if Claudette hadn't stolen anything herself, she almost certainly had known about it. Had Suzette somehow been blackmailing her to ensure her silence? If so, how? What had she known about Claudette? And had Claudette finally determined to be rid of Suzette's hold over her life?

Those were the obvious suspects, but what about the others? What about Lord Chesterhaven? Perhaps Suzette began to make demands on him and threatened to tell Mademoiselle Chanel about their affair. Would he see that as enough of a threat to commit murder? What about Mademoiselle herself? She had claimed that even an artist might commit murder if pushed hard enough. Perhaps she discovered Chesterhaven and Suzette's affair and took measures to end it once and for all. Mademoiselle had already proven herself to be of erratic temperament, not to mention someone whose loyalties could never be counted on.

Then, of course, there remained the one person who seemed blameless in all the bitter goings-on between the guests at Allerton Place—the widow, Françoise Deschamps. Eva felt hard put to suspect the poised woman of any wrongdoing, much less murder, but appearances were not always as they seemed. Eva had been fooled before.

Sitting on the side of the bed, she leaned over and rested her head in her palms. The middle of the night was never a good time to work through a perplexing puzzle. Her mind merely went round and round, leaving her dizzy and no closer to the truth than before.

A cup of tea, perhaps. Her bare feet searched the floor for her house shoes, found them, and slid into their warmth. Then she lit a candle and let herself out of the room.

She had gone only a few steps along the corridor when the sounds of weeping reached her ears. It wasn't coming from the back stairs, but the other direction, where the corridor turned a corner. Eva followed the low sobs and sniffles. Rounding the corner, a lick of brisk air grazed her cheeks. The window at the far end stood wide open, a figure perched on the sill.

The closer Eva got, the more the silhouette formed itself into familiar plump lines and rich dark hair that fell to the shoulders. "Marcelle? What are you doing here?"

The young woman straddled the sill with one leg inside, the other dangling out the window. She wore only her night shift, a loose cotton affair that couldn't possibly shield her from the bite of the night air. "Leave me alone, Miss Huntford."

"I'm sorry, but I won't do that, Marcelle." Eva's skin

prickled a warning. She ventured closer, coming to stand only a few feet from Marcelle, and set her candle on the floor. She wanted to reach over, grasp Marcelle's hands, and pull her the rest of the way inside. But she stood with her hands at her sides and spoke in a calm voice. "It's cold. Why are you sitting like this? You'll catch your death." To make her point, Eva wrapped her arms around herself with a shiver.

Marcelle gave a bitter laugh and raised a forearm to swipe away the tears on her cheeks. It didn't help. More fell, streaking her face. "As if it matters."

"Don't be silly. Of course it matters. Won't you tell me why you're here and not warm in your bed?"

Marcelle shook her head and turned to stare out into the darkness. Eva took another step closer, prompting Marcelle to whip her head back around, her face gripped by a scowl. "Do not. Just go away. Go back to bed." She grabbed the window frame on either side of her and pulled herself farther out the window.

Eva froze, not daring to breathe. "You can't mean to . . ." What should she do? Instinct told her to run for help, but what would happen in the meantime? If she left Marcelle alone, would she jump? It was three stories to the ground, nearly certain to kill. Did Marcelle truly mean to?

"Please, Marcelle, whatever it is, you can confide in me. You can trust me." She didn't stop to analyze her claim, didn't consider whether Marcelle's confidence might include having murdered Suzette Villiers. She only knew she needed to draw Marcelle away from the window. "What could possibly be so terrible you'd contemplate . . ." She didn't wish to put such a terrible possibility in words.

"Jumping?" Marcelle said for her. "There is no one who can help me. Not you, not anyone."

"How can you be so sure of that if you won't tell me what's wrong?" Eva stretched out a hand with a silent prayer the girl would grasp it. Instead, Marcelle's own hand came away from the window frame and drifted to her belly. A shock went through Eva. Marcelle rested her hand there a moment before giving herself a shake, as if waking from a dream, and turning again to stare out the window. She leaned forward. The wind stirred her hair and billowed the sleeves of her nightgown.

"Marcelle," Eva said in a fierce whisper. "Please don't. If what I think is true, you haven't merely yourself to consider, but an innocent life. Is that it? Are you with child?" This could explain the argument Lady Phoebe had witnessed in the garden this evening between Marcelle and Narcisse. Had she told him about the child and he denied it?

Marcelle didn't turn back around. She didn't say a word. But she gave a single nod and a loud sniffle.

"Are you certain?" Eva asked her breathlessly.

Another nod.

"Then you're wrong, quite wrong. Lady Phoebe and I can help you." Eva spoke quickly, before she could think twice about the promises she was making. "And we will."

"How?" Marcelle's voice was flat, devoid of any show of interest in what Eva was telling her. That made Eva try all the more.

"With whatever you need. A place to stay, visits to a doctor, money to cover the cost of the birth."

"Oh? And then what?"

"Then, whatever you decide. We'll help you if you decide to keep it, or if you decide to place the child with a family, we'll help you arrange it."

Marcelle turned partly around, showing Eva her profile as she spoke. "Are you magicians, you and your Lady Phoebe?"

"No, but we have resources. And connections." Well, Lady Phoebe did, so Eva did by extension, but she didn't consider that worth explaining at this precise moment.

"And perhaps Mademoiselle would be willing to help you as well."

"Mademoiselle." The word came out on a sigh, accompanied by a shake of Marcelle's head. "Mademoiselle cares only for Mademoiselle. Did you know she grew up in an orphanage? Oh yes, her father stuck her in one after her mother died. I am not supposed to know. No one is, but you know how it is with secrets."

Eva nodded.

"Chances are, she would try to persuade me to hide my own child away in an orphanage, because it would be too *inconvenient* otherwise. And Mademoiselle can be very persuasive when she wishes to be."

"We won't let that happen. Please, Marcelle, you mustn't end this child's life before it's even begun. Surely you couldn't bear to do such a thing." Eva moved closer, and when Marcelle didn't jerk away or order her to back up, Eva placed her hand on the young woman's forearm. Even through her cotton sleeve, Marcelle's skin felt like ice. "That's not what you want to do, is it?"

Marcelle heaved out a long, onerous breath. Then, her face turned fully toward Eva, her dark eyes gleaming and large in the dimness of the corridor. "No, it is not. If only . . ."

"If only what?" Eva thought she knew the answer, but she waited for Marcelle to say it.

"If only he wanted it. If only he would do what is right by us both."

His name hovered between them. Marcelle didn't have to identify him. Disgust coursed through Eva. He had been with Suzette, and he hadn't returned Marcelle's feelings, not in the way she wished. No, instead he had taken advantage of a vulnerable, innocent girl, took his pleasure, and then turned his back on her. The cruelty of it burned through Eva's veins.

But she had more important things to do than brood over the wrongdoings of an unscrupulous, cold-hearted man.

Her hand closed around Marcelle's. "Please, come with me now. I'll stay with you tonight and keep you company. In the morning, things will look better, you'll see."

"They will not *be* better. They will be the same," Marcelle insisted, but she had already begun shifting her body, turning back into the corridor. Finally, she swung her leg over the sill and back inside.

Eva didn't waste a moment in retrieving her candle from the floor, keeping hold of Marcelle with the other hand. Guided by an urgency to keep moving, she didn't bother to close the window.

CHAPTER 16

Phoebe pressed her ear to the door—her own door—half expecting it to rumble with vibrations. It didn't, but muffled voices still made their way past not only this slab of solid oak but that of the guest room across the hall. She straightened, held her breath, and opened her door. Just an inch. Peeked out. Opened the door wider.

The voices were louder now, though still subdued by the other closed door. A man's and a woman's. First Narcisse and Marcelle earlier this evening, now this? Did these people never sleep? Never allow a day to pass without some form of squabble? She thought she and Julia were contrary. These people, these guests at Allerton Place, didn't seem to know the meaning of the word *civil*.

She knew from glancing at the clock on her bedside table that the hour had just passed three. Who had the energy at this late hour to be yelling so loud as to draw her from her bed? Not that she'd been asleep. No, she'd been too busy going over suspects and motives and opportunities to allow her mind a chance to rest. The voices revealed all she needed to identify the couple in question: Coco and Chesterhaven. What were they fighting about?

Phoebe glanced up and down the corridor, saw no one, and tiptoed across. Now she pressed her ear to Coco's door, and the anger formed itself into words she could hear and comprehend.

"You cheated on me with her."

"I never did. Coco, darling—"

"Do not *dare* 'Coco, darling' me. Swine. And with *her*, of all people. You toss me aside for a semi-literate girl from off the farm. I should not be surprised. You have no taste."

Phoebe covered her mouth to prevent a laugh from bubbling out. Not that this argument was funny, but leave it to Gabrielle Chanel to use taste as a measure of a person's character. The words continued to fly back and forth, her voice shrill, his grating. Phoebe backed away from the door. It wasn't any of her business, as long as—

Something smashed against the other side of Coco's door and shattered to the floor. Phoebe flinched, her hands flying to her mouth. She went still, uncertain what to do. Something else hit the wall beside the door. Chesterhaven swore. Loudly.

"Stop it, Coco!"

"Oh, I should stop? It is you who should have stopped before you put your hands on someone else and then thought you could put them on me."

Good heavens. Phoebe's eyes were wide. She jumped back as something else hit the wall and clunked to the floor. Footsteps in the corridor startled her, then filled her with relief as both Julia and Theo headed toward her, their dressing gowns flying out behind them in their haste.

"What in the world is going on here?" Julia gasped as yet another object apparently flew through the air and hit the door. Another oath exploded from Chesterhaven's lips.

Then he said, "Do you want to wake the entire house? What would Julia and Theo think?"

"They will think you are a swine and *un bâtard*!"

Phoebe knew enough French to know what that last meant.

"Do something," Julia hissed at Theo, who drew in a deep breath and went to Coco's door.

He rapped his knuckles good and loud, and the voices within went silent. An instant later, Coco opened the door an inch or two and peeked out. Shards of glass crunched under her slippered feet. "Yes?"

"Yes?" Julia went to stand beside Theo. She spoke sharply, but then immediately softened her tone. "We could hear you all the way in our suite. Are you . . . all right?" Julia didn't look down, but she, too, must have heard the glass grinding beneath Coco's house shoes. Phoebe wondered what Coco had smashed against the door. She hoped it wasn't something costly and irreplaceable.

"Ah, *oui*. We are fine. Sorry to have wakened you." Coco started to close the door.

Theo stuck his toe across the threshold. "I'd like to speak with Chessy, if you don't mind." He pressed his face in the gap between the door and lintel. "Chessy, a word, if you please."

"Now, Allerton? Really?"

Even from behind him, Phoebe could see Theo's jaw tighten. "Now."

At the sound of Chesterhaven's footsteps crossing the room to the door, Julia pushed Phoebe back toward her own door. "Go inside. You don't want them to see you've been listening."

"How could I have helped it?" Phoebe murmured, but she retreated to her room and closed the door. She was about to shed her wrapper and climb back into bed when her door opened again and Julia slipped in.

"You mind?" she asked, looking very much as if she had something to say.

"Of course not." Phoebe gestured to the settee, then went to switch on a lamp. They settled next to each other. "I wonder who else heard those theatrics."

Julia shook her head. "Everyone, I'd imagine. You'd have to be deaf not to. Good grief, Phoebe, what am I going to do?"

"What do you mean? It's Coco and Chesterhaven's problem."

Julia scoffed. "Oh, I couldn't care less if they ripped each other's throats out. Just not in my home. How *am* I going to get these people out of here?"

"Perhaps they'll leave of their own accord before much longer."

"One would have thought they'd make other arrangements as soon as Suzette died." Julia half collapsed against the cushions behind her. "But no. For them, it's business as usual. I've never seen a more mercenary bunch, and I thought I'd seen just about everything."

"They certainly don't hold back when they're angry with one another."

"That's putting it politely." Julia chuckled and shook her head again. "It's been sobering, I can tell you that. I have admired Coco Chanel these past several years, only to find out she's nothing but a self-absorbed shrew. Brilliant, but a shrew. No wonder Chessy played her for a fool."

"I wouldn't call Coco a fool, not under any circumstances. And as for Chesterhaven . . ." Phoebe hesitated. She hadn't planned to make this revelation, especially not now, at three o'clock in the morning. But . . . "He deserves whatever she throws at him. Literally. It's a shame whatever she was hurling hit the wall and not him."

"My heavens, Phoebe, what *do* you mean?" Julia shifted to search Phoebe's face. Her own features pulled into stern lines. "What happened?"

Phoebe leaned her head back against the frame of the settee. "She called him a swine and a you-know-what. I couldn't agree more."

"Phoebe." The word held both entreaty and admonishment. "What has Chessy done now?"

" 'What's he done now?' So, you won't be altogether surprised, will you? After our ride the other morning, when I stayed behind with him to see the filly . . . well . . . let's just say the filly wasn't the only piece of horseflesh he wanted to get his hands on."

Julia's gaze locked with hers. Her dark blue eyes turned darker still and seared with anger. And with something Phoebe hadn't seen in years, since before their father died. They'd been to visit family friends in Oxford, and one of the sons had taken a dislike to Phoebe and teased her ceaselessly. Until Julia had stepped in, issued a thorough dressing-down, and shoved him to the floor for good measure. Julia had stood over him and told him in no uncertain terms that no one, but no one, treated her brother or sisters in that manner.

Phoebe's heart swelled and contracted and swelled again, both at the memory and to see that look again now. But she hastened to speak before Julia did. "Don't tell Theo. Not yet. I don't want to make matters worse with these people here. Wait till they leave."

"Why? Why shouldn't Theo throw Chessy out on his ear this very instant? He deserves it."

"He does. But really, Julia, did he do anything you didn't already know he's capable of?"

That had the effect of cutting off what Julia had been

about to say. Her lips compressed and she frowned. "No, blast it. I do know what he's like. And I'm sorry I subjected you to him. I just didn't think he'd get up to anything while he was here with Coco." She whistled a breath between her teeth. "The man has no shame."

"Don't worry." Phoebe patted Julia's hand. "He didn't get away with anything. I didn't let him."

Julia's guilty expression melted away and she grinned. "No, I don't imagine you did. Good." She slapped her palms against her thighs. "Now, apart from causing a scene and ordering them all out, how am I going to dislodge this wretched group from Allerton Place?"

Eva must have dozed off, although how she could possibly fall asleep in the stiff-backed chair in Marcelle's room was a mystery. Marcelle, on the other hand, had slept almost instantly, leading Eva to wonder if alcohol had played a part in her sojourn in the window. Now, as Eva's eyes flickered open, she was surprised to see Marcelle sitting up in bed, a shaft of moonlight falling across her face. A wary expression hovered in her youthful eyes as she in turn watched Eva.

"I am sorry," the girl whispered. "I did not mean to wake you."

"You didn't. Are you all right? Can I bring you anything?"

Marcelle shook her head. Her lovely hair, the color and silkiness of warm chocolate, swished over her shoulders. "I'm sorry about before. I must have caused you quite a fright."

"I'm only glad I was on hand when you needed someone." Eva rose from the chair and sat at the edge of the mattress. She took Marcelle's hand. "You must never do anything like that again. Please, promise me you won't."

"I promise. I do not know what came over me. Everything seemed so . . . hopeless."

"Do you wish to talk about it?"

"No, not now. It will not help."

"Do you want to go back to sleep?"

Marcelle shook her head again. "I do not think I can yet. But you can return to your own bed. I will be fine."

"No, I'll stay." Despite Marcelle's claim, Eva couldn't trust her not to do something rash again. If only she could find out more about what happened between her, Narcisse, and Suzette, but the girl was obviously disinclined to confide right now. But perhaps . . . "Tell me about yourself, then. I'd like to know where you're from, where you grew up."

"In Lorraine." She shrugged. "Mine was not an illustrious beginning. My village was small, unremarkable. My parents farmed. During the war my father and brothers went off to war, and my mother and sisters and I kept the farm going as best we could. For extra money, we embroidered."

"Embroidered?" Lady Phoebe had told Eva about the Society for Employment of Women, details she had learned from Françoise. It seemed the three women—Suzette, Françoise, and Marcelle—had lived in the north when the war broke out and had shared similar experiences.

"Yes," Marcelle went on. "In our home. Sometimes with the bombs falling around us. At those times, we huddled closer, or went into our root cellar, but we kept working."

Françoise had shared nearly the same details with Lady Phoebe, except the women of Françoise's village had gathered with their handiwork in the cellar of her château.

"You were all remarkably brave." Eva shifted into a more comfortable position. "And after the war, you went to Paris? How did you meet Mademoiselle?"

"Yes, I went to Paris. You see, because of our embroidery work, I discovered I had a talent for artwork. I drew many of the designs we worked on. When I went to Paris, I planned to do whatever work I could find, but meanwhile I hoped to study and become an artist. Then I read an advertisement that a fashion house needed a makeup artist. I knew little about cosmetics at the time, but I had a steady hand and skill with shading and contour. It proved sufficient, and Mademoiselle hired me."

"You were lucky. It must have been frightening for you to go to the city all by yourself. You're so young now. What could you have been then? Eighteen?"

"Nineteen." Marcelle gazed into the darkness beyond Eva's shoulder, looking wistful and sad. Eva had a hunch.

"And you knew no one? I understand Suzette and Madame Deschamps were also from Lorraine. You didn't know them from there, did you?"

"Lorraine is a large region." Marcelle pulled back, her expression becoming almost defensive. "Many people from the north came to Paris after the war to start over. The Germans left so little of our lives intact."

"I understand," Eva hastened to assure her. "Are you sorry you haven't become the sort of artist you wished to be?"

"There is still time." She flattened her hand against her belly through the bedclothes. Her voice became petulant. "Or perhaps not. Life has taken a new turn, yes?"

Eva nodded. "It has, but a no less rewarding one."

"We shall see." Marcelle's mouth widened on a yawn, and she sank into her pillows.

Eva came to her feet. "You sleep now. In the morning, and in the days to come, we'll figure out what is best to do." Leaning, she ran her fingers through the strands of hair beside Marcelle's face, as a mother would do, and Eva felt an unexpected pang.

Phoebe rang for Eva, pushing the buzzer three times in the signal they had devised to indicate an urgent matter. Then she made her way to Julia's private sitting room on the first floor. Hetta had found her minutes ago to say Amelia was waiting on the telephone, and Phoebe had hurried upstairs, well aware that telephone lines in the country left something to be desired when it came to dependability.

The room, though decorated in cool floral tones, nonetheless declared this an office more than a lady's parlor, as its desk, an inlaid cherrywood affair with curved legs and a bowed front, dominated the space before the window with an air that said important work was done here. Such a room did not exist at Foxwood Hall, nor did Grams desire there to be. Offices were for men, she always insisted, and she made do very well with the secretaire in the Rosalind sitting room for attending to her daily correspondence, thank you very much. But not Julia. It didn't surprise Phoebe one bit that Julia would take an active interest in the estate and its day-to-day functioning, and that she would want her own space for doing so.

The telephone sat on the desk, gleaming brass with a rotary dial—goodness, Julia *had* been using her money to bring improvements to Allerton Place. Phoebe went round to sit in the high-backed desk chair and picked the receiver up from where Julia had left it for her on the leather blotter.

"Amelia?"

"Yes, Phoebe. I have news. Good heavens, do I ever have news!"

"Don't tell me yet. I'm waiting for Eva. I want her to hear it, too. For now, tell me how you are. How is London? Are you staying out of trouble? Or are you rather enjoying your freedom?"

Amelia's laughter tumbled across the lines. "Both, I suppose. I had tea two days ago at the home of the Duchess of Linnsbury and you'll never guess who attended." Before Phoebe could speculate on possibilities, Amelia rushed on. "Princess Mary! Oh, Phoebe, she was lovely, *just* lovely. Not at all what one would think of a princess. Not a bit haughty, but quiet and thoughtful and she has the most expressive eyes. I wanted to talk to her in the worst way, but of course I was seated at the other end of the table, and she never directly spoke to me other than in greeting, so I hadn't the chance. Have you heard she's engaged?"

Amelia finally stopped for a breath, giving Phoebe a chance to reply. "Yes, I'd heard that. And apparently the king and queen are enormously relieved."

"Yes, I suppose so, but he's fifteen years older than her." Phoebe could all but see Amelia wrinkling her nose. She was no doubt thinking of Julia's first husband, but Gil Townsend had been older than Julia by much more than a mere fifteen years. "Oh, I do hope I'll find myself in her company again. She's only a few years older than I am and she looks as though she could use a friend—a real one."

"Just stay away from her brother," Phoebe warned, only half in jest.

"Oh? Which one?"

Phoebe shook her head at her sister's naïveté. "David, you goose. Or haven't you heard of his exploits?"

After a knock at the door, Eva stepped inside. "Is that Amelia?"

Phoebe nodded and waved her over. "Amelia, Eva's here

now. I'm going to hold the receiver so we can both hear you. Eva, why don't you bring that chair over." Once Eva had carried over the small side chair and settled in, she and Phoebe tilted their heads on either side of the receiver and told Amelia to go ahead.

"Well, it seems Miss India Vale is no proper young maiden," Amelia began in a droll yet erudite voice. "She has been expelled by no fewer than four finishing schools, the latest being only last spring. It seems her parents have finally given up on the idea and now want her married."

"Yes, I'd gathered that when I . . . *overheard* her conversation with her mother." Eva blushed at her own reference to having eavesdropped on India's call home.

"Oh, and incidentally, she's seventeen, not eighteen." Before Phoebe and Eva could digest this, Amelia went on briskly, "but young as she is, she's a favorite among the London debutants. The wilder set, of course. Seen out late at parties, and even . . ." Amelia paused and drew a breath. "At certain clubs that are only open at night." Amelia spoke as if this were the most shocking of scandals.

"Nightclubs?" Phoebe suggested with a grin at Eva.

"Indeed." Amelia's voice dropped to a whisper. "Have you heard of a woman named Kate Meyrick?"

"I . . . er . . . have, yes," Phoebe said after a startled pause. "But I'm shocked that you have."

"Apparently, she recently opened an establishment here in London called the Forty-Three Club, and, Phoebe, it's already notorious."

"I should think so." Phoebe had heard about both the woman and the club from her friend Olive Asquith. While Olive was not the sort of young woman to frequent such establishments or associate with London's bohemian set, she seemed always to be informed of the latest gossip.

Where Amelia had heard of Miss Meyrick and her club, Phoebe couldn't begin to guess. "But surely you're not suggesting . . ."

"I am. India Vale has been seen there."

Both Phoebe and Eva raised their heads from the receiver and traded a look, their eyebrows arcing and mouths gaping. "India?" Eva mouthed with a grimace of disbelief.

"But speaking of brothers," Amelia continued, "it's not only the debutantes India is popular with. It's their brothers, too."

Phoebe groaned.

"Oh yes." Amelia's voice held the self-satisfied note of someone who considered herself an authority on a subject. "The most recent incident occurred with the heir to Viscount Morlane. It seems they were caught in compromised circumstances by his parents—and no one has seen India since. Except you and everyone at Allerton Place, of course."

Phoebe moved her mouth closer to the transmitter and weakly asked, "Is this all?"

"Essentially."

"I'm not going to ask where you found all this out, but whomever you spoke to, I don't think you should spend much time in that person's company. Or any time. They know far too much for their own good or yours." Phoebe sighed. "I rather wish I hadn't asked you to make inquiries."

"Oh, Phoebe, now who's being a goose? I'm not a child anymore. You don't need to protect me."

Yes, you are, and I do. Amelia would always be Phoebe's innocent baby sister, and Phoebe would always feel responsible for her. They spoke a few more minutes, and then Phoebe rang off. She sat back and stared into space.

"It's so much worse than we imagined," she finally said.

"It's barely believable." Eva fingered the collar of her dress as if to loosen it. "We detected a rebellious streak, but *this*."

"What it seems to say is that we can't rule out anything when it comes to our dear Miss Vale." Phoebe came to her feet, and Eva did likewise.

"No, indeed. She certainly warrants closer scrutiny."

"We need to make a plan."

CHAPTER 17

After Lady Amelia's telephone call, Eva climbed to the second floor to return to Marcelle's room. She hadn't told Lady Phoebe about what happened last night. She didn't like the omission, but Marcelle had entrusted her with a delicate secret, and Eva didn't feel she could break that trust. If carrying Narcisse's child had caused Marcelle to murder Suzette, her rival in his affections, well, she was already a suspect based on her obvious jealousy. What they needed now was solid proof of whether she, or another guest here at Allerton Place, had committed the deed.

She found the girl still sleeping, as she had been when Eva left her a little while ago. She resumed her place in the inhospitable chair, wondering how long before Marcelle awoke. She hadn't long to wait.

Only minutes passed before Marcelle's eyes fluttered open and she stretched her arms over her head with a leisurely yawn. The color had returned to her lovely, rounded cheeks, and she looked so carefree she might have been awakening from a refreshing nap. Her gaze landed on Eva, and her expression sobered.

"You are still here." She pushed up on an elbow. "*Merci.* For everything."

Eva smiled at her. "Not at all. I confess, I did leave you for a few minutes not long ago, but you were sleeping so soundly I didn't think you'd need me."

"I should get up. Mademoiselle might be wondering where I am." She sat more upright, tilting her head back to shake out the glossy length of her hair.

"Are there to be more photos taken today?"

"I am not sure. Mademoiselle was uncertain yesterday. She will decide after she sees more of Nar—of the developed photos." In that little hesitation, Eva heard the name Marcelle chose not to speak: Narcisse. What would happen now? she wondered. How would Marcelle find the strength to continue working with him without letting the others in on her secret? And how long could such a secret be kept?

"If you wish, I could tell Mademoiselle you're indisposed today, that you're feeling ill and are resting," Eve offered. She stood and went to the window, glancing back as she grasped the curtains. At Marcelle's nod, she opened them to emit the morning sunlight, weak though it was through a gauzy haze of clouds.

"No, I'll go down. Better to distract my mind. I can always help Claudette with the clothing."

That sent a little wave of relief through Eva. If Marcelle had chosen to remain in her room today, Eva would have felt obligated to check in frequently to make sure she didn't try to harm herself again. Perhaps Eva should ask the housekeeper to keep watch on her. She could tell Mrs. Bristol that Marcelle had been under the weather last and might need a bracing cup of tea or a chance to put her feet up.

With Marcelle taken care of for the time being, Eva could focus on other matters, namely, India. Her mind still reeled with what they had learned from Lady Amelia, and now she and Lady Phoebe would take turns watching her and speaking with her at every opportunity; Lady Phoebe if she found the girl abovestairs, and Eva whenever India ventured outside in the gardens. Between the two of them, they hoped to bring out more of India's true nature, the one hidden beneath the schoolgirl enthusiasm and sunny smiles.

Yet, none of that could happen if they couldn't find her. And Eva couldn't. Neither could Lady Phoebe, who had called belowstairs on the in-house telephone to say she hadn't seen India anywhere either.

She asked the chambermaids, the only servants likely to have seen India either in her room or in the upstairs corridors, but both women shook her heads and went on their way. It wasn't until lunchtime that Eva realized Narcisse was also missing—or at least absent. Her heart pattered as she considered whether the two were together. They had certainly established a friendly working relationship, and considering India's ambitions in the fashion world, it wasn't a far stretch to imagine her wanting to be more than friendly with the only fashion photographer she knew. On a hunch, she headed into the main kitchen.

A couple of minutes later, armed with new information, she made her way outside.

The cook had told Eva that Narcisse had requested a picnic hamper earlier. The woman had obliged by handing him an empty basket and having one of her assistants accompany him into the larder to show him what he could take and make sure he wasn't overly generous with himself.

But where had he gone with it, and was India with him?

If she was, they couldn't have gone far, not with her still needing crutches. The most likely place suddenly occurred to her—somewhere close by that offered a modicum of privacy. Hurrying out to the garden, she walked through the grass rather than on the graveled pathways to muffle her footsteps. She passed the fountain, the symmetrical flower beds, and the sculpted foliage until the semicircle of hedges rose up through the trees. She heard their voices before she got very near the place, and even heard a splash as apparently one of them tossed a pebble into the reflecting pool. Eva skirted the opening and came up behind it, where she could hear them and even see slivers of them through the branches. She could tell they were sitting on one of the benches, and the brown blob at their feet must be the picnic basket. But unless they knew she was there, they mostly likely wouldn't notice her.

Once again, she found herself eavesdropping. Not that there was much to hear, and certainly nothing surprising.

"So you'll convince Mademoiselle to keep me on," India said, the eagerness bubbling in her voice. She once again sounded like an ingenuous teenage girl, and not at all like the out-of-control carouser Amelia had described. Eva had a devil of a time reconciling the two.

"She would be a fool not to, *non?* One has only to look at you to know you alone can sell the winter collection."

Had India told him of her desire for independence, her need for an income sufficient to render her parents unnecessary? Eva very much doubted it.

"You really think so?" India exuded youthful innocence with just the right amount of self-doubt. *Oh, she was good.*

"Of course, *mon amie.*"

And so it went, with India laughingly fishing for reassurances and Narcisse smoothly delivering them.

And then she heard him murmur, "You are cold? Come closer . . ."

Eva heard their shifting and could only imagine India snuggling against him. She backed away. It wasn't anything they said, or that they'd met for a picnic that troubled her. And never mind that he was obviously too old for her. It was that Narcisse had been with Suzette until so recently, and even if her actions had ended their relationship, she had died only days ago. How could any man move on so quickly, and under such circumstances? What could his heart be made of?

Without an answer to that, Eva traipsed back to the house.

With little else to do, she turned her attentions to Marcelle and Claudette, although she learned nothing new from either of them. Marcelle went about her day in a subdued state, hardly speaking, and when Claudette asked about it, Marcelle murmured that she had a headache.

At midafternoon, Mademoiselle called her employees to the drawing room for a meeting. Eva silently bemoaned the inclusion of India in their gathering, as this would have provided the perfect opportunity to steal time alone with her. She wondered if they were going to pack up their clothing and equipment and finally leave Allerton Place. If they did, there would go any opportunity to discover who closed the flue in Suzette's room.

It wasn't until she went up to help Lady Phoebe dress for dinner that she learned the answer to that question. "They're apparently not going anywhere yet, however much Julia and Theo would like them to. Julia would never kick them out. She'll endure them to the very end of her sanity."

India didn't show up for dinner that evening, leading Phoebe to wonder what she had gotten up to now. Coco had sent Remie to her room to check on her, but India hadn't been there, and Phoebe itched to run belowstairs and see if Narcisse was also missing from the dining hall. Then again, after what Eva had told her she witnessed this afternoon, was there any question about their having stolen off together again? Would the pair be as obvious as that? Or did they think that since they took their meals separately no one would notice?

Not that it was any of her business. Or, it shouldn't have been, and Phoebe would happily have let it go and left them to their own devices, come what may, were it not for Suzette's death.

"Perhaps we should have the footmen search for her," Julia suggested during a lull in the conversation.

"Who, darling?" Theo asked from the other end of the table.

"India." Julia took on a look of annoyance, as if Theo should have been able to follow the thread of her thoughts. "Perhaps we should be looking for her. She might have fallen and hurt herself again."

"Her ankle is much better." Coco flapped a hand in the air. "She is probably down at the stables. You know that girl and horses. They are in her blood."

"Alone?" Julia sounded unconvinced. She glanced around the table to assure herself the rest of the company was present. "And in the dark?"

"There are grooms down there, and the horses to keep her company." Chesterhaven sounded bored. His gaze accidentally met Phoebe's and a rush of blood turned him pink.

"Stables aren't always safe places to be," Phoebe said offhandedly. She enjoyed watching his complexion heat to an even brighter shade. "*Are* they?"

Chesterhaven coughed and quickly raised his wineglass.

"Perhaps you're right, my dear." Theo had sliced into a medallion of chateaubriand but left it uneaten on his plate. "In light of . . . well . . . things, perhaps we shouldn't dismiss her absence out of hand."

"If she is not hungry, why should we fret? She is not a child."

Phoebe opened her mouth to contradict Coco's statement, but on second thought, let it go.

Theo turned his attention to Owen. "What do you think?"

Owen cleared his throat. On the way down, Phoebe had confided in whispers about India's tryst with Narcisse beside the reflecting pool. He had responded with a mixture of amusement and mild concern, not so much aimed at the pair themselves but at what might come of their being found out. Would Coco sack Narcisse for mixing business with pleasure? Would India's parents find out and make the photographer's life a living hell? He had seen it before, this mixing of poor tradesmen and the daughters of wealthy families. It only ever led to regrets and broken hearts.

Now, Owen dabbed his lips with his napkin, shot Phoebe a quick look, and cleared his throat. "It might be best all around if we minded our business."

"What on earth does that mean?" Julia gave a laugh. "You make the matter sound terribly mysterious, Owen. Is there something we should know?"

Phoebe wanted to groan and sink lower in her chair. As soon as the words had left Owen's mouth, she had cringed, already anticipating Julia's likely reaction. And she hadn't been wrong. She caught Owen's gaze and shook her head minutely.

Then she turned to Julia. "He means exactly what Coco said. India's not a child, and we shouldn't treat her as one."

"Hear, hear." Françoise raised her wineglass. "Our Miss Vale has conducted herself most admirably, sprained ankle and all. If she wishes some time alone, we should respect that. It is a big house. There are plenty of rooms one might lose oneself in. She is probably curled up with a book and a tea tray."

Curled up, perhaps . . . Phoebe only just managed to stifle a chuckle.

Following the dessert course, they had just come to their feet to retire to the drawing room when Coco's maid, Remie, appeared in the doorway. "Mademoiselle," she began, and rambled something in such rapid French Phoebe couldn't comprehend it.

"Remie?" Coco stared at the lady's maid as if not quite recognizing her. Then, in French, she demanded, "What are you doing in this part of the house? Have you lost your mind?"

"*Non, Mademoiselle. C'est Mademoiselle Vale.*" Pale and shaking, she made beckoning motions with both hands "Come quick, *s'il vous plaît.*"

"What about Miss Vale?" Phoebe demanded.

Once again, Remie chattered away in French, her slender hands gesturing wildly. Phoebe made out enough this time. With a gasp, she turned to the others, all of whom spoke some amount of French, but given Remie's frantic state were having trouble understanding. "India's been found in her bathroom, unconscious."

"Dear heavens." Julia's eyes rounded. "You left her alone?"

Remie shook her head in glazed-eyed incomprehension. Phoebe translated, heard the reply, and told her sister, "No, it seems the chambermaid found India and cried out for help. She's there now with her."

That set the room in motion. They streamed out of the dining room and up the staircase. Remie took up the rear, her running steps thudding behind them.

At the door to India's suite, Phoebe came to a halt, her heart pounding. Blocking the way of the others behind her, she hesitated for the briefest instant before quite determinedly crossing the unoccupied room to the open bathroom door. The light was on, and the chambermaid sprang up from India's side and gripped Phoebe's hands.

"I was bringing in the towels for Miss Vale's evening toilette, and I found her . . ." She released one of Phoebe's hands, half turned, and pointed at the prone India. "I don't know what happened. She seems to be coming round now. Been moaning a bit, stirring like." Indeed, India let out a weak groan and turned her head slightly. The maid's gaze darted to the others filing in behind Phoebe, and as if only then realizing the familiarity of holding the hands of her employers' guest, she quickly released Phoebe. "M'lord, m'lady." She tipped a curtsy. "I don't know what happened to her. I was just—"

"It's all right, Tilly, you can go," Theo told her.

Before she took two steps, Julia added, "Ask that a pot of strong tea be sent up. And have Mrs. Bristol telephone the doctor."

The young woman nodded and scurried out.

By then Phoebe was already crouching beside India. Her crutches lay at angles on the floor on either side of her. She had dressed for dinner in a low-waisted moiré silk gown, a feathered headdress, and low-heeled satin pumps. She had obviously had every intention of joining the rest of them in the dining room. Someone, either Remie or Tilly, had slipped a small pillow beneath her head, but the rest of her lay sprawled on the cold marble floor. Phoebe took her hand and patted it. "India? Can you hear me?"

Owen crouched at India's other side. "Let's get her inside, onto the bed."

"Yes, of course." Phoebe moved out of the way while Theo and Owen lifted India off the floor, one on either side of her, doing their best to keep her level. Chesterhaven proved useful in cradling her head in his hands to prevent it from falling back and straining her neck. Phoebe gathered up the crutches and brought them into the other room.

"What could have happened?" Julia followed them into the bedroom, where Coco and Françoise had remained, watching through the doorway. She quickly turned down the bedclothes, and after the men laid India down, she drew them up nearly to her chin. The others ranged themselves around the bed. "Could she have slipped on wet tiles and hit her head on the tub?"

"She's fully dressed," Phoebe pointed out. She dredged up whatever shreds of patience she could find. "She obviously hadn't been taking a bath."

"She might have spilled some water on the floor while washing her face," Julia replied with an obvious effort to restrain a huff.

Coco slipped into the bathroom. "I don't see any water on the floor."

"This probably happened before we sat down to dinner," Julia said. "Any water would have been dry by now."

"It's possible." *But not likely*, Phoebe thought. Not as India was dressed. Why would she have gone into the bathroom to throw water on her face *after* dressing for dinner? No, more likely she had gone back in to use the mirror, or perhaps to give herself another spritz of perfume. Or . . .

Or someone had attacked her in her bedroom, and dragged her into the bathroom to prevent her being found too soon. Phoebe looked her over, lying pale and still on the four-poster bed. There were no bleeding wounds. No bruises she could see. Had she been coshed on the head?

She searched Owen's features, his frown of concentration, his narrowed eyes. Was he entertaining similar thoughts?

India stirred again and murmured something unintelligible. Julia, standing at the girl's shoulder, leaned down low.

"India? Are you all right, dear? Do you know what happened?"

"Nar . . ." India gasped a breath, coughed, and opened her eyes. "Wh—what . . . happened? Why . . . are you all here?" Her voice rasped like a rusty hinge.

"India," Julia said more loudly this time, "we found you unconscious in your bathroom. Do you remember what happened? Did you slip and fall?"

"I don't know . . ." came her hoarse murmur.

"What were you about to say when you woke up?" Phoebe had distinctly heard her say *Nar*. "What was the rest?"

"Oh, Phoebe," Julia scolded, "it hardly matters what she was going to say. What *does* matter is what happened to her. How she fell. And if she's in any pain now." She leaned over India again. "Are you, dearest? In pain, I mean?"

India's features contracted as she apparently scanned for pain. "Not sure. My head . . . a little fuzzy."

Phoebe glanced at Chesterhaven to get his attention, but he looked away before their gazes met. Nonetheless, Phoebe asked him, "Did you feel a lump as you supported her head?"

"I—er—couldn't tell. Her hair and all."

"Well, let's wait for the doctor." Theo smiled down at India. "In the meantime, are you comfortable now?"

India nodded. But then her hand went to her throat, and she winced. She wore a velvet choker with a small cameo pinned to it. Perhaps when she fell, it had somehow tightened around her throat.

At the clinking of porcelain, Eva came into the room carrying a tea tray. A few digestive biscuits sat on a plate beside the teacup. "I heard what happened. Is she all right?"

"We think she'll be fine," Julia said, "but we've got the doctor coming just in case."

Eva nodded and set the tray down on the bedside table. She took up the pot and poured a steaming, dark brew into the cup. Strong, just as Julia had asked for. "Cream and sugar, Miss Vale?" At India's nod, Eva finished preparing the cup.

"Let's see if we can't sit you up a bit." Julia slid an arm beneath India's shoulders and helped raise her, while Françoise went to her other side and did likewise. Between the two of them, they had India half reclined against her pillows. "There now." Julia helped her take her first sip.

While they were thus busy and the others looked on, Eva sidled over to Phoebe. In barely a whisper, she said, "Narcisse never came down for dinner."

Phoebe's eyes widened as she remembered that clipped *Nar* India had uttered as she'd awakened. Had he been here with her? Snuck up behind her? Had they argued? She glanced about her for signs of a struggle. There were clothes several layers thick tossed across the back of a chair, a jumble of shoes, some lying on their sides near the wardrobe, and a tangle of scarves and stockings spilling from a half-open bureau drawer. Indications of an untidy occupant, yes, but not of a fracas. "Was anyone else unaccounted for?"

"No, not that I noticed."

"Who else knows about this?"

"Only Mrs. Bristol so far," Eva replied. "And the maid who found her."

Phoebe gave a roll of her eyes. "Which means everyone belowstairs knows by now."

Eva conceded this with a nod and a shrug.

"What are you two murmuring about?" Owen had come up beside them. His hand hovered at the small of Phoebe's back.

"Narcisse, the photographer, didn't come down for dinner tonight," Phoebe whispered. She noticed Chesterhaven watching them and turned her face away from him as she went on. "Someone needs to find out where he is, and where he's been all night."

Owen grasped her shoulders. "Leave it to me. I'll find him."

The doctor arrived about a half hour later. He came into the room with his leather bag in hand, took one look at his patient, and shook his head. "You again, Miss Vale? We really must stop meeting like this."

"Sorry, Doctor," she replied with an attempt at a smile. She coughed. "Can't seem to help myself. It's that handsome face of yours."

The others chuckled, and Chesterhaven said, "She's had a run of rotten luck. Haven't you, old girl?"

"The rottenest," India agreed with a groan.

Phoebe wanted to tell him luck had nothing to do with it. It hadn't been ill luck that sent India's horse stumbling over the wall that morning they were out riding, and Phoebe didn't for a moment believe tonight's incident had happened by accident. Owen had made his excuses and left the room some minutes ago. Phoebe yearned to go after him, to help him search for Narcisse, but when he had requested that she let him handle it, her nod of acceptance had been a pledge of sorts, and she intended to keep that pledge. Besides, she still hoped to learn more from India.

"So you apparently fell," the doctor was saying, "and you were found on the floor, on your back. Is that correct?"

Theo cleared his throat. "I think Chesterhaven and I should make ourselves scarce for the time being." With a little nod to India, he led Chesterhaven out of the room.

"I'll go, too." Coco hurried after them.

"That's as much as I know, Doctor," India replied when only Phoebe, Eva, Julia, and Françoise were left. She calmly endured his prodding, letting him lift her arms to scan them for bruises. He took her pulse, listened to her heart, and examined her eyes. Finally, he ran his fingertips through her hair, searching for lumps.

"Yes, she was on her back when we found her," Phoebe added for good measure. "Near the tub. But not so near she could have hit her head on the rim, I would say."

The doctor nodded and emitted an *mmm*. His brows surged together as his fingertips went still. "My word, young lady. That's quite a lump you've got there on the back of your head. Must have hit it on *something* on your way down. Can you remember?"

India's face tightened in concentration, and then she shook her head. Françoise crossed to the bathroom and looked inside. When she returned, she said, "Judging by where she was found, there is really nothing she could have struck her head on. Not unless she moved herself across the floor before passing out."

India wiggled lower in the bed again, relaxing back against the pillows. "Hardly bloody likely, is it?" Then, realizing what she'd said, she pressed a hand to her mouth. "Sorry. Don't much know what I'm saying."

Phoebe knew better. Perhaps well-brought-up girls didn't utter words like *bloody*, but after what she'd learned from Amelia, Phoebe wasn't surprised by it.

"One more thing," the doctor said. "I notice your voice is hoarse. Can we remove this choker?" When India fumbled with the tie at the back, Phoebe helped her with it. The velvet and cameo came away to reveal small bruises.

"Doctor, look," Phoebe exclaimed with a gasp.

"I see." The man touched the skin gingerly, eliciting a grimace from India.

Françoise leaned over the bed for a better view. "What does this mean? Was she . . . ?"

"I'd say the police had better be called in," he replied tersely. "There is more here than a simple fall."

"Indeed." Phoebe sat at the edge of the bed opposite the doctor. "India, think. What was the last thing you remember doing?"

The girl's hand returned to her lips, and her eyes darted back and forth as she glanced at each of them—Phoebe, Eva, Françoise, Julia, and the doctor—in turn. "Other than preparing to go down to dinner, I . . . really can't remember."

Phoebe considered her a moment, suddenly unconvinced of what India actually did and did not remember. "Were you alone the whole time you were here in your room? Did the maid or Remie come in? Did either of them help you dress?"

"Ah . . . no. Neither of them came in."

Phoebe caught India's slight hesitation, and she again wondered about the half word she had uttered upon awakening. "Did someone else?"

As Phoebe scrutinized every twitch and every tinge of color as she awaited India's answer, Eva drifted across the room to the end table beside the overstuffed chair near the window. She picked up a spray of flowers—bright yellows and soft purples—and held them up for the others to see. "Where did these come from?"

"I suppose the maid must have brought them in earlier. Anyway, Doctor, I'll be all right, yes? No serious aftereffects or anything?"

"That lump is going to be sore for a few days, and you've probably suffered a mild concussion. I'll come by tomorrow afternoon and check on you." He folded his stethoscope and slipped it into his medical bag. "Good day for now, Miss Vale." To Julia he said, "I'd advise someone keep a close watch on her."

"You can be certain of that, Doctor." She walked him to the door.

Silence fell after he left, until Eva brought the little bouquet she had found over to the bed. She sent a significant look at Phoebe, one Phoebe understood. Eva and India had established a rapport these past days. If there was more to learn, Eva would learn it.

"Françoise, Julia, why don't we let Eva settle India more comfortably and go tell the others about this new development," Phoebe said.

"Good idea," Julia agreed. "India, we'll check on you later. I'll have Lord Allerton assign a footman to stand outside your door."

With that, Phoebe and the other two women left the room.

CHAPTER 18

Eva sat at the edge of India's bed, holding the flowers in her lap. "They're lovely," she remarked.

"They are." India reached out to finger a petal. "I suppose they'll need a vase."

Eva smiled, then met the girl's gaze. "India, we both know the chambermaid would never leave a spray of flowers on a table like that. If she had brought them to brighten the room, she'd already have put them in a vase herself, wouldn't she?"

"Perhaps she was called away suddenly."

Eva smiled again, more indulgently this time. "You know, I've been in the hothouse. I don't remember seeing bluebells and hawkbit growing among the roses, begonias, and pansies. These look more like something found near the stables, or at the edge of the woods."

India's face glowed pink against the stark white of her pillow. "I don't know where she got them."

"She didn't bring them at all, did she? Someone else did. Why don't you tell me who it was?"

India studied the counterpane, her brows tugged low.

"If I tell you, do you promise not to tell anyone? It's no one's business, after all."

"You know I can't promise that. Not after what happened to you. India, you were attacked. Don't you think whoever was here might be the person who did it?"

"Oh no. He wouldn't." India snatched at Eva's free hand, her fingers closing around it and squeezing. "I mean . . ."

"India, was Narcisse here?"

"Maybe . . ." She dragged in a breath. "He wouldn't hurt me. And he left before I started dressing for dinner. It couldn't have been him."

Eva didn't respond immediately, but rather contemplated what India had just divulged. A seventeen-year-old girl, entertaining a man at least ten years her senior, alone in her bedroom. She forced herself not to shake her head at India's recklessness and her folly in thinking she was old enough and sophisticated enough to handle every situation.

Finally, she said, "How do you know he didn't come back in? Had you locked your door?"

"No, I didn't bother, but why would he? We were . . . I mean . . . we were both preparing to go down to dinner, me in the dining room, and he belowstairs." She scoffed. "I don't think it's at all fair he has to eat with the servants. You either, for that matter."

"It's how things are done." Eva smoothed back strands of red hair from India's face. "I really think when this is all over, you must go back home."

"Home? Are you mad? After all the freedom I've enjoyed, I'm not about to crawl back into the cage my parents want to keep me in."

They don't do a very good job of it. "Since you've been here you've been in a riding accident—"

"It was no accident."

"Precisely," Eva said forcefully. "A riding *incident*, and

you've been struck on the head and possibly strangled. Doesn't that frighten you? Doesn't that tell you what a dangerous place the world can be for a young girl on her own?"

"I don't care. And why would anyone want to strangle me?"

"I don't know." *Yet.* Eva surrendered to the futility of trying to talk sense into the girl. "Is there something you know about someone, something they wouldn't want getting out?"

India frowned. "Such as what?"

"Such as, for instance, who closed the flue in Suzette's bedroom."

"You mean, who murdered her?" Eva nodded, and India shook her head. "I have no idea. All I know is it wasn't me."

Eva studied her a moment, searching for signs India was holding something back. "All right. Getting back to what happened, do you remember hearing anything at all right before you were struck? Do you remember exactly what you were doing?"

India seemed to make an effort to remember, but after a moment shook her head.

Eva stayed with her a while longer, attempting to jog her memory. Then Lady Allerton knocked on the door and beckoned Eva into the hallway.

"The police are here. The photographer is suspected of the attack, if that's really what it was."

Surely Lady Allerton couldn't still be denying that a murderer stalked the halls of Allerton Place. "There is evidence someone tried to strangle her," Eva reminded her.

"Well, Owen Seabright found him in his darkroom and hauled him belowstairs for questioning. Has she said anything about what happened?"

"Only that she doesn't remember. And that Narcisse wouldn't hurt her."

Lady Allerton wrinkled her nose. "His name came up? If she doesn't remember, why would she mention him?"

Eva steeled herself with a breath. "Because she admitted he was here before dinner. She says he left before she prepared to go down, and that he would never hurt her."

Lady Allerton took several moments to absorb that. "What was she saying? That he and she are . . ."

"I didn't have her explain the particulars, but yes, one can assume that if he was alone with her in her bedroom, they've formed an attachment."

"Good heavens. He's old enough to be her . . . very much elder brother."

Eva could only nod.

After another pause, Lady Allerton said, "I'll go in and sit with her. You're wanted downstairs, to make a statement."

The police had Narcisse under guard in Mr. Tewes's pantry. Everyone else was being questioned one at a time in Mrs. Bristol's parlor, and awaiting their turn in the servants' hall. Eva walked in to see Claudette and Marcelle there at the table, along with Tilly and two of the footmen. Who was missing? Remie, she realized, who must have gone in for questioning. Were any of the abovestairs guests being questioned as well?

She considered the faces ranged around the table. She discounted any of the footmen; they would have been far too busy preparing and serving at table upstairs. Tilly would have eaten earlier, then gone up to the first floor while the guests had dinner, to deliver fresh towels and turn down the bedclothes. Remie, Claudette, and Marcelle had been last to appear in the servants' hall, each coming in alone, a minute or two apart. Narcisse, on the other hand, never came down at all. But, she realized with a start, any of those latter four could have had time to steal into India's room, do the deed, and race down here. But why had the culprit left the job undone? Why strangle India, hit her on the head, but leave her alive?

Perhaps because he or she hadn't realized India *was* still alive. Because really, if one weren't a seasoned assassin, the difference between death and unconsciousness wasn't always immediately apparent. She halted in mid-thought. Remie had been sent by Mademoiselle to check on India, and had believed her room to be empty. But perhaps both India *and* her attacker had been there in the bathroom?

Eva stared hard at the table in front of her as she tried to work it out. Someone could have sneaked into the room, found India in the bathroom, rendered her unconscious and attempted to strangle her—and then heard Remie entering the bedroom. With India already passed out, her attacker might have panicked at the sound of Remie's voice and decided to flee as soon as Remie left, rather than risk taking the time to make sure the crime had been completed.

But who? Narcisse himself, possibly. It was of no consequence that India insisted he would never hurt her. Young women had been fooled by devious men since time began. But why would he wish to hurt her? Did she know something about him, and were his romantic overtures simply an excuse to get close to her? Did she know, perhaps, that he had closed the flue in Suzette's room? His shirt, after all, had smelled of smoke.

But if not Narcisse . . . ? Once again, she studied the faces around her. Marcelle—pretty, youthful Marcelle with her round cheeks and dimples and large dark eyes. Claudette—also pretty, slender like Mademoiselle, and stylish in a very modern way with her close-cropped curls. Each had reasons to want Suzette gone.

What about Remie herself—long-suffering Remie, who

had more to complain about in Mademoiselle's employ than any of the others. Could she resent India her sudden place in Mademoiselle's favor? Eva considered her fellow lady's maid. Drab in every way, her hair flat and pulled back into a dreary bun; her clothing as plain and nondescript as Eva's; her shoes sensible, clunky, devoid of all feminine adornments. But if one were to redo her hair, brighten her dress and shoes, apply some subtle cosmetics . . .

Yes! Good heavens, Remie would be an attractive woman. Perhaps she yearned to be in front of the camera and despaired of always being overlooked. Worse than overlooked, treated as though she were of no significance at all, barely an individual in Mademoiselle's sphere.

She shook her thoughts away, realizing she had incriminated everyone in her mind without being able to single out any one of them. Surely they couldn't all have done it.

Could they?

Phoebe, Julia, and Françoise sat at the table on the terrace, admiring the sprinkling of stars that braved peeks through the scudding clouds, presided over by a half moon haloed in silver. Owen had found Narcisse in his darkroom up on the third floor, and he had been arrested and taken away. It seemed Eva had finally persuaded India to tell the police the truth about Narcisse visiting her earlier that evening. That, combined with his not coming down to dinner and the smoky shirt found in his laundry, convinced the local constables they had enough evidence to hold the photographer on suspicion of assault and murder.

"They're calling in a detective from Gloucester," Julia said with a shake of her head. She lifted the crystal cordial glass of sherry to her lips and sipped delicately. "This is getting rather out of hand."

"Julia, it's long been out of hand." Phoebe sucked in a lungful of night air, laden with the scents of well-tended flowers and foliage and tinged with a dewy nip of autumn. Julia stared down into the shadowed gardens, pretending she hadn't heard, and Phoebe didn't bother repeating her remark. It was pointless. Julia believed what she chose to believe, and nothing short of a declaration of guilt from Suzette's killer would change that. Phoebe turned to Françoise. "What do you think? Could he be guilty?"

"I do not wish to believe it of Narcisse." Françoise sat with her ankles crossed, a cashmere shawl pulled tight across her shoulders. She sipped from her cordial glass. "But I believe the police are correct in that a murder and an attempted murder have taken place."

Julia let out a long sigh. "The bruises on India's neck were negligible at best and could have been caused by her choker when she fell. As for the lump on her head, again, she *fell*."

Julia's denial left Phoebe speechless. Her ire boiled inside her, yet she pinched her lips together, knowing her words would fall on deaf ears.

"Perhaps you are right." Françoise combed her fingers through strands of her silver-blond bob. "If the police can find no solid evidence, they should release Narcisse and let us all get on with our lives."

"Hear, hear," Julia exclaimed, raising her glass in a toast.

"What?" Phoebe couldn't believe what she'd just heard. Surely, sensible Françoise couldn't be as deluded as all that? Or was the notion of one of her fellow employees being a murderer too much to bear? After all, they had worked together since the war ended, had rebuilt their lives together, even if they weren't all the best of friends. Despite the many disagreements among the group, they couldn't help but share a special bond.

Françoise appeared about to say something more, but then suddenly came to her feet, her sherry abandoned on the table. "Excuse me. I am going in. It has been a very long day."

"Good night," Julia called after her. Then, after a brief pause, she too stood up from the table. "I'm going to turn in. Phoebe, are you coming?"

"Not yet. You go ahead."

"You're going to sit here in the dark all by yourself?" Her hands went to her hips. "Doesn't the idea of that frighten you, what with a killer on the loose?"

"Julia . . ."

"She won't be alone, because I'll be with her." Owen stepped out from the drawing room. "Good night, Julia. See you in the morning."

"Good night, Owen." Julia pecked his cheek on her way inside.

Once he'd pulled a chair closer and seated himself beside her, Phoebe leaned in to give him a kiss of her own, but not on his cheek. "Thanks for rescuing me."

"Glad to be on hand. What was all that about just now?"

"Oh, you know. Julia's ongoing denial of everything that's happening under her nose."

"Ah." That single word expressed a world of understanding. He reached for her hand and held it between them over the arms of their chairs.

"Odd thing, though. Just before Françoise left us, she seemed to be swayed to Julia's point of view." She explained Françoise's aversion to the notion of Narcisse's guilt.

"And you? Do you think he's guilty?"

Phoebe sat back and considered. "I think it's entirely possible. He's was undoubtedly involved with Suzette and now appears to be involved with India."

"You're joking."

"'Fraid not. The question is, *why* is he involved with India? Is it because she knows something about him?"

"For instance, that he killed Suzette?"

"Precisely. But he wasn't the only person to have reasons to resent Suzette. Marcelle and Claudette did as well. Good reasons. And here's what's nagging at me: Suzette and Marcelle were from the same region in the north of France. Lorraine. They were there during the war, and both went to Paris immediately following the war and found work in the same place."

"Phoebe, my dear, coincidences aren't always diabolical. Lots of people were in the north during the war, and countless numbers of them went to Paris afterward to build new lives. Why should it be hard to accept that two women from the north ended up working at a Paris fashion house? Besides, didn't you tell me Françoise was also from the north? What about her?"

Phoebe waved the notion away. "I don't see that she and Suzette were ever at odds, but Marcelle and Suzette? By Marcelle's own admission, yes. And Claudette, too, for that matter."

"Forgive me for eavesdropping." Theo stepped outside and joined them at the table. "Am I intruding?"

"Of course not," Phoebe assured him. "Julia's gone up."

"I know. I told her I'd be up presently." He swirled his glass of whiskey before taking a sip and setting it down. "Needed some air first. And another nip of this." He nodded at the glass. "What a night. Don't know how much more of this sort of thing we can take."

"There *will* be more of it, if the police are wrong about Narcisse." Phoebe smiled grimly at her brother-in-law. "I'm sorry. You don't want to hear that."

Theo hesitated, working the fingers of his left hand open and closed. Like the skin on his face, his hands had been burned by the mustard gasses at the Somme. When he'd first come home, he'd had trouble using them, but the past few years of therapy had made the skin and tendons much more pliable again. Still, Phoebe knew sometimes they tightened up and pained him. "I overheard what you were saying about two of the women being from the north."

"Three," Owen said. "The makeup artist, the clothing mistress, and Françoise."

"Could one of them have played traitor during the war?"

"What?" The notion startled Phoebe.

Theo nodded. "Yes, it happened, much more often than one would like to think. People in the villages, especially in the occupied northern regions, sometimes resorted to helping the enemy as a way to keep themselves and their families alive. They were traitors, and it was unforgivable, but they were desperate. At least most of them were. Some were merely greedy."

"That's beastly." Phoebe suddenly felt a need for a drink of her own, though she hadn't brought one outside with her. In fact, she had had nothing more than a glass of wine at dinner. "I don't care how frightened or desperate one is, to aid the enemy . . ." From the corner of her eye, she caught Owen's stoic expression—and she understood.

She rounded on him. "You knew of this. Of course you knew, you were in France during the war. And yet minutes ago when I brought up Suzette and Marcelle both being from the north, you said nothing. Oh, except that not all coincidences are diabolical."

"Thanks, Theo," he murmured, and then louder, he said to Phoebe, "It's still in all probability a coincidence. Are you going to accuse this Marcelle of murdering Suzette merely because they both hail from Lorraine?"

"What if one knew something about the other? What if one of them betrayed their country, and the other knew about it?"

"Phoebe, think about this," he said so patiently she felt as though he were patting her on the head. "Why now?

These women have been working together since the war ended. Why would this suddenly come out now, and here in the English countryside, of all places?"

"He's got a point," Theo put in. He lifted his glass and gave it another swirl.

Some of Phoebe's indignation subsided. "Yes, I suppose he has." She met Owen's gaze. "Sorry. But you still might have said something."

"Had the enemy ever dared set foot in England, I'd have died rather than betray our countrymen," Eva avowed after Lady Phoebe had told her what Lord Allerton had revealed about betrayals in France during the war. The very idea of turning traitor made her shudder with icy revulsion. She understood there had been spies on both sides, and double spies—bad enough—but these were ordinary individuals, like herself, her parents, her fellow residents of Little Barlow. It seemed unimaginable.

"I agree, and although we can't know the terror of living under an occupation, I'd like to believe we're made of sterner stuff than that." The sight of Lady Phoebe, sitting at her dressing table with her hair released from its pins and hanging in a braid down her back, and her silk wrapper cinched over her embroidered linen nightgown, made Eva smile with pride and affection. She might presently look like a dainty scrap of a girl, but Eva knew Phoebe Renshaw possessed every bit of that sterner stuff of which she spoke.

"Of course we are," Eva heartily agreed. "And let's not forget that most people living in the north of France were courageous and did *not* turn traitor."

"You're quite right. And I would like to dismiss the notion entirely. But could Suzette or Marcelle have been guilty of treason? That's a pressing question."

"If either one was, then Marcelle murdered Suzette either to punish her or to silence her." Which would make Marcelle the person they had been trying to identify. A murderer.

She thought of Marcelle, looking as vulnerable last night as Lady Phoebe did now. No, much more so. Younger. So very lost. And carrying the child of a man who cared nothing for her. Could such a woman muster the cold calculation to commit murder?

Perhaps, if she thought it might protect her child. Or at least avenge the injustice of the adults who had wronged that child.

Lady Phoebe nodded pensively, gazing down at her satin house shoes. "Yes, that would mean Marcelle, wouldn't it?"

"To be fair, there is also Françoise Deschamps. She's also from the north," Eva reminded her. "How does she fit into this?" She gathered up Lady Phoebe's evening things and began putting them away.

"Can you imagine a woman like Françoise committing treason? I can't. Besides, she didn't stay long in the north. She spent most of the war in Provence. She wouldn't know what went on closer to home." She fell silent again, before adding, "Perhaps the police are right about Narcisse. Perhaps he did it—killed Suzette and attacked India." Her features tightened as she stood and went to sit on the settee.

"You don't look convinced of that." Eva sat beside her. "And I'm not either. That he might have murdered Suzette to be rid of her, perhaps, but why attack India? When I questioned her, she was adamant that she didn't know anything about Suzette's death."

"Those are my reservations as well. Why attack India? And also . . . the night Suzette died, the way he knelt beside her and took her hand. His regrets were palpable, but they didn't seem the regrets of a murderer. More like . . . a lover faced with the reality of never being able to make things right."

"If it isn't Narcisse, I truly don't think the police will find enough evidence to formally charge him. A shirt that might or might not have been his, and the fact that he skipped dinner in favor of working in his darkroom?" Eva shook her head decisively.

"Whose shirt is it, then?" In Lady Phoebe's tone Eva heard no challenge, merely curiosity. "It's not Owen's or Lord Allerton's. It isn't large enough for either of them."

"Must it be a man's?"

"It *is* a man's shirt." Lady Phoebe's shadowed expression revealed the doubts she wished she could deny. "You think it could be Françoise's?"

"I know you don't want to think it." Eva patted her wrist. "And I understand your reasoning. But Madame Deschamps is as much a possibility as the other two, as Narcisse or Marcelle."

"You're right. I *don't* want to believe it. I want to resist the very idea. Because I've grown quite fond of her. But I realize you've grown fond of Marcelle and India and the others. And once we feel we know someone, envisioning them in the worst sort of light becomes a near impossible task."

"It's growing late, and there's little we can do tonight. Tomorrow, perhaps we'll learn more about how the police are proceeding, and if they've uncovered any other evidence." She offered her hand to help Lady Phoebe up, then followed her to the bed. "Try to get some sleep. Perhaps something we've overlooked will come to you."

"In my dreams?" She chuckled.

"You never know."

CHAPTER 19

Phoebe was up before the sun rose. Eva had been wrong last night. No answers or even suggestions had come to her in her sleep. She awakened several minutes ago just as muddled as when she'd gone to bed.

She opened her curtains to a tarnished pewter sky and a foggy garden below, the crawling mist so dense she could make out nothing of the flower beds beneath it, nor the paths or anything but the highest tips of the trees, and only just.

No one else would be up for the next two hours at least, but the kitchen staff would already be preparing baked goods for breakfast, and she might beg a scone or two and a cup of tea. She chose a warm jumper in soft lambswool and a woolen skirt, and just in case she found her way outdoors, her snap-on woolen half boots to keep her feet warm. Her hair she left in its nighttime braid, as she planned to be back upstairs and readying herself for the day with Eva's help before the others stirred.

Downstairs, a soft glow pooled just inside the drawing room, and she could hear movement within. Soft scrapes of metal against metal suggested someone was sorting through the clothing racks, and her first thought was that Claudette had risen early to get a head start on her day.

She hesitated in the doorway and peeked into the room. It wasn't young Claudette's brunette curls she saw at the far end, among the dresses and ensembles, but Françoise's silver-blond bob. Phoebe expected to see the efficient clipboard again, but Françoise's hands were empty as she slowly slid each piece of clothing along the rack that held them, pausing to study each before pushing it along and running her gaze over the next. Her sigh drifted through the room. She half turned, and Phoebe caught sight of her face. Françoise didn't appear to be inspecting the clothing at all. She looked, but with an absent expression, her eyes barely focused on her immediate surroundings.

Phoebe started to back away, but at that moment, by sheer chance, Françoise's gaze lighted on her. "Phoebe. Good morning. You are up early."

"As are you. I didn't mean to disturb your work. I'll leave you to it."

"No, please. Come in and keep me company."

Phoebe ventured inside. "Deciding on which dresses must be photographed again?"

"No. I woke early, troubled. About Narcisse, I suppose. Going through the clothing always helps settle my mind."

"I see." Phoebe traversed the room, stopping just beyond the fireplace. "Have you breakfasted yet?"

"I am not hungry. In a little while, perhaps." She continued sliding hangers across the rack, until she reached the last frock and moved on to the next rack. "Coco has been working on the tweed. She is very excited about what will come of it."

"It was very comfortable." Phoebe perched at the end of the long settee that faced the fireplace. "I would love to see a collection of country tweed for women. How soon do you think that might happen?"

"I could not say. Coco works at her own pace. She cannot be rushed."

"No, I wouldn't think so. Will you work on it with her?"

"Perhaps." She worked her way listlessly from one end of the rack to the other. "Or perhaps not. I . . . may not return to France with her."

"Not return to France?" Phoebe couldn't help the rise in her voice. "You mean you'll stay in England?"

"*Oui*," she replied softly. "In England. France holds little for me now."

"I don't understand."

"I told you of the war, how the Germans overran our homes and our lives. How we helped the local people around our home to hide the crops they managed to grow, their livestock, so that the Germans would not steal them. How the women stitched and embroidered to make money to feed their families, even as the shells exploded."

"Yes, you did explain all that to me," Phoebe said, her throat tight with compassion. "I can't imagine the fear you lived with daily."

"Four years of terror." Françoise tsked bitterly.

"But you weren't there for the entire four years, were you?"

As if Phoebe hadn't spoken, Françoise went on in a toneless voice, "And then we were betrayed. Someone told the enemy about the hidden stores, and the work the women were doing. They raided Château des Champs, stole what they could, and burned the rest. The house, the outbuildings, the vineyard . . ."

"And your husband died in the flames," Phoebe murmured, her voice as flat as Françoise's. A cold realization gripped her very bones. "You told me the fire was an accident."

Françoise came away from the clothing racks. Taking Phoebe's hand, she sat on the settee and drew Phoebe down beside her. Phoebe braced, ready to spring to her feet. Françoise smiled sadly. "You need not be afraid of me. I mean you no harm." With a deep sigh she glanced to the end of the room, to the terrace doors. "The sun will be up in a little while. Then I will do what I must."

Fear sent a spiking pain through Phoebe's neck and shoulders. "And what is that?"

"Turn myself in to the police."

"You killed her." Phoebe's whisper caught in her parched throat. "Suzette. Because she betrayed you, didn't she?"

"She betrayed everyone she had known since birth. She deserved to die. To die by flames as my husband did. I am not sorry." She released Phoebe's hand, and although logic told Phoebe to run, instinct persuaded her to stay and hear the woman out. "I cannot let an innocent man take the blame for what I did." She gave a bitter laugh. "Not that he deserves any woman's pity. He is a cad of the worst kind, preying on pretty faces and then casting them aside once he grows bored. But I cannot let him hang for my crime."

"The shirt, it was yours."

Françoise nodded. "But I did not put it with Narcisse's things. I do not know how it got there."

Phoebe had trouble believing that, but instead of dwelling on it, she asked, "When did it happen? The betrayal, I mean."

"In the third year of the war."

Phoebe finally understood something. "You didn't leave for Provence when you said you did. Your work with the Society for Employment of Women—it was ongoing throughout the war."

Françoise nodded.

"But then why now? Why wait all these years for your revenge, and why here?"

"I can answer that."

Both women turned toward the drawing room doors in surprise. Marcelle hesitated on the threshold. She wore a simple skirt with a woolen jacket buttoned over a shirt-waist, and with her hair tied back with a colorful scarf she appeared even younger than she was, almost childlike.

She stepped inside and closed the doors behind her, locking them for good measure and slipping the key into the pocket of her jacket. "You see," she said as she came closer to them, "Françoise left Lorraine immediately after the raid, so she never learned the truth. Although my family's farm was well outside the village, we heard of the raid, not only of the house but the entire village. The horror of it. People were executed—taken out and shot. Suzette got away before word of her treachery spread, but people discovered the truth. Oh, but her name was not Suzette Villiers then. It was Suzanne Vallerand. Clever, *non?*"

Marcelle's expression implied she found it anything but. Phoebe glanced from one woman to the other. "I still don't understand why this all came out now."

"You will." Marcelle's hand remained in her jacket pocket, her fingers fidgeting inside the fabric. A muffled clinking came from inside, as if she played with two keys instead of one. "Like so many others, I went to Paris after the war to find work. I went to the fashion district hoping to put my stitching skills to work, or my art skills. It did not matter, I needed money to live and to send home.

"It was pure coincidence that Suzette and I met, but I recognized her immediately, even with the changes in her appearance—the way she had coiffed her hair, the cosmetics, the costly clothing. Then I learned she was working for a fashion designer, someone who had already proved her talents with ladies' hats and who was poised to become important in the fashion world. I gave her no choice but to see that I was hired."

"And Françoise?" Phoebe held herself very still, her attention riveted on Marcelle. "Did Suzette also arrange for her employment at Maison Chanel?"

"*Oui*. She had such sway over Mademoiselle in those days. She was the favorite, the star of Maison Chanel. Ah, but how wonderful it was to see Suzette squirm beneath the threat of exposure. She did not know at first that Madame Deschamps had no idea who she was. You see, she was not one of the hardworking women who gathered at Madame's estate, and they had never met face-to-face. Even so, Suzette tripped over her own two feet to please Madame Deschamps, always afraid Madame would expose her."

"You used your knowledge about Suzette to blackmail her." Phoebe realized she had clutched her hands in her lap and forced them to relax. "I still don't understand why her death happened now." She darted an accusing gaze at Françoise. "And why did you attack India?"

"First questions first." Marcelle's brows converged. "You ask why Madame Deschamps closed the flue in Suzette's room? Because I told her only days ago what Suzette had done during the war. And yes, even now, Madame hated the person who destroyed her home and murdered her husband. I finally told her the truth because of what Suzette did to me and Narcisse. He could have loved me if not for her—would have been a father to our child."

Phoebe's eyes grew wide at those words. Marcelle pressed a hand to her belly. "Yes, I carry his child. Before Suzette played with him and made him out to be a fool with her dalliance with Lord Chesterhaven, Narcisse was an honorable man. Now, because of her, he has no heart, no honor. He used me because of her, and he cast me away."

"It sounds to me as if Narcisse took advantage of what he could get, whenever he could," Phoebe reasoned. "You can't blame Suzette for his lack of honor."

"I can!" Marcelle lurched closer, prompting Phoebe to press against the back of the settee.

Françoise held up a hand as if to hold Marcelle in place. "My dear, calm down. We do understand the unhappiness and disappointment you have suffered at Suzette's and Narcisse's hands. And we—"

"It was Suzette's fault," the girl insisted. The clinking inside her pocket continued, setting Phoebe's nerves on edge.

Her mouth fell open with understanding. "Françoise didn't attack India. Neither did Narcisse. It was you, Marcelle."

"She deserved it, did she not? She is another Suzette. She destroys everything and everyone she touches."

"And you have assigned yourself the task of punishing her and Narcisse for betraying you." Françoise ran both hands through her hair, holding it back from her face before letting it swish forward. "You put my shirt with Narcisse's laundry. I had stowed it in the bottom of my trunk, and I had not known it was missing until it was said to have turned up among Narcisse's things."

"I knew any self-respecting laundress would recognize the scent of smoke and feel it her duty to report it. Better Narcisse hangs for Suzette's death than you." Marcelle's eyes were lusterless, like two gemstones covered in grime. "I tried to save him. I gave him a choice, but he flung it back at me. Let him hang, then."

As Marcelle rambled on in her condemnation of all three of them—Suzette, India, and Narcisse—the clinking in her pocket became faster and louder. Her fingers worked furiously beneath the woolen weave, until Phoebe became so absorbed in it she was no longer able to focus on the words.

"What are you doing? What have you got there?" she blurted, her nerves raw and jangling.

Marcelle went silent, her nonstop stream of words cut off in mid-syllable. She slid her hand from her pocket. "This."

Phoebe went rigid and Françoise gasped as Marcelle held up a pistol so small her hand nearly swallowed it. With a curving hardwood grip and a nickel barrel, it looked decades old, not something a soldier would have carried in the war. Phoebe envisioned the handgun collection at Foxwood Hall, which she had seen only a handful of times because her grandfather hid them away, choosing to display only the estate's hunting rifles in his study.

But she knew enough about handguns to understand the danger this one posed, and the opportunity it presented. "It's a single shot pistol," she said, sounding infinitely calmer than she felt. "So which one of us do you intend killing?"

"It is loaded and ready to be fired. A single shot is all I need to ensure your silence, Lady Phoebe, but for now, I am going to aim my weapon at Françoise, because I know it is the only way to persuade you to do as you are told."

"Marcelle, put that away." Françoise came to her feet, then went still when Marcelle took aim at her. "Where did you get it?"

"It is Suzette's. Did you not know? She slept with it under her pillow, because she knew one day someone would come for her. Silly Suzette, she should have known better than to drink herself into oblivion that night. Or did she?" She compressed her lips as she studied Françoise. "Or did you slip something into her wine when no one was looking to make sure she slept soundly that night? It is all right if you did. I cannot blame you. She deserved it."

"What is it you want, Marcelle?" Phoebe came to her feet beside Françoise. "This makes no sense. If you fire that in here, everyone will hear it. You'll be caught and go to prison. Is that what you want for your child?"

"Do not speak of my child." Marcelle's eyes sparked with a burst of fury that set Phoebe's limbs trembling. "I want to ensure Françoise's escape. She suffered enough during the war. She deserves to go free. And I will go free with her. We are all leaving today once everyone is up. Mademoiselle decided late last night. We shall take care of this business quickly and be gone before anyone notices you missing."

"Marcelle, listen to reason, please." Phoebe took a step but halted when Marcelle stretched out her arm to center her aim more narrowly on Françoise's chest.

"You will not shoot me, Marcelle." Françoise reached out a hand. "You know you will not, so give me the gun. You have done nothing so far that cannot be forgiven."

"No? I tried to strangle the life out of that trollop, India. But even if I do go to jail for it, it will be worth it." Marcelle turned her mouth down at the corners. "It would have been more worth it if I had succeeded."

"Do not do this, Marcelle. I am guilty of Suzette's death and I will pay the consequences. It is right that I do." This time, Françoise reached out with both hands, as if to embrace the younger woman. "You are not guilty. Lady Phoebe is not. There is no reason to harm her or for you to destroy your own life."

"She is a most troublesome creature." Marcelle cast a contemptuous glance at Phoebe. "Even if you had not told her what you did, she would have discovered the truth because she never stops asking questions. She and her maid."

"You'll leave Eva alone." Phoebe didn't recognize the forcefulness of her own voice. Her fingertips shook with rage. With desperation.

Marcelle studied her a long moment, and then shrugged. "I will. I have no desire to harm her. She has been kind to me. I only wish to distract her. She'll be frantic searching for you, as will the others. Your sister, your gentleman friend. Françoise and I will have our chance to get away."

"There is no reason to kill her. We will take her out—far into the forest." The words tripped from Françoise's tongue in an eager rush. "We'll tie her feet and hands so she cannot return to the house until she is found. You and I shall have our escape."

To Phoebe's astonishment, Marcelle began to laugh. Though her pistol never lost its aim, she pressed her other hand to her belly to contain her mirth. Phoebe had a moment's indecision. Should she lunge forward, make a grab for the pistol? The moment passed. All too soon, Marcelle's laughter faded, though her smile remained, one that incongruently brought beauty to her features. "Silly Françoise. I am not planning to kill her. I am planning to do exactly what you have said. Unless she forces my hand. Come. Let us be quick, before people stir from their beds."

With her pistol she pointed the way between the racks of clothing. At Marcelle's prompting Phoebe opened the terrace doors, and they stepped out into the swirling mist that turned the gardens dull and sooty. From the windows above, they would be little more than faint blobs, easily blending with the autumn foliage. The air spread its clamminess across Phoebe's face and down her neck. She shivered as Marcelle hurried them along, skirting the length of the house to the north lawn and beyond, where oak and birch trees and rhododendrons dotted the landscape, before gradually thickening into a dense canopy overhead.

They walked until Phoebe's legs began to ache. If anyone had been trailing them, their job would have been made infinitely easier by the thrashing of leaves underfoot, and the cracking of twigs as the three of them forged a path where none existed. But no one would be following them; they were alone here in the woods, so thick the morning light wouldn't penetrate the trees and fog for hours yet.

"Haven't we gone far enough?" she asked through lips gone stiff from the cold.

"A little more," Marcelle said from behind her. "Françoise, go to the right. That will take us farther away from the house."

As they turned, Phoebe determined that they headed west, judging by where the moss covered the bases of the trees. They turned direction several more times, and she tried to keep a map in her mind's eye. Though the riding trails were somewhat familiar to her, she didn't know this part of the estate at all. How long would it take the others to find her? Perhaps if she managed to untie whatever they bound her with, she could find her own way back.

She stepped through a break in the trees and stumbled down a rocky incline. Several boulders soared up from the ground, forming an overhang that extended back into darkness, like a small cave. Saplings and underbrush surrounded the rocks, with the larger trees closing in high above.

Marcelle told them to stop. "This will do."

Her heart racing from exertion, Phoebe scanned her surroundings. This tiny clearing, if one could call it that, lay in a depression in the forest floor, undetectable from a distance. Even if she had worn more colorful clothes and not dull beige and brown, she would not be seen.

Marcelle shook the silk scarf from her hair, which tumbled forward in a sea of dark waves. She gestured to Françoise. "Here, take it, and use yours as well." She pointed to the scarf encircling Françoise's collar. "Tie her good and tight. I will check the knots when you are done to make sure."

"Marcelle, it is enough that we brought her here," Françoise protested. "Why must we tie her?"

"We cannot have her strolling back to the house before we are gone."

"If they don't find her for a very long time, she could succumb to exposure." Françoise hugged herself to prove her point. "The days have been growing colder. The nights more so."

Marcelle shrugged. "That is a chance we will have to take."

After a brief hesitation, Françoise nodded. She turned to Phoebe. "I am sorry about this. Turn around."

Phoebe turned and allowed Françoise to secure her hands behind her back. Once that was done, Marcelle ordered her to sit on the ground. Phoebe lowered herself to the forest floor. The dampness penetrated her skirt and stockings but she refused to let herself shiver.

"Make sure you tie her tight. Above the boots so she cannot slip her feet free."

With another murmured apology, Françoise bound her ankles together. When she had finished the job, Phoebe's wrists and ankles throbbed. As promised, Marcelle had Françoise back away so that she herself could test the knots. Her sharp tugs sent fresh needles of pain through Phoebe. Marcelle nodded with apparent satisfaction.

"All right, we have done it." Françoise rubbed her hands together, then tugged her sleeves over them. "Let us get back to the house and prepare to leave."

"One more thing." Marcelle reached into her pocket and drew out a handkerchief. She shook out its folds, crumpled it into a ball, and then crouched before Phoebe. "Open your mouth." At first Phoebe compressed her lips, but the gun against her forehead convinced her to do as Marcelle commanded. The girl stuffed the handkerchief into her mouth. Phoebe gagged; her stomach took a precarious jolt upward. Despite myriad other dangers, she fervently hoped the handkerchief had come fresh from the laundry.

Marcelle stood and backed away. Phoebe half sat, half lay in shadow beneath the rocky overhang, the dampness seeping through her clothing and the dank air filling her nose and threatening to make her sneeze. Marcelle stared down at her and made no move to leave.

"Marcelle, please, we must go," Françoise urged.

Marcelle glanced down at the pistol in her hand.

"Marcelle, we must off. What are you doing?" Françoise gripped her shoulder from behind.

Marcelle shook her off. "Thinking. Perhaps it would be better if, when she was found, she was not—"

"No, Marcelle." With a long stride, Françoise placed herself between Phoebe and Marcelle. "You said you would not harm her."

"If we leave her alive, she will tell them too soon what has happened, and we might not have time to leave the country. And then—" She broke off, her chin hefting in the air, her eyes wide. "What was that?"

Phoebe heard it, too. Footsteps. As loud as their own had been. Louder, even. A single pair, though, she judged. And headed straight this way.

Without further warning, Eva came shuffling through the trees.

CHAPTER 20

"Phoebe Renshaw, whatever are you doing out here? You'll catch your death of cold. What *would* your grandmother say?" Despite the gun now pointed in her direction, Eva marched into the tiny clearing, bordered by trees on three sides and a ledge formed of boulders on the fourth. In her hands she clutched Lady Phoebe's belted wool coat. For one panicked instant, she didn't see Lady Phoebe, only Madame Deschamps and Marcelle. And the pistol in Marcelle's hand.

Then she saw Lady Phoebe huddled beneath the overhanging rocks.

Both Frenchwomen looked thoroughly bewildered, and Eva knew there was nothing for it but to continue her ruse. If nothing else, she might keep the barrel of that pistol trained on her and not Lady Phoebe.

Neither woman had yet to find her voice. Eva strode between them as though she were a stern governess and they her wayward charges. "I fail to understand what game you are playing, but I insist you all return to the house at once. I am tasked with my lady's well-being, and I can tell you that traipsing through the forest at dawn never did anyone a lick of good, except perhaps for hunters hoping to bring home a covey of grouse, or the early bird hoping to catch the worm. And you, ladies, are neither."

Her pulse throbbing in her temples, she kept going, despite Marcelle extending the pistol toward her as if to sharpen her aim. "What on earth are you playing at? Marcelle, put that ridiculous thing away. Wherever did you find it? Lady Phoebe, come out here at once and put your coat on. I promise you the countess is going to hear about this childish behavior." Eva got all the way to the boulders and began to crouch. She heard Marcelle's promise of "I'll shoot" behind her, and, coat and all, threw herself on top of her dear lady.

The blast shook the forest and sent Eva's heart slamming against her ribs. Before the reverberations faded, voices filled the air. Male shouts. Feminine shrieks. The next thing Eva knew, Madame Deschamps was beside her, squeezing into the depths of the overhang.

"Phoebe, Eva, are you both all right?" The Frenchwoman reached out and pulled a square of linen out of Lady Phoebe's mouth.

She coughed and sputtered. "I am. Eva, are you all right?"

"Yes, fine." Eva waited another five seconds at least before she eased off Lady Phoebe, using the spongy ground and Madame Deschamps's shoulder for leverage. As she crawled into the open, Madame Deschamps began working at the knots that secured the bindings around Lady Phoebe's ankles. Eva braved a peek behind her.

Marcelle was on the ground, with Owen Seabright and Lord Allerton on either side, pinning her down. Her shrieks continued, wordless utterings that conveyed only rage.

Lady Phoebe wiggled out of the rocky enclosure, and Madame Deschamps steadied her while she struggled to her feet. She half turned her back to Madame Deschamps. "Free my hands."

"Of course. I am so sorry." Madame Deschamps struggled with the knots while Lady Phoebe worked her arms until she was finally able to slide her wrists free. As her arms fell to her sides, Eva threw her own arms around her. Lady Phoebe's relieved laughter was the most delightful sound she had heard in a long while.

"How are you here? How did you know to follow?" Lady Phoebe looked beyond Eva's shoulder. "Owen, Theo. Thank goodness you're both here."

Marcelle's gun lay in a heap of leaves several feet away from where she lay pinioned by Lords Owen and Allerton. Madame Deschamps took the scarves that had held Lady Phoebe and handed them to Lord Allerton. He secured Marcelle's hands behind her back and allowed her to sit up. Satisfied she could go nowhere in any sort of a hurry, Lord Owen reached Lady Phoebe in two bounds and wrapped her in his arms.

He did not let her go during the trek back through the woods, into the house, and onto the morning room settee.

By now the others had begun rising from their beds. Lady Allerton strolled into the morning room with a gurgling Charles tucked against her side. His cold seemed much better, his cheeks pinker and his nose clear. At the sight of his father and the others, he let out a happy howl and began a singsong chatter while reaching for the gold chain hanging around his mother's neck. Barely missing a beat, she caught his chubby hand in her own, saved the necklace, and began a fierce interrogation.

"Theo, Phoebe, where on earth have you been, and why so early? You, too, Owen. I woke up to find my home virtually empty." The exaggeration nearly made Eva chuckle. Lady Allerton perused them from head to toe. "I want the truth. You weren't out riding, that's certain." Her scrutiny fell on Eva. "Please tell me my sister didn't have the temerity to wake you at such an ungodly hour to go traipsing across the countryside."

"Julia, of course I didn't," Lady Phoebe protested from the newfound safety of the settee.

"No, my lady, I was already well up before your sister needed me." Eva released a breath that trembled with relief that such had indeed been the case. What might have happened if she hadn't remained vigilant last night and this morning?

"Eva, sit and tell us how you *did* happen to be up, and how you all found me in the woods." Lady Phoebe patted the settee beside her, while she kept her other side pressed against Lord Owen. "Julia, could we have coffee and perhaps something to nibble on brought in here rather than the dining room?"

With a quizzical look, Lady Allerton tugged the bellpull beside the fireplace. Within moments, Mr. Tewes appeared. He tossed Eva a curious gaze but turned his attention immediately back to his employer. "Yes, my lady?"

"Tewes, could we have a light breakfast brought in here this morning?"

"Of course, my lady. Presently." He started to stride off, but paused and turned. "It seems Miss Renault," he said, referring to Claudette, "arrived in the drawing room some minutes ago expecting to meet her fellow employees there and begin packing the clothing. She is both confused and perplexed to find herself alone, my lady."

Lady Allerton nodded, her expression neutral. "Thank you, Tewes, I'll let Mademoiselle know." The moment the man left them, she rounded on her sister and husband. "Which one of you is going to tell me what's going on?" She smoothed a hand over Charles's pale curls, and then

brought him to his father. Theo took him readily and settled himself in one of the easy chairs opposite the settee,
his son on his knee. Charles responded with delight and
tugged Lord Allerton's nose. His wife turned to Eva, an
eyebrow reaching for her hairline. "Eva, I suppose I
should appeal directly to you. I know you'll tell the truth,
whereas the rest of these miscreants . . ." She shrugged
again and waited.

"Yes, well, there is much to be explained, and I suppose
I am the person to start with." Eva drew herself up against
the settee. "I hadn't slept much last night, not because I
couldn't but because I deemed it prudent to stay awake.
Awake and listening." She went on to describe the events
of the night before last with Marcelle and the open window. Both Lady Phoebe and Lady Allerton were aghast,
and Lord Allerton demanded to know why Eva hadn't
told anyone, albeit in a gentle tone that would not startle
the child on his lap.

"Because, sir, I believed I'd defused the situation—
averted the crisis, as it was—and I didn't think I had the
right to divulge what the girl had told me in strictest confidence. But last night, I began to fear a repeat of her de-
spondency, and I stayed awake listening for sounds that
she might be leaving her room. About a half hour before
dawn, I heard just such a sound, and I peeked into the corridor to discover her slipping from her own room, fully
dressed, and tiptoeing to the stairs. I followed.

"When she headed for the drawing room, I very nearly
went back upstairs. I knew Mademoiselle and her people
were leaving today, and I thought Marcelle went early to
help with the packing." Eva paused and turned to lock her
gaze on Lady Phoebe's. "But then I heard your voice.
Yours and Madame Deschamps's. I admit I felt a stab of
guilt for staying and listening, but something about the

way Marcelle lingered in the doorway, also listening to the two of you . . . well, there was something in her bearing that set me on the alert."

Lady Phoebe reached for Eva's hand. "I promise I will never fault you for listening in on anyone's conversation under such circumstances."

Eva was about to continue her tale when Mr. Tewes reentered the room. Robert, the footman who had been accused of neglecting to open Suzette's flue, followed him, wheeling in a cart that rattled with china and cutlery. Together they set out cups, saucers, and plates on the sofa table. Without making eye contact with anyone—anyone but Eva, that was, and then only briefly—Robert placed two covered platters, coffeepot, and cream and sugar beside them. Then he stood at attention while Mr. Tewes asked, "Will there be anything else?"

"This should do for now, thank you, Tewes. Thank you, Robert. Oh, and when Mademoiselle Chanel and Lord Chesterhaven come down, do send them this way." She began pouring tea and handing round the cups. To Eva, Lady Allerton urged, "Please go on."

"As soon as Marcelle closed the doors behind her and I heard the key in the lock, I knew something was very wrong. I hurried over from my hiding place near the library and pressed my ear to the door."

"Resourceful Eva," Lady Phoebe murmured in admiration.

Eva accepted a cup and saucer from Lady Allerton and after adding a lump of sugar and a trickle of cream, she took a bracing sip. The effect was immediate. Warmth traveled through her and steadied her nerves. "What I heard sent me running upstairs to do something I never in my life thought I would do: knock at a gentleman's door and urge him from his bed."

Here, Lord Owen pushed out a grim laugh. "And thank

the stars she did. I got Theo up—sorry, Julia, there wasn't time to tell you anything and you were sound asleep anyway. The two of us pulled on clothes—" He gestured at the trousers and shirts they both wore. No vests, no neckties, nor any of the trappings that typically distinguished a gentleman even in the country. "We shoved our feet into boots, grabbed coats, and followed Eva downstairs. Theo brought along an extra key to the drawing room. By the time we got inside, Marcelle had already nudged you and Françoise out onto the terrace."

"Françoise?" Lady Allerton stopped midway as she reached for the coffeepot. "What's she got to do with this?"

"Everything," Lady Phoebe said. "Julia, it was Françoise who opened Suzette's flue. She did it deliberately, and Marcelle knew about it."

Lady Allerton paled. "That's impossible. Not Françoise. She's so . . . normal."

Lady Phoebe and Eva spent the next quarter of an hour explaining all they had learned, not only that morning but in the days following Suzette's death. The three-sided affairs, the dark secrets to be found in each individual's past, even India's rebellion against her parents. With each revelation, Lady Allerton's expression wavered between indignation and dismay.

"Theo stayed behind long enough to telephone the constable," Lord Owen added. "Then he followed Eva and me into the woods."

"How did we not hear you?" Lady Phoebe asked him.

He chuckled. "The three of you were making enough noise to flush every last bird in those woods out of its nest. Professional beaters at a pheasant hunt couldn't have done a better job. On the other hand, Theo and I served in the war. We learned a thing or two about stealth."

"And I just made sure to walk carefully," Eva put in.

"The ruse you used." Lady Phoebe stared down at her

hands, and when she looked up, her eyes had gone large and shiny. "It was terribly risky. To simply come walking along, complaining about my lack of good sense and catching my death of cold could have gotten you shot."

Eva grazed her lady's cheek with her fingertips. "It worked, though," she whispered. Louder, she said, "I wagered on Marcelle being so distracted by my ridiculous tirade that for at least a good several seconds she wouldn't make a move to stop me, and that would give Lord Owen and Lord Allerton the chance they needed to disarm her."

"And where are Françoise and Marcelle now?" Lady Allerton seemed alarmed that perhaps they might still be on the loose.

"Did you not follow, my dear?" Lord Allerton dipped his finger into the clotted cream he'd dolloped onto his plate and offered it to his son. "I telephoned over to the constable's office before following Owen and Eva outside. They've taken the pair to the village. They'll be handed over to the Gloucester main station tomorrow."

"What is this? Françoise has gone to Gloucester? And Marcelle?" Mademoiselle Chanel, with Lord Chesterhaven by her side, sauntered into the room, stopped, and fisted her hands on her hips. "We are to leave for London today. I cannot abide a delay."

Lady Allerton set her teacup aside and came to her feet. "You'll have to go on without them. I'm afraid their delay will be of a rather permanent nature. Although you may have your photographer back, as he's presently being released."

"What do you mean?" She pierced Lady Allerton with a glare obviously meant to intimidate, the sort she used with her lesser employees, Eva guessed. "What is this all about?"

"Françoise and Marcelle have broken the law," Lady Allerton calmly informed her. "One is a murderer, the other . . . well . . ." She glanced at Phoebe and Eva over her shoulder. "It sounds to me she is quite insane."

"By gum, you don't say?" Lord Chesterfield scratched his chin, tugged at his tweed coat, and ambled over to the sofa table. "Got any extra cups?"

Lord Allerton pointed to the two that had been left stacked together. "Help yourself."

"So poor Suzette's death really wasn't an accident," Lord Chesterhaven said after pouring his coffee. He leaned over the platters of scones and fried bread, his hand circling over them before he made his selections. When he perhaps thought no one could see his face, his expression changed to one of remorse, communicated to Eva in the tuck of his lip between his teeth and the rippling of his brow. For Suzette?

He shook the emotion away and brought his cup and plate to the small table in the corner. His mouth half full and a dab of jam at the corner of his lips, he continued. "That'll be a relief for your footman, won't it, Theo? I suppose Julia has some apologizing to do. And the photographer's certainly having a better day today than yesterday. Lucky chap."

"I most certainly will apologize to Robert," Lady Allerton murmured, looking and sounding so wretched Eva wanted her wrap her arms around her. "I only hope he can forgive me."

"Never mind any of that." Coco remained rooted to the spot just inside the doorway, as if coming any closer might be to accept circumstances she obviously found insuperable. "I need my people back."

"Coco, they are not going to be released. Both will be going to prison for a very long time." Lady Phoebe didn't say the obvious, that Françoise would possibly hang for her crime, committed in cold blood. Eva found herself hoping the authorities would take into consideration what Françoise had suffered during the war at Suzette's prompting.

Mademoiselle still would not be budged, her dark brows slashing across her forehead and her mouth a harsh red line. "Who is going to pack up my clothing? Who will help me once I reach London?"

"You still have me, old girl." From across the room, Lord Chesterhaven waved his bread knife in the air to catch her attention.

"*Och.*" Mademoiselle folded her arms and turned her back to him. "I'll need your servants to help me, Julia. It is the least you can do."

Baby Charles chose that moment to decide something in his tiny world simply wasn't right, or comfortable, or perhaps he sensed his parents' attention had wandered too far from himself for his liking. He let out a howl.

Mademoiselle's hands flew to cover her ears. "Make it stop that awful noise!"

The admonition made Eva want to jump up and issue a scathing rebuke. But Lady Allerton proved capable of defending herself—and her son. She went to her husband and took the baby in her arms, rubbing his back and bouncing him up and down. Above his squalls, she said, "I've done quite enough for you. We all have. Now I must ask you to leave. At once. My servants *will* pack your clothing for you, not as a favor but to facilitate your vacating Allerton Place, to which you will never return. We'll have it all shipped to London wherever you want it."

Mademoiselle trembled from head to foot, her dark eyes blazing. Her hand stiffened, and for one appalling moment Eva feared she might slap Lady Allerton—and perhaps Mademoiselle actually considered it. Her nostrils flared, and then she pivoted on the heel of her leather pump. "Chessy, are you coming?"

It was far more an order than a question. He looked forlornly down at his breakfast, shoved one last bite into his mouth, washed it down with coffee, and came to his feet. On his way to follow Mademoiselle, he paused by the others. "Sorry to eat and run. Women." He held out a hand toward the receding clack-clack of Mademoiselle's heels on the marble floor. "Well, thanks a ton, and see you."

His heavy footfalls and Mademoiselle's sharp staccato were replaced by a quieter step-thud, step-thud. India shambled in on her crutches, stopping to say good morning to Lord Chesterhaven and looking puzzled when she didn't receive an answer. She took in the group on the settee and ranged around it.

"Hullo, everyone. What was that all about?"

"They're leaving," Julia told her. "And so are you, young lady. You're going home. I'm calling your parents to let them know where you've been."

India's mouth dropped open, and then she launched into an urgent diatribe on why Lady Allerton shouldn't do that. Her words went unheeded.

The next day, Phoebe leaned back against the leather seat of Owen's Morgan Runabout motorcar and closed her eyes to the breeze streaming in through its open sides. To prevent her hat being blown out into the passing fields, she had removed it and tossed it onto the seat between them. Her hair would be an utter disaster by the time they reached Foxwood Hall, but so be it.

They had left Allerton Place only minutes ago, with Eva having gone in Phoebe's Vauxhall with Robert, newly restored to his position as head footman, at the wheel. The trip to return Eva and the Vauxhall to Foxwood Hall was part of a small holiday Julia and Theo had offered the young man as part of their apology to him. Upon leaving Little Barlow, he would catch the train to Oxfordshire to visit with his parents. He had been so delighted with the prospect, one might have thought he was setting out on an adventure across the world.

"I'm so happy things worked out for Theo and Julia's footman," Phoebe mused aloud as Owen negotiated a turn so narrow it took them perilously close to a hedge-row. "And for Narcisse, I suppose. But I can't help being sorry about Françoise. One can almost sympathize with what she did."

"Murder?" He glanced over at her, then set his gaze back on the road. "But I know what you mean. What Suzette did to her—to her husband. To the entire village. It was unconscionable."

"And then there's Marcelle. I hate to think it, but Julia was right when she said the poor girl has lost her mind. And the child she claimed to be carrying." Here Phoebe paused to draw a breath and acknowledge the great tragedy of a life wasted. "It was a figment of her imagination. Right before we left, Julia told me the police had a doctor examine her, and he concluded she was not and never had been pregnant."

"I suppose that redeems Narcisse somewhat."

"Yes, I suppose. Though only marginally. His conduct has been less than honorable, nonetheless."

"And me, Phoebe?" He glanced over again, this time lingering over her features before pulling his gaze back to the twisting road. "Have I redeemed myself for being such an overbearing blighter?"

"You weren't."

"I was." He gave a shake of his head. "We both know it."

"Well, maybe you were, a bit."

"I treated you like a child." His fist tapped the steering wheel. "I only want to keep you safe, but I know that's not the right thing to do. Especially not with you. I'm slowly learning to overcome my fears and trust your instincts. They've rarely failed you."

"They almost failed me *this* time, didn't they? If not for you, Theo, and Eva . . . Well." She scanned the roadside and pointed to where the verge widened along the straight-away they'd entered. "Pull over there."

"Why?"

"Just pull over, please."

A look of concern etched itself across his features. When he'd pulled the motor up onto the grass and set the brake, Phoebe leaned to take his face in her hands. "I'm slowly learning to take your feelings, even your fears, into consideration before putting myself in danger. It's only right, isn't it, that we learn to compromise." Before he could answer, she pressed her lips against his and kissed him soundly. "Thank you for being on hand when I needed you."

"I always will be, if you'll let me." His grin was infectious, and they suddenly found themselves laughing. Laughing and kissing, right there on the roadside with several sheep staring at them from over a stone wall.

After several minutes, they wiped tears of mirth from their eyes and leaned back against the seat. Owen took her hand. "When we get to Foxwood Hall, would you mind very much if I closeted myself awhile with your grand-father? There's something rather important I'd like to speak with him about. If you're agreeable, that is."

Suddenly as light as air, her heart lifted, and then settled with an unfurling sensation of warmth. Her eyes teared all over again, but for a very different reason. "Why, Owen Seabright, is that your idea of a proposal?"

"Oh no, Phoebe. Not yet. When I propose, you certainly won't have to ask me if that's what it was. You'll know."

He put the motor in drive and eased back onto the road. Holding the wheel one-handed, he reached the other around her shoulders and drew her to his side, where she happily stayed for the remainder of the trip home. Her hat suffered from being crushed between them, but what, after all, was a hat?

One month later

As she had been doing for the past several weeks, Phoebe smiled down at the ring encircling the fourth finger of her left hand. The square diamond, surrounded by sapphires on a platinum setting, might be a smidgeon larger than she would have chosen for herself, but it *was* a lovely ring and the beaming look of joy on Owen's face had precluded her saying anything but how happy he had made her.

Standing on the terrace now, a thick cardigan buttoned nearly to her chin, she gazed out over the grounds beyond Foxwood Hall and thought back to that evening. It had been sunset, and they had walked out past the tiered flower beds, across the footbridge, and to the edge of the ornamental pond, coming to stand beneath the sheltering sweep of the old willow. She had known why they had gone there. Been prepared for it. Yet for all that, her tears had overflowed at his question, and his figure had blurred as he'd gone down on one knee, and her lips had barely been able to form her reply.

How perfect, to come to this crossroads in her life, there beneath the willow. The same willow where her father had once tasked her with looking after the family while he went off to war. It had been a turning point in her life then, an entirely new course she had faithfully followed ever since, but as Eva had assured her, the time had come for another change. One not thrust upon her at a time of urgency, but which had dawned gradually yet inevitably in the natural course of events, like the change of the seasons.

Where they would make their home, how she would continue to be a vital part of her family, what arrangements she and Eva would make—all that had yet to be decided. But there was time yet. Time to think and to plan. And in the meantime, there was simply this newfound happiness, this treasure, of seeing a future of their own making—hers and Owen's—stretching before them.

When the door behind her opened, she barely heard it. She hoped it was merely another member of the family coming out to enjoy the late afternoon sunlight before the evening chill set in in earnest. Amelia or Grampapa, who would come to stand beside her and gaze out over the landscape—the gardens that gave way to the more pastoral grounds, bordered by forest, then farmland, and finally, in the farther distance, the surrounding Cotswold Hills. Yet it wasn't Amelia or Grampapa, and when she heard her name formally spoken, part of her wished to ignore the intrusion. Whatever it was, couldn't it wait?

"Lady Phoebe, I'm sorry to disturb you," Douglas, the footman said, "but Miss Huntford said it was important."

Phoebe spun around to face him. "Eva? Yes, I'll come right away. Is she belowstairs?"

"No, waiting for you in Mr. Giles's upper pantry."

Eva was so much more to Phoebe than a mere lady's maid, but it would be highly unusual for a lady's maid to be seen in the public rooms of the house. No wonder, then, that Eva, who rarely broke protocol, had sent Douglas to find her.

Phoebe wasted no time in crossing the house to the dining room and letting herself into the pantry through the door hidden within the wall panels. Inside were tiled workbenches lined with glass-fronted cabinets holding all manner of china, from teacups to soup tureens and everything in between. Eva waited beside the center worktable, a troubled look on her face.

Phoebe came to a trembling halt. "What is it? Has something terrible happened?"

"This." She lifted something off the table, held it up a moment, and then slapped it back down. "An utter betrayal. Though hardly a surprising one."

"Good heavens, Eva, I don't understand. That's only a magazine. Which one is it?" Phoebe ventured closer to glimpse the title: *Vogue.* It looked to be an English edition. They tended to come regularly. The maids loved thumbing through them, and Eva used the fashion plates to keep up on the latest trends from London and Paris. Although Mrs. Sanders, the housekeeper, strictly forbade the scandal rags from entering the house, she tolerated the fashion magazines as basically harmless.

Eva, her lips tightly compressed, flipped open the cover and skimmed through several pages.

"Oh, is that India?" Phoebe pointed at several black-and-white photos spaced across two pages. She even recognized the gardens of Allerton Place in the background.

"It is," Eva said through clenched teeth. She flipped another page.

The blood leached from Phoebe's face, instantly leaving her light-headed. She moved closer to the table, reached out, drew her hand back, placed it on the open pages, and slid the publication closer. "Surely not."

But it was. Photos of her and Julia, posing in the sunshine, Julia in signature Chanel pieces, and Phoebe in her makeshift country tweeds meant to introduce a whole new look for women.

"She promised she wouldn't."

"She lied," Eve replied tersely.

"Has . . . has Grams seen this yet?"

"I don't know. I don't think so."

"Then we must make sure she doesn't. Please get rid of this immediately, Eva. Burn it, and make sure there are no other copies in the house."

Eva readily agreed, and a minute later Phoebe crossed the grand hall thinking she could use a bit of a lie-down before dinner. From upstairs came the ringing of the telephone in Grampapa's study. Phoebe went still. It could be his solicitor, his estate manager, or any number of other individuals telephoning about ordinary matters. But somehow, Phoebe knew.

And was therefore unsurprised when Grams appeared at the top of the staircase, her nearly six-foot-tall figure swathed in black crepe, looking for all the world like an avenging angel, her eyes ablaze with indignation. "Phoebe Renshaw, what in heaven's name were you and your sister thinking?"

Phoebe steeled herself with a breath and started up the steps, preparing to explain what, in Grams's world, could never be adequately explained. It was going to be a long evening.

Author's Note

With the exception of Gabrielle "Coco" Chanel, the characters in this story are entirely fictional.

Coco Chanel was born Gabrielle Bonheur Chanel in 1893, into a home marked by extreme poverty. After her mother's death, her father, a peddler, placed her in an orphanage, where the nuns taught her how to sew. As a young woman, she discovered she could earn a living by singing in cabarets, and it's said her nickname came from this time, from a particular song she sang onstage. Chanel, however, was known to explain that Coco was short for coquette. Young, attractive, and intelligent, she also secured her fortunes by attaching herself to wealthy men. One of those men, Étienne Balsan, a socialite and heir to an industrialist (and later the brother-in-law of Consuelo Vanderbilt) helped her start a milliner's shop in Paris before WWI, where she would put those sewing skills to good use. Her hats were innovative, and wealthy women wanted them.

It was during her affair with Balsan that Chanel also became involved with Arthur "Boy" Capel, an English aristocrat who helped her expand her business beyond hats and into the world of haute couture. Their affair lasted nine years, even after Capel married. It's said the two intertwining Cs of the Chanel logo are a combination of their last initials. He died in a car accident in 1919, and by Chanel's own admission many years later, she never fully recovered from his death. But there were other influential men in her life. Igor Stravinsky, the Prince of Wales, and the Duke of Westminster were among her conquests, as well as Grand Duke Dimitri Pavlovitch, first cousin of Czar Nicholas, who had escaped Russia during the revolution.

Chanel's association with the latter two men would influence her clothing designs. With Pavlovitch, she embraced the square necklines and elaborate embroidered trim of Russian peasant clothing. Thanks to the Duke of Westminster, with whom she traveled in England, she saw the potential in men's classic tweed attire for creating comfortable yet sophisticated clothing for women. I took a liberty by creating a fictional character in place of the duke, and also with the timing, setting the relationship and trip a few years earlier than in actuality. But by the mid-1920s, Chanel had cloth manufacturers in the UK producing what would become her signature tweed fabrics.

So, why did an intelligent, ambitious woman with brilliant business sense and an innovative eye for fashion need to align herself with one powerful man after another? One might suppose it was because for a woman to succeed in those days, she needed the help of men. However, with Chanel the reasons went deeper. Her early life, with its poverty and what she perceived as abandonment, was, for her, a source of humiliation she sought to conceal behind a fictional narrative she constructed later. Through the men she associated with, she hoped to find the stability, protection, status, and esteem she lacked as a child. Was there something of a delusional quality to these relationships in that she hoped to elevate herself, through marriage, to a position where she would no longer be vulnerable—such as a duchess, or, in the event the Russian Revolution failed and Pavlovitch took the throne, czarina? There is evidence to suggest she entertained such ambitions. However, Coco Chanel never married.

What was she like? As I mentioned above, she was ambitious and brilliant, and fiercely focused on her goals. She could be generous to a fault, supporting friends and opening her homes to them. She could also be selfish, indifferent, and ruthless. She was less than sympathetic toward her many employees, who referred to her simply as Mademoiselle. She was a homophobe. An anti-Semite. During WWII and the years leading up to the war, she proved herself to have no loyalties except to her own profits, no sense of morality but what benefited herself.

So why make her integral to the plot of this book? A couple of reasons. For one, the Coco Chanel of the early 1920s was still a largely unknown quantity. She had yet to show her true colors, but she was unmistakably an important component of society's post–WWI push into the modern world, where women could be comfortable in their own clothing, and where, despite lingering obstacles, they were venturing out into the business world in ways never seen before. Such themes are in keeping with those I've been following throughout this series.

And two, the notion of hero worship always gives me pause. Whether it's a sports figure, celebrity, politician, etc., I have come to feel the worshiper will always find reasons, in the end, to be disappointed. Even to feel a sense of abandonment and betrayal on the part of the person they had admired. Just as Julia does by the end of the story.

Coco Chanel spearheaded a business that has lasted more than a century, that more than once changed the very nature of women's fashion, in ways that both reflected and facilitated the changes in women's roles in society. That part of her story is admirable, remarkable. The brilliance of her vision is undeniable.

And yet.